THE GREAT CELESTIAL THREAT

Sun-Tzu shook his head. *I can't afford to lose control. Ever. Can't you see that?*

Isis stopped kneading his shoulders, stepped around and perched herself against the corner of his desk. "So what do you intend to do about Kai?"

Kill him, if I can, Sun-Tzu answered silently. Kai would forever be the greatest threat to his position as Chancellor, despite any self-avowed denial that he did not want the Celestial Throne. *Neutralize him, if I cannot.*

"I'll think of something," was all he said. *If I am to regain control of this war, I will have to.*

Isis smiled. . . .

BATTLETECH®

THE KILLING FIELDS

Book Two of *The Capellan Solution*

LOREN L. COLEMAN

A ROC BOOK

ROC
Published by New American Library, a division of
Penguin Putnam Inc., 375 Hudson Street,
New York, New York 10014, U.S.A.
Penguin Books Ltd, 27 Wrights Lane,
London W8 5TZ, England
Penguin Books Australia Ltd, Ringwood,
Victoria, Australia
Penguin Books Canada Ltd, 10 Alcorn Avenue,
Toronto, Ontario, Canada M4V 3B2
Penguin Books (N.Z.) Ltd, 182–190 Wairau Road,
Auckland 10, New Zealand

Penguin Books Ltd, Registered Offices:
Harmondsworth, Middlesex, England

First published by Roc, an imprint of New American Library,
a division of Penguin Putnam Inc.

First Printing, August 1999
10 9 8 7 6 5 4 3 2 1

Series Editor: Donna Ippolito
Mechanical Drawings: Duane Loose and the FASA art department
Cover art by Bruce Jensen

 REGISTERED TRADEMARK — MARCA REGISTRADA

*This book is dedicated to
my editor at FASA, Donna Ippolito.
For her patience and support.*

Acknowledgments

The list keeps on growing. Without the following people, *The Capellan Solution* would either not have happened or not turned out so well as it has.

Jim LeMonds, for those first classes. My parents, who remain two of my best supporters. The Orlando Group, with a big "welcome back" to Ray Sainz and thanks to Russell Loveday for the chem/bio/rad details (blame him).

Mike Stackpole, who continues to be a good friend and advisor. Always, Dean Wesley Smith and Kristine Kathryn Rusch, without whom I'd have given up too early.

The FASA BattleTech team of Bryan Nystul and Randall Bills. Jordan Weisman and Ross Babcock, for creating such a fun universe in which to play. Chris Hartford, Chris Hussey, Chris Trossen—for their comments. Annalise Raziq, for her Internet assistance. Donna Ippolito, my editor at FASA, who lets me get away with murder—literally, that is.

BattleTech fans Maurice Fitzgerald and Warner Doles, who contributed to charity for their appearances. Samuel Fang, for his help with Chinese terminology. Group W and Khorsakov's Cossacks, for the loan of their units. Robert Kyde, for miniatures support.

My agent, Don Maass, and his staff.

My family—Heather, Talon, Conner, and Alexia. For putting up with me through this project, and the next.

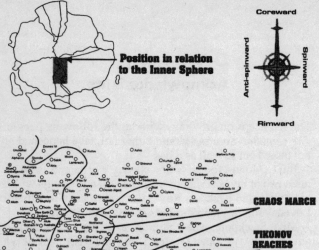

Coreward

Anti-spinward | Spinward

Rimward

Position in relation to the Inner Sphere

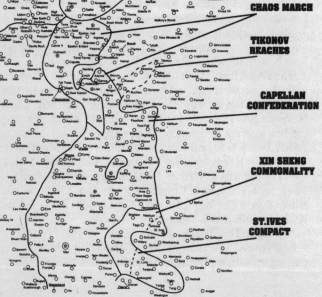

CHAOS MARCH

TIKONOV REACHES

CAPELLAN CONFEDERATION

XIN SHENG COMMONALITY

ST. IVES COMPACT

CENTRAL INNER SPHERE

· CIRCA 3062 ·

Prologue

Ho-lu Lowlands, Denbar
Xin Sheng Commonality, Capellan Confederation
21 February 3062

The blue-white arc of particle projection cannon fire snaked into the thick stand of trees and sliced low into a large elm. Moisture in the wood flashed to steam, splintering the bole in its rush to expand. The energy stream ate up the splinters and carved deeper, cutting through to scorch earth on the far side even as the majestic tree began to topple.

Sitting ten meters off the ground in the cockpit of his new *Emperor* assault BattleMech placed Major Warner Doles nearly at a height with the tops of the trees. Certainly he outmassed them. The falling elm brushed against the Battle-Mech, branches snapping off with rifle-shot echoes and leaving smears of green moss against the *Emperor*'s dull bronze finish. The ninety-ton machine barely shook, its widespread stance keeping it firmly rooted to the ground while the equilibrium feedback from the major's neurohelmet dealt automatically and easily with the light tremor. Major Doles noted the event but otherwise paid it little heed. BattleMechs, war machines built mostly along humanoid lines, heavily armed and armored, had reigned supreme on the battlefields for well over three hundred years. Nature couldn't compete. And in an assault-class machine especially, about the only thing a MechWarrior had to be concerned with was another BattleMech.

Dragging his targeting reticle over a distant stand of trees, mostly elm and cypress so close to Denbar's Huai Bayou, the major searched his head's up display and also through the ferroglass cockpit viewscreen for a target. The *Emperor*'s targeting system apparently found something among the trees and hanging moss that his own vision missed, the reticle flashing the alternating red and gold pattern of a partial weapons lock. He returned fire with twin large lasers, not surprised to see the ruby streams miss wide. A few more scattered bolts of gemcolored laser fire flashed between the trees as his Blackwind Lancers and equally hidden members of the Third Confederation Reserves sniped at each other.

We only need to buy a few more seconds, he thought, dismissing the errant laser fire as he gauged the final moments of his battle plan. *Keep them pinned down.* He knew that the Third Reserves had nowhere to go; outnumbered, their backs to the bayou and his Lancers pressing in on three sides. They simply waited for the final charge and watched for a miracle. *A position not wholly unlike that of the St. Ives Compact.*

Doles swallowed against a suddenly rancid taste. Now *there* was a thought he could have lived without, at least for a little while longer.

The St. Ives Compact had once been a Capellan Commonality until splitting off from the Confederation during the Fourth Succession War thirty years prior. The war against Houses Davion and Steiner left the Capellan Confederation in shambles, too weak to prevent the loss of the Compact. So Candace Liao had ruled her small state in relative peace, separate from the madness that had later reigned in her sister Romano's larger realm and sharing only the common Asian heritage of their family and national culture. Later, under the relative stability Romano's son Sun-Tzu finally brought to the realm, the Compact again began to worry over the possibility of Confederation aggression.

The Compact realized those fears soon enough. Barely two years ago—Doles could hardly believe it so recent—Chancellor Sun-Tzu Liao, then also First Lord of the resurrected Star League, announced his intention to tour the Confederation-Compact border. Doles had been executive officer of the Blackwind Lancers' second battalion, serving under Major Tricia Smithson. Her near-fanatical hatred of Sun-Tzu had only been intensified by the Chancellor's repeated slurs against the Compact and the pro-Confederation fervor raised by his tour. Smithson had jumped the border with her battalion in an attempt to remove what she considered the final threat to the Compact's sovereignty.

An event that might be entered into the Compact's history as the beginning of the end, Doles thought, his grip on the *Emperor*'s control sticks knuckle-white. Despite what was shaping up to be a victory here, he knew the Compact was not faring well in its fight to remain a free and independent state.

Sun-Tzu Liao's entire tour had been a setup, the Capellan Chancellor looking for any pretext or provocation to bring forces against the St. Ives Compact and so reclaim the territory for his Confederation. The first wave came in as "Star League peacekeepers" occupying six Compact worlds, with a second and third wave already in motion. In hindsight, few people no longer doubted that Sun-Tzu would have found or engineered some excuse. But the belated rationale helped Doles and his warriors not at all. None could forget the capture of Smithson by House Hiritsu forces, followed closely by Duchess Liao's condemnation of the Lancers and their return to the Compact in disgrace. Black days for the Lancers. Bad karma.

But the gods, if they existed, took pity on the Lancers. *Or perhaps they are not yet tired of the amusement we provide*. The very speed that had helped the Confederation establish a solid presence in the Compact also allowed the remnants of the Lancers' second battalion to slip away and begin a resistance effort on Denbar. Militia armor and BattleMechs were quickly supplemented with captured machines. Duchess Liao's daughter Cassandra, a fine MechWarrior in her own right, made contact then and began irregular supply runs. Usually the supplies consisted of salvage from the guerrilla campaign her St. Ives Lancers were waging against the occupation forces. Occasionally she smuggled in brand new equipment, like the *Emperor* that was Doles' current BattleMech.

And so the war continued. A civil war, delayed three decades but finally being waged as days melded into weeks and then weeks became months. Doles often wondered when it would end, and how, but then doubted he would live to see it.

As if summoned by the thought, a quick burst of static sounded over the comm set built into his neurohelmet before the filters cut in and dampened it.

"Major, we're set," a voice made tinny and distant by transmission whispered in his ear. Captain Samuel Fang, his exec, reporting that the final units had moved into place to box the Third Confederation Reserve against Huai Bayou.

"Wo dong le." Understood. Major Doles punched up an increased magnification on one of his auxiliary screens, focusing in on the heavy stand of trees hiding the Third Reserves to the east of him. *Now we see how confident they are.* "First units, forward," he commanded.

From screening cover north and south of his position two BattleMech lances broke from the treeline at a full run, heading into the no man's land that separated the opposing forces. Two *Wraith*s led the southern charge, Free Worlds League machines captured by Cassandra Allard-Liao on Indicass and delivered to his Lancers. A *Nightsky* led out the northern lance. *If the Third has any real fight left to them, or if there is more than the single company* I think *we have trapped, they'll break cover to meet the charge.*

Response from the Reserves was quick, but lacking in commitment. A small flurry of brightly colored streams and pulses flew out from the woods down-range, the machines remaining in the cover of the trees. A single PPC arced out with its manmade lightning to score against the lead *Wraith*, the coruscating stream of energy particles sloughing away armor from the *Wraith*'s right side. Autocannon tracers sparked briefly in flight, one set marking the stream of depleted uranium slugs that chewed into the *Nightsky*'s right leg.

Then an older *Catapult* design broke cover long enough to launch a single spread of missiles at the second *Wraith,* paying for its temerity when no less than a dozen Lancer BattleMechs opened up from their places of concealment to slice away the remaining armor protecting its torso. Three converging streams of autocannon fire ripped across the *Catapult*'s open chest, probing deep and chewing away engine shielding as well as cutting free its gyro. As if his Lancers had reached in and pulled the still-beating heart from some monster of fable, the *Catapult* took two faltering steps and crashed to the ground.

Doles overrode his warrior's cheers and comments by cutting in the master circuit on his comm panel. There was still work to do—a battle to be won.

"All units, advance," he ordered, throttling the *Emperor* into what passed for running speed among assault 'Mechs.

At roughly fifty-five kilometers per hour, Doles knew his machine set no speed records but crossed a battlefield quickly enough. His first step snapped more branches off the fallen elm and brought ninety tons down on its thick bole, crushing it. The tree shifted slightly, throwing a quick hitch into his second step, but the bulky neurohelmet he wore fed his own sense of equilibrium down into the massive gyro that kept so much metal upright and moving.

Four more lances surged forward, paced by the *Emperor* and bearing straight in on the Third Reserves' position. Two lances fielded only three 'Mechs, short one machine each due to previous battlefield losses. The faster lances running ahead now angled out to bracket the eastern stand of woods, in preparation for curling in at the back of the Reserves and effectively boxing them.

With the Lancer force exposed and the Third still in hiding, the Confederation force possessed a slight tactical advantage that Warner Doles believed negated by his superior strategic position, or at least would be very soon. Still, the

Reserves used what they had. No enemy MechWarrior repeated the *Catapult*'s mistake and broke cover, instead pouring intense fire into the Lancer formations from concealment. One Lancer *Wraith* stumbled to the ground, its left leg amputated at the knee by laser fire, then the light lances were around the edge of the treeline and making for the rear. A furious assault combination of autocannon, lasers, and a PPC gutted a Lancer *Blackjack,* its fusion engine releasing a fireball that disintegrated the medium-weight machine. Its pilot ejected safely, but a vicious Confederation warrior turned his lasers skyward, burning the Lancer MechWarrior and his parafoil to a cinder.

With no time to mourn his lost warrior as the *Emperor* gained the eastern treeline, Doles knocked smaller trees aside in search of targets. A wash of moss smeared against his viewscreen, but not so much that he couldn't see the enemy *Vindicator* looming before him. The *Emperor* shrugged off the PPC discharge leveled at it while its own large lasers cut deep into the smaller BattleMech's right side and leg. Fragmenting slugs from the *Emperor*'s twin LB-X class autocannon scoured off more armor, and a few fragments searched out flaws and gaping wounds in the armor. The *Vindicator* fell under the barrage, and a savage kick from the *Emperor* caved in its torso.

Doles left it behind, broken and out of the battle.

He continued to wade forward through foliage and weapons fire, at times fighting alongside one of his warriors, then beset by two of the struggling Third Confederation Reserves before the tide of battle swept him into another dense maze of massive tree limbs and hanging moss, which he tore down with gargantuan hands. Heat levels in the cockpit slowly crept higher as the fusion plant driving the Battle-Mech continued spiking in order to meet the constant demand for power. Sweat runneled from his brow and down his arms and legs.

The *Emperor*'s sensors screamed out a warning only an instant before two Gauss slugs tore into the 'Mech's right side, rocking it onto one foot and nearly sending it down to the moist earth. Warner Doles wrenched against his control sticks, manipulating the wide-bore barrels that made up the *Emperor*'s arms to help balance himself. If not for a nearby cypress that caught his 'Mech's shoulder, he likely would have gone down.

A *Pillager* shouldered its way through a light stand of fir trees and into Doles' rear right quarter, firing its powerful Gauss rifles. An impressive assault machine produced by the Compact, it was no doubt salvage from a previous battle. This was no 'Mech for a company commander either. *Could we have run a battalion or even the regimental command company to ground?*

Two more of the heavy Gauss slugs streaked across the short distance in silvery blurs, slamming into the *Emperor*'s right arm and left leg even as Doles returned fire with everything at his disposal. His lasers chewed ruby light deep into the *Pillager*'s arms and torso. Autocannon spat out twin streams of depleted-uranium ammunition, one stream careening off the shoulder and into the side of the *Pillager*'s head but not penetrating the armor to anything vital.

Both machines sagged back under the respective onslaughts, but neither succumbed to gravity and so another trade of hellish weapons fire ensued. In the near-scorching atmosphere that flooded his cockpit, Doles' breathing came in ragged gasps. He selected cluster munitions for his LB-X autocannon, hoping to force the breach he'd carved into the *Pillager*'s head. Around them the battle continued, with smaller 'Mechs occasionally nipping in for a strike that was mostly ignored by the monolithic assault machines. With over thirty tons of armor between them, both Doles and his opponent could absorb an incredible amount of damage. But in the next trade only one of the *Pillager*'s Gauss rifles fired. Depleted of ammo, now both rifles fell silent as the Reserves warrior relied on other weaponry. For Doles, whose ammunition load was much fresher, that made the battle only a matter of time.

It was a laser shot, not his clusters, that finally worked its way past the armor protecting the *Pillager*'s head and decapitated the assault 'Mech.

Gasping for breath as his heat levels dropped, Warner

Doles first noticed the clusters of Blackwind Lancer 'Mechs on his HUD. They were all around him, with no enemy unit to be seen. Staring out through the green-smeared viewscreen, he turned the *Emperor* in a slow circle. He spotted almost every one of his Lancers visually, through great gaping holes and pathways that other 'Mechs had ripped into the woods. The devastation stretched for hundreds of meters in any direction, and was not limited to vegetation. The hulks of downed 'Mechs could be seen as well, some in pieces and some still burning after fusion engine overloads, the flames scorching nearby trees but not yet setting them ablaze. Impossible to tell which had been his people and which the enemy, though by rough count he couldn't have lost more than three or four warriors while the Third Confederation Reserve had lost a dozen at least.

They really had no chance, Doles thought, but did not feel sorry for them. *Confederation or Compact, we are all* janshi. *Warriors. Our trade is death and destruction, and no one of us can afford sympathy if we hope to survive. Today, we owned the numbers, and when the time came we rolled over them with barely a hitch. They would have done the same to us.*

But again, this only brought to mind the similarities between this battle and the Compact's situation, and the thought robbed him of what little satisfaction he might have known from the victory.

A House Divided

Invincibility lies in the defense; the possibility of victory in the attack.
—Sun-Tzu, *The Art of War*

If it is not possible to be victorious, what is left but to lose? Mankind has yet to see a war in which a draw did not demand a similar price as a defeat.

With these options laid before you, then, it is always better to be on the attack.
—Sun-Tzu Liao, in a speech to the Sian War College, 21 February 3062, Sian

1

Celestial Palace
Zi-jin Chéng, Sian
Sian Commonality, Capellan Confederation
25 February 3062

Memories of his mother plagued Sun-Tzu Liao as he slowly paced an aisle within his strategic planning center, the Confederation's war room located several levels beneath his palace on Sian.

The folds of his silk robes of state rustled softly as he moved, barely audible against the background noise of whispered conversations and the occasional flurry of keystrokes. Dimly lit, the room discouraged any feel of the casual workspace, while overhead spotlights threw down islands of brightness around consoles and tables isolating the officers present. No technicians here, everyone an officer of *sao-shao* rank or greater—what would have been a captain before Sun-Tzu's Xin Sheng program worked its way into Capellan military ranking conventions and replaced them with proper Chinese titles. Talon Zahn and Ion Rush, the Chancellor's top military advisors, stood in the center of the room, their backs toward their lord as they continued to study the large holographic map displayed there.

Everything orderly and everyone about the business of

running a war. Mother would be so proud, Sun-Tzu thought
bitterly. Though ten years dead, Romano Liao was never far
from his thoughts these days, and had not been since entering into this second year of open warfare with the St. Ives
Compact. Her spectral presence sat in judgment over every
action or decision, and he sensed her smiling far too often.

The approval of Romano Liao was not something Sun-
Tzu sought.

The urge to quicken his pace, to flee Romano's presence,
was incredibly strong. But Sun-Tzu's deeply imbedded
scorn for spiritual nonsense allowed him to recognize and
explain the intrusive thoughts. Old memories, he told himself. Vivid ones, brought forward by the stresses of the three
months since the last Star League conference. He deliberately varied his pace and stopped at random intervals to
check a console's information from over the shoulder of a
suddenly nervous officer.

He sensed the tensions generated by his unexpected visit.
Felt it radiating from nearly everyone present and read the
confirmation in their frequent glances in his direction, fear-
ful and uncertain. Most were old enough to remember service under his mother. All of them knew that the madness
had been passed on to his sister, Kali, who embraced her insanity, believing herself the reincarnation of the death goddess and worshipped as such by her cult of Thugee
assassins. Sun-Tzu knew that those around him vigilantly
watched for the first evidence of similar madness from him.

He almost laughed. Seldom did he allow anyone to see
past the protective masks he wore. To think that they would
recognize madness in him . . . Yes, he could *almost* laugh, if
it weren't his own greatest fear as well.

Sun-Tzu possessed very few recollections of his grand-
father. He remembered him as a physically failing and
mentally crippled old man, the once-great Maximilian Liao
broken by Hanse Davion in the Fourth Succession War
much the same way as Hanse's Federated Commonwealth
armies had crushed the Capellan Confederation. Romano
had inherited a shattered realm and the duty to help it sur-

vive. But the near-destruction of the Confederation and the desertion of her elder sister Candace Liao, followed by the secession of the entire St. Ives Commonality, had tipped the balance of her sanity. Rampant paranoia and a ruthless nature drove her to massive purges of the government, the military, and even the civilian sectors. Romano ruled her nation with an iron fist, and controlled the population through fear, lest any other think to follow Candace in desertion of the Confederation. Perhaps she had preserved the state through that time of crisis, but Romano's legacy now tainted Sun-Tzu's reign and would likely dog him to his final days.

And how have you done differently? It was a question Sun-Tzu routinely asked of himself, though he often heard it with a tinge of Romano's icy tone. Violence, intimidation, and intrigue were still mechanisms of common employ. Executions and assassinations were other tools he wielded when their results served him—he had pulled the trigger himself on Demona Aziz when she'd tried to bring Word of Blake against him, and more recently he'd ordered the same action to resolve a building crisis within the Periphery. *And during my three-year reign as First Lord of the new Star League, I started a war.* The specter of Romano Liao grinned, and he brutally thrust the image aside. *I am not my mother.*

"So it is confirmed," Sun-Tzu said, voice pitched low to hide any sign of his discomfiture. "The Third Reserves regimental command is lost?"

Ion Rush, Master of Warrior House Imarra, was first to respond. "To the last man," he said, voice gravelly from damage to his larynx. Surgeons had repaired most of the physical damage caused by the explosion in which he'd been caught last year, but some things were still beyond their ability to reconstruct. Of course, some things could also now be improved . . .

Rush turned from the map slowly, carefully, and still Sun-Tzu noticed the large man's shoulder muscles quiver and knot as if preparing to handle a heavy load. Impressive.

"The Blackwind Lancers caught the Reserves down in Denbar's Ho-lu Lowlands with no nearby support. Our people did not take the threat of the Lancers serious enough."

An easy assignment on a world in space I supposedly control. Two battalions of a newer Confederation Reserves regiment on site with Marshigama's Legionnaires should have been more than enough to deal with the Blackwind Lancers' resistance, and it typified to Sun-Tzu just one of the ways in which the fight to reclaim the Compact seemed to be slipping from his grasp.

That problem at least was close to being neutralized once Zahn returned Smithson to her unit. Only three people on Sian knew that Tricia Smithson was a deep-cover Liao agent. One of several Sun-Tzu had ordered into the Compact years ago—and only two people on the capital world knew *that.* Smithson would neutralize the Lancers, just as she had delivered them for his needs to start the war.

Sang-jiang-jun Talon Zahn, senior general of the Confederation Armed Forces, had yet to turn around. He glanced at the Imarra Master and nodded absently in support of his comment, then returned his attention to the holographic display. After a few moments' reflection he added, "*Sang-shao* Oravey was wrong for the position. A shame he cost us eleven good warriors."

The Chancellor covered his agitation by carefully smoothing a pleat in the sleeve of his tan silk robe. Only the leeway Sun-Tzu was used to granting Zahn delayed a sharp reply at the general's seemingly cavalier attitude. Young as Zahn was—at thirty-six only six years older than the Chancellor—the man still possessed the sharpest strategic mind Sun-Tzu had ever found. Zahn had won the Chancellor's notice by speaking his mind, regardless of what he thought Sun-Tzu might *want* to hear. Sun-Tzu knew better than to discourage this trait in his chief general. Still, he could not permit the privilege he allowed Zahn to infect the other officers present.

"I remind you, *Jiang-jun* Zahn, that Petyr Oravey was a Capellan citizen." Sun-Tzu kept his tone neutral, only the shortening of Zahn's title hinting at his displeasure. "As such, his death is still a shame." All Confederation members took their citizenship very seriously, since it was not a guaranteed right but a privilege that each one must earn.

This time, Zahn did turn from the holographic map to face his lord. "*Duì-bu-qui,* Chancellor," he apologized, giving a conciliatory nod. "I did not mean to suggest otherwise. What I meant to say was that it was my fault for not removing him from command. He did not truly understand your Xin Sheng movement, calling for a revitalized national effort, and so simply sought his 'hopeless battle.' "

"Foolish," Sun-Tzu agreed calmly, holding anger in check. The "hopeless battle" syndrome was another legacy of his mother's rule. In essence, a Capellan officer would seek a suicidal last stand, becoming a martyr to the realm rather than take the chance of surviving a defeat or, sometimes worse, a narrow victory. Court-martials and execution had often awaited those who failed the state in not providing a sound victory. The Xin Sheng programs had begun during Sun-Tzu's short term as First Lord, with him milking the Star League office for every gram of prestige and what little power it held. Literally translating as *New Birth,* the programs were a nationalistic effort designed to strengthen all aspects of the Capellan Confederation and hopefully defeat such problems as the "hopeless battle" syndrome. Sun-Tzu had hoped for—and expected—better results.

"And just what is the overall status of my armed forces then?" he asked.

"Fairly solid," was Zahn's quick reply, dark eyes flashing with sudden animation. Not even the Confederation's senior general, Sun-Tzu noted, was immune to the pleasure of reporting good news to his lord. "Prestige units such as the Warrior Houses are pushing to the limits of their ability for you. Our long-established support regiments are performing well, especially those committed to action in the Chaos March and against St. Ives. If a problem remains it is with units such as the Confederation Reserves, too long in garrison assignments and not much secure in their abilities."

Ion Rush nodded agreement. "And the best improvement we've seen is in the mercenary units who accepted your offer of Confederation citizenship to become regular line regiments." The dour warrior nearly smiled, the edges of his mouth twitching. "Little Richard's Panzer Brigade is better disciplined than ever, trying to prove they are just as worthy of the privilege as the Tau Ceti Rangers." The twitching stopped. "Of course, they would decline if offered."

The Chancellor took mental note of the subtle warning. Not that he ever intended to offer the Brigade citizenship, but knowing that they thrived on competition with the Rangers could be exploited in other ways. "What of Mc-Carron's Armored Cavalry?" he asked, naming the impressive five-regiment mercenary outfit that had been the first to receive his offer, and accept.

"Three regiments holding our rearward lines," Zahn said, indicating the display. "They represent the bulk of my strategic reserves right now along the St. Ives Front. One regiment holds Brighton in the Xin Sheng Commonality. And the Nightriders"—he paused, obviously for effect—"are on Nashuar."

Sun-Tzu moved up to study the large holographic display. On it the St. Ives Compact stretched from the floor to a height of almost two meters, its coreward and rimward arms now split by the Confederation presence on Denbar and Indicass. Green arrows programmed into the holographic map labeled the two arms the "St. Ives" and "Teng" Fronts, named for the two furthest worlds along each arm. Confederation worlds that lined the Compact's spinward border glowed dark green, and the seven occupied worlds of the Compact, the so-called Xin Sheng Commonality, a lighter shade. A few worlds, such as Denbar, occasionally flashed between light green and red, showing armed resistance to the return of the Confederation. The eleven remaining Compact worlds glowed solid red.

"The Nightriders regiment?" Sun-Tzu asked, taking the offered path.

"They're making a mess of things on Nashuar," Zahn said matter-of-factly. "Highest casualty rates among civilian populations of any of our forces. Peaceful civilian interference is treated as military opposition." His steady gaze faltered for a moment. "The deathwatch is at two and a half minutes, down from three last week."

The deathwatch was a term Sun-Tzu's father, Tsen Shang, had taught him and which the Chancellor had explained to Talon Zahn. As head of Romano's Maskirovka intelligence service, Shang had been responsible for implementing many of the purges she'd ordered. "They were so swift and violent that first year of her *official* reign," he had explained over a rare glass of plum wine shared with his son, "that the deathwatch was down to eight minutes. Every eight minutes, another Capellan citizen died by the Mask's hand. Where we failed to protect the realm from outside treachery, we were ruthlessly efficient among our own people."

This war is averaging a Capellan citizen every two and a half minutes, counting the people of the Compact, who are Capellans even if they are not of the Confederation, yet. Sun-Tzu found no pleasure in the fact, especially with over ninety-five percent of those casualties civilians and all his efforts to curb the carnage so far producing no results. Last week it had been at three minutes.

What's thirty seconds? Romano's specter asked.

Almost thirty-five thousand Capellan citizens, Sun-Tzu replied. If he was to establish a difference between his rule and Romano's, it would have to be on such distinctions. Where his mother would have thought little of sacrificing so many of her own, Sun-Tzu at least acknowledged their deaths and hoped to ensure that the gains would be worth their sacrifice.

"It is hard to fault them for being somewhat overzealous when it comes to protecting themselves," Ion Rush offered softly.

Zahn nodded but Sun-Tzu kept his own counsel. The Nightriders, deployed the year before to end resistance on the Chaos March world of Wei, had been greeted with a nerve agent the rebellious government had dredged up from an old CBR graveyard. A battalion of elite warriors lost in a few minutes without a shot fired. And not easy deaths either, from the holopics the Maskirovka had provided. Sun-Tzu understood the Nightriders' vicious behavior, but he would not condone it when it cost Capellan lives.

"Send another message to *Jiang-jun* Lord Baxter over my signature," he said. He doubted it would do any good, but a direct order to pull the Nightriders from combat duty risked alienating the Cavalry. "Can we drop another Cavalry regiment onto Nashuar, to help pacify the world?"

Both Zahn and Rush shook their heads, but it was Zahn who fielded the question. "That would endanger our logistics network. We're stretched thin as it is, focused in too many directions."

By which Zahn subtly criticizes my decision not to pull troops back from the Chaos March. Over fifty old Confederation worlds had thrown off the Federated Commonwealth yoke in the turmoil raised by the Marik-Liao offensive of 3057. Most of those remembered their Capellan heritage and had returned easily to the Confederation. But a large area of space near Terra resisted the return of the Confederation, proclaiming themselves independent of any Great House, and the drive to reclaim them continued to sap strength away from the St. Ives conflict.

Sun-Tzu did not care. Those were Capellan worlds, and they would be his again. *We will not back away.* He wanted to lash out in frustration, but he allowed only a touch of irritation to creep into his voice. "I will find you more troops," he promised, jade eyes hard and unblinking.

If Talon Zahn noticed his lord's hint of anger, he did not let it touch him. "I'll need them. With Star League forces arriving, it gives the Compact more freedom in tactics than I'd like to allow." He brushed a hand over the holographic map, through Confederation space bordering the St. Ives Compact. When he spoke again, his tone was strong yet unhurried. "The concept of a 'frontline' in interstellar warfare changes significantly, Chancellor. JumpShips can too easily bypass the occupied worlds to strike into Confederation territory. I don't want more Compact regiments duplicating your cousin Kai's efforts. He's already enough a problem."

"Most of Candace's offspring are a problem," Sun-Tzu said. "And Kai is the worst of them." He recognized Zahn's attempt to shift away from the touchy subject of the Chaos March but still make his point. Thinking of his various cousins, Sun-Tzu knew the point was a valid one. Kuan Yin and her humanitarian efforts in the combat zone constantly upstaged Sun-Tzu's own efforts along those lines. And Cassandra's hard-hitting guerrilla campaign continued to blunt his advances and even caused small reversals along the Teng Front.

Kai Allard-Liao was his Aunt Candace's eldest son and heir to the Compact. He was also one of the deadliest Mech-Warriors the Inner Sphere had ever known, and his First St. Ives Lancers threatened to collapse the entire St. Ives Front. With Star League and ComStar forces bolstering the Compact's sagging defenses, Kai had gone on the offensive, taking his Lancers over the border and into Confederation space. For the last two months he had moved about, striking at the support infrastructure on which Sun-Tzu's military depended. His latest strike, against the Necromo shipyards, had temporarily crippled the Confederation's ability to produce or repair many classes of military DropShips so critical to landing troops and BattleMechs on planets. In effect, he had created a third front to the St. Ives conflict. The "Kai Allard-Liao" Front. And since no one could predict where he would strike next, he forced Sun-Tzu to tie up good troops in an effort to keep him contained.

So many against me, yet all of Liao blood. "And what of my uncle?" Sun-Tzu asked. Tormano Liao had been disowned by Maximilian before the outbreak of the Fourth Succession War. His Davion-sponsored Free Capella Movement had remained a thorn in the side of the Confederation ever since, opposing Romano and then Sun-Tzu. Kai took it over for a few years, running it as a humanitarian support effort while Tormano served Katrina Steiner-Davion directly as her aide-de-camp. After the Star League Conference Tormano had taken a leave of absence from Katrina's service. That suggested trouble.

"Just as we suspected," Ion Rush said. "The Maskirovka

confirmed that the resurgence of the Free Capella Movement on a military footing was his doing. For the most part they have been involved mainly in the escalating Tikonov conflict, likely as part of a deal cut with Katrina to prevent an open declaration of rebellion."

Zahn nodded. "Warfare by proxy," he said, a thin, hard line to his mouth. "The Free Tikonov Forces that we support against a large portion of Free Capella."

With only Capellan lives lost on either side, Sun Tzu noted. *Yes, that is Katrina's style.* Tikonov was another old Confederation Commonality that broke away during the Fourth Succession War, subjugated by the Steiner-Davions rather than existing as an independent state. Tikonov was the long game Sun-Tzu played against Katrina, but Tormano's involvement there and in the Compact was an issue to be considered now. *You do not fool me, Uncle.* Tormano did not care for the Compact's independence or Tikonov's rebellion. *He wants the Celestial Throne, and this is his bid to establish legitimacy.*

Sun-Tzu wasn't ready to give up the throne quite yet.

But how to deal with him? How to deal with them all?

Romano whispered in his ear, and Sun-Tzu visibly started.

Kill them, came the answer. Blunt and brutal, much as Romano had been herself. He began to shake his head, then noticed the questioning looks from both Ion Rush and Talon Zahn. Clearly they had noticed his moment of weakness, and that must be addressed.

"I have some ideas," he said slowly, lying, passing off his visible shock as insight. He smiled, his eyes hard and cruel, because it would be expected of him. "Keep me informed of developments," he ordered, then turned to withdraw.

"Any requests in the meantime?" Zahn asked, interrupting his Chancellor's departure.

Unsure if his general was merely being efficient or might be probing the lie, Sun-Tzu turned an icy stare on him. "A few solid military victories would be nice," he said, tone coldly neutral. *In the meantime, I will deal with the family.*

How? his mother asked from within the dark recesses of his mind.

I am not sure, he replied. *But there must be a way.*

Zahn's dark eyes blinked back, but showed no other sign of discomfiture. "*Duì,* Chancellor." *Of course.*

Sun-Tzu answered Talon Zahn's bow with a curt nod, then turned and walked off without further ado. Romano's ghost followed.

2

Heisang
Pardray, St. Loris
St. Ives Compact
5 March 3062

Lien-zhang Aris Sung piloted his *Wraith* with a deft and easy touch, mainly working foot pedals and throttle as he marched his fifty-five-ton BattleMech along the expressway that ran through the heart of the city of Heisang. At the head of his 'Mech company and trailing the final 'Mech of the forward company by sixty meters, his position put him at the middle of House Hiritsu's parade column. Easily distinguished, since the armor on Aris' *Wraith* had been treated to give it a blued-steel finish. Armored vehicles, with Warrior House infantry riding atop and on sideboards, cruised along at regular intervals, one vehicle pacing every 'Mech on the left. Over ten thousand tons of armored war machines on formal procession.

People had gathered along both sides of the expressway, some as far out as the spaceport but the majority crowding the grassy banks that followed the expressway through the city. Most sat on their parked cars, but others had decided to take advantage of St. Loris' spring weather and the informal holiday that House Hiritsu's arrival had afforded them and

THE KILLING FIELDS 23

sprawled on picnic blankets to watch the "landing day" parade. They cheered for each passing BattleMech and some waved flags. The occasional school marching band performed the Capellan Confederation national anthem, making up in enthusiasm what they lacked in recent practice.

Aris possessed no burning desire to participate in the parade, and doubted any other House warriors did either. The Confederation's eight Warrior Houses existed to serve in the state's defense, not to provide entertainment. *And certainly there has been nothing for us to celebrate lately.* But *Shiao-zhang* Ty Wu Non, their House Master, had ordered the traditional parade. Two companies, his own included, while the third remained on guard at their landing zone to protect the DropShips. A tribute, he'd called it, to the people who had proactively hastened the return of the Confederation to St. Loris. Selection of Aris' company would normally be an honor.

Aris Sung thought of it otherwise.

Four weeks earlier, his Warrior House had been stationed on Nashuar, fighting a never-ending series of battles against St. Ives Compact forces. Units rotated in and out on both sides of the conflict, but House Hiritsu remained on station, spearheading the so-called "St. Ives drive," though the Confederation had failed to move past Nashuar or Taga in the last nine months. There would be—could be—no entropy-based warfare here, the style of combat that had recently proven so effective against the Clans. No simple smash-and-destroy tactics, leaping forward and leaving an unsecured line of retreat. This was a slow war of complete subjugation. To reinstall the Confederation with sufficient strength so that never again could the worlds of the St. Ives Commonality be wrested from it. No pockets of resistance would be left behind, ready to flare up behind the main drive and so cause unnecessary reversals. At least, such was the concept of the St. Ives conflict.

Fresh coolant shot through the tubes of Aris' cooling vest, the chill raising gooseflesh on his arms and briefly interrupting his reflection. Technically, the vest was not required for parade, but Aris never relaxed from battle conditions when piloting a 'Mech. *A bad habit to fall into, and St. Loris is a hostile world. Or at least, it will be soon enough.*

He glanced at his head's up display, the tactical screen projected across the top of his viewscreen. His practiced eye scanned it in a fraction of a second, checking the position of his company and finding everything in perfect order. *As should only be expected.* Pride sparked within him briefly and he enjoyed its fleeting pass. These days there was little enough of it.

Nashuar had been a rough time for Aris. It was a world full of Capellan citizens who had followed Duchess Candace Liao in defecting from the Confederation years before but otherwise remained true to their heritage. And where pro-Confederation sentiment was beginning to appear on other Compact worlds, Nashuar remained completely supportive of their Duchess. They did not want the Confederation back and fought it at every turn. The entire planet a battlefield, they suffered for their resistance—warrior and civilian both.

Two years ago Aris had been ready to war against these people, confident of his nation's superior morality and proud of his own Asian ancestry, though he knew that being Asian did not make someone a Capellan, just as being a Capellan citizen did not necessarily give one an appreciation for the nation's Asian heritage. These days, on the rare occasions he could bring himself to look in a mirror, he saw a face that could just as easily belong to someone he had called an enemy, but now also thought of as his victim. Somewhere along the way he had lost his dreams of glory. What remained was a sense of duty, and at times that felt to be eroding as well.

He had not been sorry to see the end of Nashuar, though he did not see an answer to his troubles on St. Loris' horizon either.

The Confederation's arrival on St. Loris had been precipitated by the Pardray militia publicly declaring in favor of Chancellor Sun-Tzu Liao. The island continent of Pardray, running parallel to the main continent of Layting for several hundred kilometers, made for a good staging base. Pardrayans took control of the system's one recharge station, at the zenith jump point, making travel into and out of the system much easier for Confederation forces than for the Compact.

Sang-jiang-jun Zahn had dropped in the 151st Air Wing to hold the island country against Compact loyalists, and then called up BattleMech units to begin the drive to take the world of St. Loris. House Hiritsu had been relieved at Nashuar by a regiment of McCarron's Armored Cavalry and sent to spearhead this new drive along the Teng Front, currently supported by the 151st Air as well as the mercenary Little Richard's Panzer Brigade.

But they still faced an opposition that was joined to them by a common heritage—nothing had truly changed. Cassandra Allard-Liao had brought her Second St. Ives Lancers to oppose House Hiritsu. One regiment of the mercenary Korsakhov's Cossacks, Rubinsky's Light Horse, remained on planet to help defend the massive territory. From intelligence reports, Aris recognized Cassandra to be the life and soul behind Compact resistance along the Teng Front. She accomplished as much as her brother, though few remarked on it. And the people of Layting would be just as opposed to them, and bitter over the perceived betrayal of Pardray.

Nashuar may be behind us, but the war's not over yet. Starting tomorrow, House Hiritsu will begin to visit the same destruction against St. Loris. It was a warrior's privilege to serve the Chancellor, and an additional honor to belong to a Warrior House. But for the first time in his life, Aris felt doubts that being *janshi*, a warrior, was worth the price it extracted.

No, he thought, hands tight on the *Wraith*'s control sticks, *there is certainly no cause for celebration on St. Loris.*

The day's celebrations also bothered *Ban-zhang* Li Wynn. In full field uniform, the green and black patchwork camouflage pattern of House Hiritsu infantry, Li Wynn rode on the running board of a Regulator armored tank that paced Aris Sung's *Wraith*. His left arm he'd looped through a steel rung used to climb up to the turret hatch. His right rested on top of the SMG slung over his shoulder, fingers tracing the top edge of the barrel as he scanned the crowds for any potential trouble. He held himself responsible for the safety of the parade; partly out of pride for his recent promotion to *ban-zhang,* a Warrior House infantry squad leader, but mostly due to the sense of obligation he still felt toward the Warrior House that had adopted him.

But it wasn't his sense of responsibility that left him uneasy in the face of so much pro-Confederation enthusiasm. Li Wynn held mixed feelings for the very people who were celebrating his House.

Another marching band swung into view as the hovertank rounded a bend in the expressway. Better than most others they'd passed, Li Wynn still heard the fumbled notes and melodies and he hated them for it. *Citizens of the St. Ives Compact are the enemy.* Or at least they were, before planetfall on St. Loris. On Denbar and then Nashuar most civilians had acted under forced cooperation. Li Wynn had done his share of forcing. He was too used to thinking of them as traitors to the Confederation, and if civilians were injured from the war's collateral damage, then it was only justice for three decades of rebellion.

Even the recent swell of pro-Confederation sentiment in the Compact did little to ease Li Wynn's harsh judgment. *Where were you thirty years ago?* he wanted to ask them. *Or fifteen? Or even five?* Li Wynn thought of them as "closet Capellans," ready to leap onto the bandwagon now that a Confederation victory seemed assured. *Scared? You should be.* Li Wynn doubted that Sun-Tzu Liao would allow such people to hide behind false patriotism.

Pardrayans, though, had acted on their own to bring back the Confederation. Acted first, and then requested aid, knowing that if the Confederation Armed Forces had been unable to respond, St. Ives forces would roll over them quick enough. *How much should that count for?* It upset Li's sense of proportion that he could not answer that question easily.

He had approached Aris Sung about the problem, shortly

after planetfall in the hour before the parade. *Shiao-zhang* Non had named Aris as Li's *Sifu,* his Mentor. In a Warrior House, a *Sifu* was responsible for overseeing the inculcation of House tenets and military training in the cadet. Li Wynn had noticed Nashuar Aris' growing hesitation, even agitation, when it came to discussing the war with his charge. In the DropShip 'Mech bay, he had offered only the briefest advice.

"Put yourself in their place," Aris said, gaze distant as if staring into a pond, or a mirror. "See with their eyes and understand their pain. Until then, they will be the enemy."

Now what was that supposed to mean? Li Wynn could only imagine that Aris was testing him in some way. He couldn't be equating Compact civilians with Confederation citizens, that would be treason. Or at least some kind of heresy. Was he counseling moderation? Personal reflection?

Could Aris be suggesting that these people had no choice?

The thought came to him like an electric jolt. That had to be it. Li had been unable to see it because of his own origins and the way in which he had come to recognize Confederation superiority. Though he had been born and raised outside the Confederation proper, no one had ever tried to stifle his own freedom of thought. *The Pardrayans are true Confederation citizens, who have been repressed for years and awaiting their chance for freedom.* In Li's mind, that lent an even darker nature to the majority of St. Loris' population. *The people of Layting have that much more to pay for,* he vowed.

As the parade continued, he actually waved to a few members of the crowd, at peace with himself again. Aris Sung certainly could have meant nothing else.

3

Subcommander Maurice Fitzgerald thought the skies over Hazlet formed the perfect backdrop for today's battle. Low-lying cloud cover dropped a seemingly endless light rain, staining the city damp gray. The heavy skies promised a more severe storm to follow, but in the meantime the occasional light rumble of thunder was lost among missile explosions, the staccato chatter of heavy autocannon fire, and the echoing footsteps of giant war machines. A lousy day, made more miserable by open warfare in the streets.

The four Nashuar Home Guard 'Mechs under Fitz' command squared off against a like number of McCarron's Armored Cavalry—the Nightriders regiment—in Hazlet's main industrial district. The newly promoted Subcommander had forced the battle here, away from the more populated areas and with the thought that the Home Guard's older but more robust machines would give them a slight edge in such wide open spaces. *Now I just wish I could remind the Nightriders that we're supposed to hold the edge here,* Fitz thought as his *Blackjack* stumbled backward under the vicious onslaught of twin blue-white arcs from particle projection cannons and a hail of autocannon fire. It fetched up against a single-story, steel-faced warehouse, splitting several sheets and warping the ceiling supports, but remaining on its feet.

The Nightriders were pushing hard today, the first time in weeks that they'd been able to penetrate the city borders. Aleisha's Mounted Fusiliers had stopped the main Nightrider assault cold, just hours earlier and well outside of Hazlet. This attack, involving a single 'Mech company supported by armored vehicles, had come in fast and furious from the western flank. Probably meant as a diversionary raid, then lucky enough to break through the lines and hit the city. The fighting had broken down into three lance-on-lance battles, and from chatter over the Home Guard frequencies, at least one Nightrider lance had already shattered and fled.

"Fitz, behind you!"

Fitzgerald flinched involuntarily, though the warning from his lancemate had been unnecessary. Sensors were already screaming for his attention by the time the final word crackled over the comm system built into his neurohelmet. A *Jinggau* had burst through an office building to Fitz' rear, raining bricks and kicking steel beams into the street that separated the offices from the industrial park. Dust billowed around the sixty-five-ton 'Mech, the residue of smashed plaster and bricks, but the light drizzle quickly swept it from the air.

"I'm on it," was all he had time to call out.

The *Jinggau*'s molded armor lent it a distinctive appearance, its bullet-shaped body suggesting a deadly grace that Fitz might have appreciated more had the 'Mech not been painted the blue and black scheme of the Big MAC's Nightriders regiment. And if it hadn't just smashed its way through an occupied building.

With no way to avoid the *Jinggau*'s fire, Fitz managed instead to turn his *Blackjack* into the stream. Where the emerald-colored laser bolts might have penetrated the lighter protection along his back, now they punched into the better armor along his left side and arm. Fitz rode out the damage, a light touch to his control sticks assisting the BattleMech's gyro in keeping the *Blackjack*'s forty-five tons upright.

"All units," he ordered, opening a channel to his lance, "draw inward and stay between me and the Nightriders." There wasn't much thought behind the order. Fitzgerald simply recognized the danger that a heavy-weight enemy 'Mech at his lance's rear represented, and knew it had to be dealt with before the Nightriders lance pressed forward with any form of coordination. He traded salvos with the newcomer, the two of them scoring against each other. But where the *Blackjack*'s wire-frame damage schematic flashed cautionary yellow in places, warning him of armor loss but no penetrations, Fitz noticed the spray of gray-green coolant that erupted from the *Jinggau*'s torso.

Heat sink. But if I got through armor already, it must have been shaved pretty close earlier by another lance. That also explains why he hasn't been firing his Gauss rifle. He's out of ammo! He shifted the wire-frame from his 'Mech to the *Jinggau*, whistling low and even when he saw the rents in the heavier Nightrider machine. *Bluffing. The Cavalry pilot is thirty seconds from falling apart.*

Only Fitzgerald didn't have thirty seconds to wait. The *Jinggau* had to come down now.

Fitzgerald was barking orders before the decision was fully made. "Cameron, post! Everyone else scrap the *Jinggau*!"

Posting a 'Mech meant charging it forward, followed by a rapid retreat. A feint. If it went off, he might buy a few seconds of redirected fire. Fitz knew that any amount of hesitation would doom the maneuver, but he trusted his people. *And, I have no choice.*

It went down so flawlessly, he almost needn't have worried. Lance-Sergeant Cameron Long ran his new *Enforcer* forward, the well-armored 'Mech bearing up under massive concentrated fire by the Nightriders. Meanwhile, the other two members of Fitz' lance turned to target the *Jinggau*, adding their firepower to the *Blackjack*. Fitz saw two more heat sinks burst, and then from several holes in its torso the *Jinggau* spat out a stream of high-velocity metal that could only be a gyro tearing itself apart. The *Jinggau* fell over backward, partially into the hole it had ripped through the office building, and it didn't move again.

"They're pulling back." That was Cameron's voice, tinny and distant from transmission, but giving off surprise and relief.

Fitz hauled his *Blackjack* around, scanning the industrial park. Having survived the posting maneuver, Cameron had retreated to take meager cover behind a low retaining wall. A few of the Nightriders continued to snipe at him with long-range energy weapons, but they were indeed falling back toward the city outskirts. Fitz wouldn't have bet on the Nightriders crumbling so easily. Personal experience over the last few months told him that McCarron's Armored Cavalry did not retreat while odds remained close to even. The answer came a few seconds later when three new symbols flashed onto his head's up display, the computer designating them as Home Guard BattleMechs.

"It's the Commander," Jason crowed happily, his line of sight giving him the information a split second before the others could read it off their HUD themselves.

Commander Danielle Singh's voice followed right on the end of Jason's transmission. "Singh to Fitz, glad to see you still in one piece." Her *Helios* broke away from her two escorts, angling in toward Fitzgerald while the others formed a skirmish line should the Nightriders decide to return.

"I'm not too worried," she said, voice stronger as she cut over to a private frequency shared only with her two lance commanders and occasionally the Home Guard's CO, Major Nevarr. "Base monitored their order to withdraw. They're gone."

Fitz nodded to his empty cockpit. "For today," he returned after switching over to the same frequency. The weariness he refused to let show in front of his own people now bled into his voice. Danielle had been his friend before holes in the TO&E bumped her up to his commanding officer. She was one of a few select people Fitzgerald could actually talk to. "Good thing you happened along. I'm not sure how much longer we'd have held."

"You'd have held, Maurice. Taking side bets on which Nightrider your team would put down first, and then collecting your winnings in volunteered charity time."

The beginnings of a smile pulled at the edges of his mouth, but couldn't fight its way completely past the fatigue. Danielle was one of the few people who could use his first name and make it work. She also liked to tease him about his old hobby of handicapping the Solaris fights. But even in the light banter they used when trying to cheer each other up, he still sensed her approval of his more recent off-duty work, volunteering for Hazlet's various emergency services. A good thing, since he had rarely been so serious about anything.

Few active-duty personnel and an even smaller percentage of MechWarriors took the time to volunteer. Most couldn't afford to, already standing double watches or on-call for the almost-daily battles. But when Fitzgerald had more than two hours of down-time back to back, and if he'd slept in the previous twenty-four, he could be found out with search and rescue, or relocation relief, or any other humanitarian service being provided to the people of Nashuar. Not even Danielle understood where Fitz' reserve of energy came from.

The answer was simple. Fitzgerald felt responsible.

Nashuar had seen a rough year. It had been one of the first worlds targeted by Sun-Tzu's "peace-keepers," then suffering continued attacks by House Hiritsu and other units. The latest assault force, the Nightriders, seemed exceptionally brutal even on a world that was growing increasingly desensitized to the concept of *daily* warfare. No one wanted to remember that a short time ago the Compact had been at peace, because then they'd have to admit that nothing could be done to bring peace back.

And it was this casual acceptance of ongoing warfare that most bothered Fitzgerald. People still suffered and died whether war was considered routine or rare. BattleMechs were designed to limit the horrors of continuous warfare. A MechWarrior should try to contain those effects, not help prolong them. It was this hope that had brought him back to the MechWarrior ranks after failing the admissions tests the first time. It was this hope that made him constantly find himself lacking.

"Anyway," Danielle continued, "we hardly happened along. We were tracking a *Jinggau* that got away from us, hoping to take it down for salvage. Did it pass by?"

In his dark mood, Fitz didn't trust himself to use the radio. Obviously she had not noticed the large hole in the building behind him, or if she did, had not wanted to look closer. He merely sidestepped his *Blackjack,* giving her *Helios* a straight-on view. People were stirring around in the rubble that had once been a large part of the building's interior, looking for survivors. He saw a few people, armed with personal handguns or even a piece of rebar, up near the cockpit just daring the Cavalry warrior to come out. *If he's at all intelligent, he'll wait for the militia.*

"Fitz," Danielle said softly, her voice almost lost in transmission noise. "Fitz, I'm sorry."

I'm not the one you need to apologize to, Fitz thought but did not say. And anyway, was it really Danielle's fault that the Cavalry MechWarrior had run through a building rather than around? No more than it was Fitz', or Major Nevarr's, or Sun-Tzu's, or even Duchess Candace Liao's.

"You weren't piloting the 'Mech, Danielle."

She signed. "Maybe not, but I still feel like hell."

"Well, then let's get our people together and head back to base," Fitzgerald said. "If we're going to be depressed, might as well make it at Major Nevarr's daily debriefing." *And the sooner begun, the sooner I might be able to get back out here and work off some more frustration.*

As if reading his mind, Danielle asked, "You coming back out here this afternoon?"

"Probably. Why?" Fitz readied himself to hear the standard CO talk about keeping rested, making sure he didn't overtax himself. *That I'm needed more in a 'Mech than I am handing out bandages.*

Danielle surprised him. "I was thinking of catching a ride with you. If that's all right."

Now Fitzgerald did smile. Not in humor, but from the hint of hope that Danielle had given back to him. Even if for a short while. *One way or another,* he promised, *the Mech-Warriors will make a difference.*

4

Royal Palace
Tian-tan, St. Ives
St. Ives Compact
18 March 3062

Candace Liao sipped at her green tea, then replaced the fine china cup onto its saucer with the softest of sounds. Back straight and dark eyes sharp and piercing as ever, she remained focused on Colonel Caroline Seng, who sat opposite her. The overcast day robbed the palace sun room of much of its charm, which made it an appropriate setting to receive the latest evaluation from the Compact's senior colonel.

"You paint a grim picture, Caroline." Candace watched Seng take a sip of her own tea, for politeness' sake, she suspected. "You're sure that there is no other hope?"

Caroline Seng smiled sadly. Dark circles under her eyes told of an all-night conference with her top aides, preparing the document she'd just summarized. "There is always hope, Duchess. Sun-Tzu might withdraw. Your son could conceivably break the back of the Confederation logistics network. What I have outlined is simply based on the facts as of this morning."

"Three months is not a lot of time," Candace said with a slight frown.

"I know." Caroline nodded agreement. "But with our forces divided along two axes, we cannot hope to hold out against the Confederation's assault. The Confederation may not field an impressive front-line force, but they have deeper reserves to draw upon, while we have almost exhausted ours. Victor's troops and George Hasek's help notwithstanding, in three months the strain will begin to show and we begin the long slide backward."

"But you do not count the Federated Commonwealth troops still within our borders."

Seng hesitated. "Intelligence analysis is inconclusive, Duchess, so I'm going off my instincts. General Devon is on her way back to St. Ives," she said, naming the Federated Commonwealth liaison to the Compact, "so we know her mission to New Avalon was a success. Katrina will honor the pledge made by her father, and the three FedCom regiments will remain within our borders. But I believe the moment it is to her advantage to remove them—and that could happen as easily as one solid concession from Sun-Tzu—she will betray you."

Candace agreed. And though Simone Devon had secretly promised to refuse any order to abandon the Compact, she could not be as sure of her troops. The Federated Commonwealth was too fragile to predict anything at the moment.

"When will Simone be back?" Candace asked.

"Just over a month from now."

"I had hoped for more time, but if three months is what we have, we must decide how to proceed." Candace paused to consider Seng's earlier statements. "Unfortunately Sun-Tzu cannot afford to withdraw; he has leveraged too much of his state in this attempt to reclaim the Compact to quit now."

"And Kai?" Seng asked.

Candace did not try to stifle the pride she felt in her son. In all her children. "Betting against Kai is a dangerous thing," she said. "He will continue to act as he sees fit, just as Cassandra and Kuan Yin will. As Quentin has done from the beginning." She shook her head lightly. "But my nephew is not to be underestimated either. I can't mortgage the future of the Compact on what any one of my children *might* accomplish." She narrowed her eyes in thought. "What if I request more troops from Victor?"

Victor Steiner-Davion, the new Precentor Martial of ComStar, had been given control of the Star League Defense Force at First Lord Theodore Kurita's insistence. He'd promised as much aid as Candace would allow, though so far she'd drawn on that sparingly. The newest arrival, forces from Clan Nova Cat under SLDF colors, she had landed on St. Ives itself as a new garrison force and strategic reserve.

Seng shook her head. "We've looked at any number of combinations, but all of them would end up being the Rasalhague Solution. We're already cutting it fine with the troops you have allowed in. All situational models show the Compact becoming a ComStar protectorate within a year if we rely on much more."

"Unacceptable," Candace agreed. Not that she couldn't see herself answering to Victor, and certainly Kai would never see fault in his friend, but Candace knew her people. *They would never accept the Rasalhague Solution. If we are to survive, it must be on our own. A Capellan Solution.*

The silence stretched out, and finally Candace spoke her thoughts aloud. "At the Star League Conference, Tormano and I discussed the price the Compact would be forced to pay rather than bow to the whims of Sun-Tzu. I hadn't realized the bill would come due so soon." She read the tightening of her friend's face at the mention of her brother Tormano. "Don't worry, Caroline. I don't trust him either. But he's opposed to Sun-Tzu, and that's all that matters right now." She took another sip of her tea, letting it warm her. "I only wish he hadn't left so much of his Free Capella Movement tied up in the Tikonov troubles."

"Katrina's influence?" Caroline asked. "You think she demanded it as part of the price for his leave of absence?"

"No." Candace folded her hands into her lap. "He would not allow Katrina to blackmail him so easily. More likely he volunteered before she could demand it. That would place her in the position to request nothing new, *and* she would then owe *him* a favor." *If ever there was a master at playing both sides of the fence, it was Tormano.*

Candace rose from her chair, and Seng followed suit. "I don't envy you your decision, Candace," Caroline said softly, breaking formality. She rarely invoked the privilege her rank awarded, and Candace knew it to be a sign of her concern. "Capitulation to Sun-Tzu, or selling off a majority of the Compact to keep St. Ives alive. I hope you find a third alternative."

So do I. Candace walked gracefully from the room, never one to hurry. She nodded politely to servants and exchanged a few words with a palace guest, but inwardly her mind bent to the task of finding a different answer to the Compact's newest problem.

How to escape a three-month death sentence.

DropShip Jin-huáng-sè Ji-dàn
Ho-lu Lowlands, Denbar
Xin Sheng Commonality, Capellan Confederation

Major Warner Doles covered his agitation under a stiff military bearing as two armed guards escorted him into a lavishly decorated office within the Overlord DropShip *Jin-huáng-sè Ji-dàn.* It bothered him that someone had known exactly where his Lancers had set up their latest camp, and disturbed him more that they'd landed a forty-story-tall DropShip within a distance of ten kilometers. If the Third Reserves or the Legionnaires had tracked the vessel, he could expect company very soon. Only the papers delivered by unarmed messenger persuaded him to postpone breaking camp—a request to extend to the embassy all courtesies and verigraphed with the Duchess' seal.

So Doles was effectively under orders to cooperate, and be polite.

Traces of incense lingered in the office, and art of Asian influence decorated the walls. But he saw no clue to the identity of his host. No papers on the desk or holographs of family. An antique sword under glass caught the major's attention, and he drifted closer to study its craftsmanship. Again, obviously Asian in its origins, but slightly dissimilar to any sword Doles knew.

"A Han ring-pommel *dadao*," a voice said quietly from the door behind him.

Doles spun about, startled, then dropped back into a defensive stance. The first thing he noticed was the man's suit, an expensive white silk number perfectly tailored to his lean frame, all the more unusual for its being worn in a combat zone. The second was his host's features, and immediately Doles came to attention and saluted. "My apologies, Mandrinn Liao. You startled me."

Tormano Liao returned the salute in an offhand manner, not insultingly but certainly not worried about military protocol. Graying hair hinted at his age, mid-sixties if Warner remembered correctly, but the Mandrinn's face retained elements of his youth. Tormano stepped over to Doles' side, staring down into the glass case that held the sword.

"Ring-pommel *dadao*," he repeated, "a hand-crafted replica of a seventeenth-century Qing dynasty weapon. This one was made specifically for Her Ladyship, Aleisha Liao, third Chancellor of the Confederation."

The history intrigued Doles, and almost drew him under Tormano's spell. Then he recalled the DropShip and its location and shook himself back to a semblance of military alertness. "Mandrinn, forgive my interruption, but before we continue, would it be possible to relocate your DropShip? I'd rather that reconnaissance flights or satellites not pinpoint the location of the Lancers' current base camp."

Tormano glanced up, smiled, and moved to his desk, where he sat down with deliberate slowness. "They already know, Major. I told them exactly where I would be landing, and why, when I arranged for planetfall." He held up a hand to forestall the outburst he no doubt read on Doles' face. "They agreed to remain out of the area, considering what I offered them."

"And what was that?" Doles asked, partially awed and partially shocked by the Mandrinn's arrogance.

"I promised to take you off Denbar," the other man replied. "The Third Reserves particularly enjoyed the idea of your absence."

Doles' head spun. The conversation was moving too quickly. *As Tormano intends it to,* he thought. *The Mandrinn obviously enjoys his revelations, so cater to it.* "Why would I want to leave Denbar?" he asked.

"Because both you and I know that the Blackwind Lancers cannot make a real difference here. Denbar has slipped too far into the Confederation's grasp. I can take you where the Lancers can make a difference. I can also help you rebuild. You will be the core unit of the Free Capella Movement within the St. Ives Compact." He paused, dark blue eyes hardening. *"My unit."*

The Mandrinn's personal unit? Careful, Doles cautioned himself. *When something looks too good to be true, it usually is.* "Why the Lancers? We're in disgrace."

Tormano laughed softly, leaning back in his chair and steepling his fingers. "Ah, disgrace. A public perception based on time, events, and a modicum of ill fortune." He waved his hand in the air as if brushing the matter aside. "I assure you, given two months under my care, no one will ever remember the debacle on Hustaing." His dark eyes narrowed. "In fact, I have a gift for you. Two of them, actually. Perhaps they will lessen some of the guilt you *perceive* as your own."

While Doles believed him when he said the disgrace could be erased from the public mind—the Mandrinn was too self-assured not to know his own business—the offering of a gift concerned him. Gifts from the Liao family were not known for their pleasant nature. So he was shocked when Tormano stood and moved to the display case, removing the sword of Aleisha Liao. He presented it to Doles, pommel first.

The Han sword felt superbly balanced and deceptively light of weight. "Mandrinn, it is beautiful. But I cannot accept this."

Tormano returned to his desk and eased back into his leather chair. "You'll accept it because it is what I wish," he said with good humor. "Just as you'll accept my offer to join the Free Capella Movement because my sister, your Duchess, has already approved and that is also my wish." He watched Doles carefully. "The Blackwind Lancers are an old Capellan unit. They will give my Free Capella Movement more legitimacy in the eyes of Confederation citizens."

"And in the eyes of Compact citizens," Doles said, then immediately wished he'd left the thought unspoken. It wasn't Tormano's reaction that confirmed the wild guess, but rather his lack of one. No dismissive gestures. No offhand remarks. Just a cold, hard mask set into place over his face. The more Warner considered it, the more logical it seemed. *The Blackwind Lancers are a traditional St. Ives unit, at one point the personal regiment of Candace Liao herself. If the Mandrinn is seeking support anywhere by our endorsement, it is within the Compact.*

Leaning forward, Tormano pressed a button on the edge of the desk. Doles heard another door open, then realized it had been hidden behind a shoji panel. Someone entered, stepping around the panel, and was followed by a guard carrying a Hollyfeld assault rifle at the ready.

All other thoughts of Tormano's motivations and intent vanished as the major recognized his old commanding officer. "Tricia!" he exclaimed, the sword almost dropping from his grip. "Major Smithson! You escaped?"

Tricia Smithson smiled sadly at Doles, then her face hardened to cold fury as she spied Tormano seated behind the desk. Tormano drew a Nakjama laser pistol from a desk drawer, and nodded a dismissal to the guard.

"Not exactly," he said, answering the question Doles had put to his old CO. "But she is the second gift I mentioned. My agents captured her after Talon Zahn arranged her little 'jail break.' "

An icy cold crept through Doles. "What are you saying?" he asked, though Tormano's meaning seemed plain enough.

The Mandrinn smiled in false cheer. "Major Warner

Doles, permit me to introduce *Zhong-shao* Daqing of the Confederation Armed Forces." He shrugged. "Likely a trained Maskirovka assassin as well." In his explanation he'd allowed the gun to drift off Smithson, and with a start he quickly corrected his mistake before continuing. "You see, it was no accident that your Lancers jumped the border when they did and where they did. The *zhong-shao* was under orders to cause the incident."

"Is it true?" Doles asked softly.

Smithson, back straight and head high, nodded. *"Nà shì duì,"* she said in flawless Chinese. "That is so, Warner."

The button on Tormano's desk summoned the guard again, who came in, rifle leveled at the captive. Tormano set his Nakjama on the edge of the desk, then leaned back in enjoyment over the situation. "You see, Major Doles, the incident can easily be construed as a scheme of my nephew's. At *Zhong-shao* Daqing's trial for espionage—"

Tormano got no further. A weapon within reach, Smithson decided to take her chance. She spun on the guard, a snap-kick knocking the barrel of the rifle away, and then lunged for the pistol sitting on Tormano's desk. She snatched up the Nakjama, then rounded on Tormano Liao rather than the guard, intent on taking the elder Liao into death with her. Her only mistake was to disregard her previous XO.

Doles slashed once with Aleisha Liao's sword. Twice.

Tormano placing a hand on Doles' shoulder was the next thing he remembered. The Nakjama laser pistol lay on the edge of the desk, having been plucked from Smithson's grasp by the Mandrinn. Blood pooled on the metal deck— Tormano had pulled a hand-woven rug away from the spreading stain—and the guard stood over the cooling body.

"Probably just as well," Tormano Liao said. "A trial would have been a messy affair." He steered Doles toward the door.

Tormano Liao returned to his office after personally escorting Major Doles to the DropShip ramp. The body had been removed and the floor cleaned. He noticed a few specks of blood on the edge of his desk, near where the Nak-jama still rested, and filed away a mental note to demote whomever had been lax enough to miss those. Tormano expected excellence from those he allowed to serve him.

Still, everything appears to be proceeding smoothly, he decided. *The Blackwind Lancers will be mine—the entire regiment, not just this one battalion. And if I do not own Doles after today, I will soon.*

There had been a bad moment in the interview, though, where an off-chance comment by Doles had almost led him along a path of thought Tormano would rather not have pursued. The Lancers did give Free Capella a certain amount of credibility within the Confederation. That much was true, and certainly Tormano was not one to ignore an advantage. It was also true that they offered him more legitimacy within the Compact. *Someone will lose this war. Somewhere a Capellan throne might end up vacant. Only a fool could ignore that.*

Tormano picked up the laser pistol, ejected the spent clip and put in a fresh one from his desk, and then put the weapon away. *I am no fool.*

5

Sun-Tzu pressed himself deeper into the Celestial Throne, the carved wooden artifact that served as the seat of power in the Capellan Confederation, as if greater contact promoted greater control. Sandalwood incense burned in a nearby brazier, the normally soothing scent providing no comfort today. Frustration and anger raged within him, the tension in every muscle urging him to do something—anything—to work off the nervous energy building.

The impulse to lash out tempted him strongly, counseled by the continued presence of Romano Liao in his thoughts. He subdued it with only the greatest effort and then willed himself to appear calm before those gathered within the court. He frowned his displeasure, natural enough, and worked to drum the fingers of his right hand against the arm of the throne in a display of ease that he did not feel.

Sasha Wanli, Director of Sun-Tzu's Maskirovka, joined Talon Zahn today. Ion Rush was absent, attending to matters back in House Imarra's Sian stronghold. *Just as well since I prefer to keep him away from Kali.* Sun-Tzu's sister had chosen to attend. She remained back by the bronze-faced throne room doors, where the Chancellor's Death Commando guards had stood before he'd dismissed them from the meeting, her ash-gray gown blending into the light shadows. Sun-Tzu felt sure there would be a deep religious significance to her choosing to stand there, but failed to see it himself. *Of course, that is also a good sign, from my point of view. The day I can understand Kali, my worries triple.*

"No, Zahn," he finally said, voice hard and resolute. "I will not authorize any reduction in the forces fighting in the Chaos March. Those are Capellan worlds. They belong in the Confederation."

"Perhaps a temporary reduction, Chancellor?" Sasha asked. An elderly woman with iron-gray hair and of small stature, it might have been easy to underestimate her except for the look in her eyes. Forty-six years in the Mas-kirovka had left their mark, draining away any animation and leaving behind two dark diamond-cutters. "Just until we can uncover who is supporting the various resistance movements."

Although Sun-Tzu usually promoted a feeling of distrust between his top advisors—the better to keep them in competition and preventing any chance of betrayal, however slight—he was not surprised to hear Sasha seconding Talon Zahn. *She needs all the support she can find until her credibility has been rebuilt.*

"That is the Maskirovka's assignment," Sun-Tzu reminded her flatly. "It bears no relation to the Capellan Armed Forces." He regarded her with cool appraisal. "With all the mistakes and failures the Mask is already responsible for in the last year and a half, I would think that by now you would have shown some progress."

Sasha's hard gaze broke from the Chancellor's and sought the carpet. No one matched their will against the Chancellor, not in the Celestial Palace. "I will redouble our—my—efforts."

In the lull, Sun-Tzu quickly sought out Kali to find her still by the doors, idly toying with a long strand of her red-brown hair. One of the mistakes Sasha's people had made was in not guarding Sun-Tzu's sister closely enough. A comment made in another such meeting had prompted her to attempt to kill Ion Rush with an explosive device. *I do not need Kali's mania interfering again.*

Zahn moved a half-step forward, physically distancing himself from the Maskirovka failures, and Sasha, in particular. He had obviously understood the warning, though he continued his appeal. "Your cousin's raids are causing increased difficulty along the St. Ives Front, Celestial Wisdom. And in his latest raid against Sarna he escaped unscathed due to a"—he paused, obviously changing what he was about to say—"a *reluctance* on the part of the Sarna Supremacy Militia to engage him."

Talon Zahn did not make mistakes in his reports. He had wanted to draw Sun-Tzu's attention to the difficulty brewing in the Sarna Supremacy. The Sarna government cooperated with the Confederation only because of the stranglehold Sun-Tzu had on their food supply. *So, in other words, the Sarnese allowed Kai to decimate the Confederation's occupation regiment, hoping that he will cause enough trouble that they can resurrect their independent Chaos March nation.*

"Kai Allard-Liao must be stopped, Chancellor." Zahn clasped his hands behind his back. "Until that happens, there will be no major advances in the St. Ives conflict."

Sun-Tzu Liao retained his composure with difficulty. When he spoke, his voice began as a whisper and crawled upward in volume only slowly. "It is the sovereign's duty to decide to attack and then respond to the needs of his generals," he said, paraphrasing the *Art of War.* "It is the general's duty to attack and, if not interfered with by the sovereign, to win battles. Now, I have given you everything you have asked for, which you guaranteed would be enough to take the Compact *and* the Chaos March. If Kai Allard-Liao were dropping onto the world of Sian itself, *Sang-jiang-jun* Zahn, I would expect you to turn him back without a single trooper more than you've already been allotted."

Sun-Tzu leaned far forward in the throne, spearing his senior general with a hard gaze. "Is-that-clear?" he asked, snapping off each word.

No one in the throne room could have doubted Sun-Tzu's anger, though his voice never rose beyond that of normal conversation. Sun-Tzu did not even bother to check Kali's position. If she had drawn a pistol right then and shot Zahn dead, he wouldn't have cared.

For the first time ever, Sun-Tzu thought he detected a trace of fear behind Talon Zahn's eyes. A similar fear that Sun-Tzu recalled from times spent in his mother's company.

"Yes, Celestial Wisdom," the general said calmly, as if answering the simplest of questions.

Sitting at the desk in his private office, Sun-Tzu pretended to relax under the ministrations of his fiancée, Isis Marik. Though her father, Thomas Marik, Captain-General of the Free Worlds League, continued to postpone the date of their marriage, Sun-Tzu's engagement to Isis had never been more than a political move. That did not keep her from trying, even with the engagement moving into its tenth year. Now Isis stood behind him, kneading his shoulders and patiently working through the knotted muscles. The massage eased some physical discomfort, but did little for Sun-Tzu's peace of mind.

"I lost my temper," he admitted in response to her question. That she did not falter in her massage or respond immediately told Sun-Tzu that she had already talked with Talon Zahn or Sasha Wanli. After her ordeal on Hustaing, caught in the first incident that Sun-Tzu had used to start the conflict, he'd granted her request for access to his advisors. A sound decision regardless, since Isis had demonstrated in the past that she possessed a solid intellect and often saw solutions or dangers that Sun-Tzu himself did not.

"That happens," she finally said, her tone light though still revealing her concern.

Sun-Tzu shook his head. "Not to me it doesn't." *I can't afford to lose control. Ever.* Romano lurked too close to the surface these days. *Can't you see that?*

She stopped kneading his shoulders, stepped around and perched herself against the corner of his desk. She'd pulled her chestnut brown hair back with a clasp, and wore the silk robes currently in high style on Sian. "So what do you intend to do about Kai?"

Kill him, if I can, Sun-Tzu answered silently. And those were *not* his mother's words, though certainly she might have echoed them. Kai would forever be the greatest threat to his position as Chancellor, despite any self-avowed denial that he did not want the Celestial Throne. *Neutralize him, if I cannot.*

"I'll think of something," was all he said. *If I am to regain control of this war, I will have to.*

Isis smiled encouragement, then said hesitantly, "I heard from my father today." Long pause. "He and his wife send their regards."

Which is all he has sent me in some time. "Did he answer my request for aid to retake the Chaos March?" he asked, deliberately skipping the usual pleasantries. A few regiments striking in from the Free Worlds League could be all he needed to break something loose in that stagnating conflict.

Isis frowned at his unusual lack of subtlety, then shook her head. "Not as such. But he did agree to my request, our request, that he visit Sian."

Sun-Tzu knew better. Isis hoped that on a formal state visit to the Confederation her father would have no choice but to finally approve their marriage. Thomas Marik had delayed for years, finding one excuse after another to prevent placing Sun-Tzu in line for the Free Worlds League throne. Then his consort Sherryl Halas had borne him an heir and, after their marriage, another. Thomas owned no more excuses, but still the marriage did not occur.

"Did he set a date for his visit?" he asked, feigning both interest and cheer.

"We'll figure that out in our next few messages," Isis said. "But within the month I'll have a date confirmed. June, I hope."

Sun-Tzu detected the note of disappointment that crept

into Isis' voice at the end. She did not believe it either. And why should she? Thomas rarely allowed her to return home anymore, too wrapped up in his new family. *He'll cancel again,* Sun-Tzu thought.

Then he said so out loud, suddenly tired of the game the three of them had been playing for too many years. *My requests, Thomas' promises, and Isis trying to exist somewhere in between because it's all she has left to her.*

A spark of fury lit in Isis' eyes that he would be so blatant about their little game. "He may not," she said, trying to return to the masquerade.

Sun-Tzu stood, leaned forward to brush his lips across her brow, and then put on a sorrowful voice. "Doesn't matter," he lied. He moved away. "It's late. Stay if you like, and we'll talk more about it in the morning."

He may even have meant it. But, then, on his way out his eyes flicked to the framed quote over his door, the Chinese script brushed out over bright white paper. He had put it there himself, as a reminder. *I go to war only when I am ready.* It taunted him with the war's recent lack of direction.

If Sun-Tzu would talk about anything on the morrow, it would be about how to retake control of the St. Ives conflict.

6

Autocannon fire chewed up the soft earth not five meters from the *Wraith*'s cockpit viewscreen. Glancing skyward, Aris Sung saw the shimmering flights of laser pulses as more BattleMechs traded intense fire. *Ty Wu Non's first mistake,* he thought, *was underestimating Cassandra Allard-Liao.* Shaking off the fall, he worked the foot pedals and control sticks to get his *Wraith* back on its feet.

Three weeks had passed since the fight for St. Loris had commenced, with House Hiritsu and the Panzer Brigade slowly beating back elements of the St. Loris Home Guard and Rubinsky's Light Horse. Suspiciously absent were the Second St. Ives Lancers. With the Confederation's solid base of operations on the island nation of Pardray and too much territory for the Compact forces to cover on the continent of Layting, large gains had been made. But every meter of territory required guarding, and now Cassandra's Second St. Ives Lancers had entered the fray with a flanking assault driving deep into Confederation-controlled territory. Two companies of House warriors and another two from the newly arrived Third Confederation Reserves now faced off with a St. Ives Lancers battalion supported by two companies of Home Guard.

Capellans all, Aris thought, the idea clenching his stomach into knots.

In the sauna-like atmosphere of his cockpit, he wiped a sweat-slick hand across the outside of his cooling vest and then returned it to the control stick. He finished bringing the *Wraith* upright, then walked it backward into a thick stand of cedar and fir to evade the stream of light autocannon fire that chased him but failed to connect. Scarlet darts hammered out from his pulse lasers and into a Home Guard *Pegasus* hovertank that had strayed too close, the energy eating away at the vehicle's armor, spattering the ground with molten drops. Then Aris spotted the *Cestus* again, its squat profile and smooth lines easily recognizable in a tangle of 'Mechs and armor pushing forward from the north. *Cassandra, and if she falls, the Lancers fall with her.*

"*Ostscout* alert," a voice hammered into his ear, loud in the confines of his neurohelmet. "Aris, clear!"

Aris cut in his jump jets, sending his *Wraith* rocketing skyward on jets of superheated plasma. He lit off without taking the fraction of a second to verify off his own HUD and even before he'd recognized the voice of *Pai-zhang* Raven Clearwater, a lance commander and his company's number two officer. The *Ostscout,* a Home Guard 'Mech equipped with a TAG spotting laser, slipped into the Hiritsu lines from a small ravine to the east. Capable of directing massive artillery strikes, a TAG-equipped 'Mech was nothing to take lightly and Aris would have chosen to evade no matter who had sent the warning. Or so he kept telling himself, though after this third avoidance of Cassandra Allard-Liao, the excuse was wearing thin.

Angling for a new stand of trees and realizing he would fall short, Aris feathered the jump jets out early to drop down behind a small hill. From the top of his arc he saw Raven Clearwater's *Huron Warrior* move up from the backfield to engage the TAG-equipped *Ostscout* she had warned him about, sniping at it with a PPC and Gauss rifle combination, but the light 'Mech avoided her and sped away down the Hiritsu line.

Zhang-si Sainz in his *Cataphract* did not clear fast enough, and two artillery barrages fell on his location. Earth geysered up from around his heavy 'Mech. The *Cataphract* fell, a direct hit by one artillery strike blasting open its right side and touching off the autocannon ammunition stored there while the other barrage tore away the right leg. The *Ostscout* ran for the safety of its own lines, not willing to chance another run and already having taken down a 'Mech twice its own weight.

A fresh wave of heat washed through the *Wraith*'s cockpit as it landed, the jump-jet load on the fusion reactor driving Aris' heat scale deep into the red. At fifty-five tons, the *Wraith* relied on mobility over armor for staying power on the battlefield. Gasping, Aris fought to breathe in the scalding air. He knew he was jumping too much, but he had continued to do it at every opportunity in order to limit his weapons fire. He wouldn't lie to himself about that anymore, not after watching one of his warriors take a devastating hit meant for him.

Aris couldn't remember when he'd first noticed a resistance to firing on Compact MechWarriors. Possibly he'd felt twinges back on Hustaing, facing the Blackwind Lancers, and certainly later on Denbar. But really it had to have been on the killing fields of Nashuar, the battles so much like this one, with no quarter asked or given as both sides sought to claim their quota in Capellan blood. And, too often, with civilians being caught in the crossfire.

I am a House warrior! My duty is to serve the will of the House Master, who obeys the orders of the Chancellor. Should it matter that my opponents—my enemies—were once Confederation citizens?

It shouldn't have, but it did. *Because they will be Confederation citizens again. And if this war isn't about bringing the Capellan nation back together, then what is it about?* All Aris could be sure of was that it wasn't his place to second-guess Chancellor Liao. *You don't have to understand why. Just act!*

The order screamed out within Aris' mind, and he instantly throttled his *Wraith* into a run and broke from the cover of the small hill. It felt like jumping back into a river of chaos, with swirling eddies of smoke and bursts of weapons fire thick and coming one after the other. Aris swallowed against the dry, metallic tang of the cockpit's recycled air, then found his best command voice.

"Clearwater and McDaniels, leapfrog your lances forward," he ordered. "First Lance on me." He cut hard to the left to swing around a burning *Victor,* avoiding two PPC arcs that had tried to track in on his *Wraith.* "We break a hole in the Compact line, and the Reserves hold it open."

The impromptu strategy showed every sign of working. With the battle reduced to a medium-range slugging match, the Compact forces appeared ill-prepared to face a full charge. Aris led his units in where the Home Guard forces joined up with the leading flank of St. Ives Lancers, hoping to exploit the natural divisiveness that existed between units. He had no thoughts beyond putting an end to this current battle of attrition. Still, he couldn't help but wince at the death of another opposing warrior when one of Raven Clearwater's Gauss slugs caved in the head of a Compact *Helios.*

Then he saw the *Cestus,* and all other considerations became secondary.

As her left flank began to crumble, Major Cassandra Allard-Liao had obviously pulled elements from her leading edge around to face the threat. *Shiao-zhang* Ty Wu Non, whose assault company had been holding that portion of the field through brute force and their 'Mech's massive armor reserves, now pressed forward as well, though at a much slower pace. Limited by the slower speed of Non's *Yu Huang* and several other designs, they fell further afield of Aris' company and the Reserves surging forward behind his drive.

The concentrated firepower of the St. Ives Lancers now began to tell on the Warrior House. Richard Smith's *Thunder* went down under a barrage of missile fire. Raven's *Huron Warrior* stumbled under a massive onslaught of lasers and autocannon, keeping to its feet but her momentum spent and her BattleMech's armor more memory than fact. And Cassandra's Gauss fire wreaked havoc all on its own, snapping arms off whole and punching through armor to smash away at internal supports. A Regulator hovertank took one against its skirt, the slug smashing away at the fans beneath. At better than one hundred kilometers per hour the vehicle tore itself apart against the ground. Aris' *Wraith* caught one as well, the blued-steel machine taking the silvery blur slug square in the chest. The last of his armor rained down to the ground in shards and splinters as the slug ricocheted off his gyro and threw a heavy lurch into the *Wraith*'s step. For the second time in as many minutes, Aris rode his BattleMech to the ground.

Thrown hard against his couch and restraining harness, Aris nearly blacked out. He held onto consciousness with grim will, using the *Wraith*'s arms to lever up off the ground. For a brief second he believed that somehow he'd gotten turned around, as his HUD showed several of the Third Reserves well past his position. Then he realized they were in between his company and the St. Ives Lancers, driving forward unsupported. A chill washed through him despite the cockpit's residual heat, and he brought his *Wraith* back to its feet firing.

Protected by House Hiritsu's drive forward, the Reserves had managed to escape largely unscathed. Now a demi-company of six light to medium-weight BattleMechs, all older designs but still lethal, threw themselves forward with no heed for their own safety as they fought to reach Cassandra's *Cestus*.

Aris couldn't be sure who led the run, so he merely shouted into his comm, "Third Reserves, abort. Pull back!"

But the lighter machines were too fast. It was too late when the order went out and Aris knew it. Home Guard and Lancer BattleMechs closed in around them, cutting the Reserves off and preventing any further breach of their lines by Aris' warriors, who now lacked the bulk to support a renewed drive. Ty Wu Non ordered Aris back with his people.

Four of the Reserves managed to come point-blank

against Cassandra's *Cestus*. But where they had only themselves to rely upon, Cassandra could call in the firepower of an entire company. And she did. In a furious exchange of weapons, all four 'Mechs went down, and Aris paused his fighting withdrawal long enough to see if the small unit had managed to bring down the Compact commander. But the *Cestus* stirred, regaining its feet and standing up to preside over the fallen BattleMech corpses.

Aris slammed one fist into the arm of his control couch, frustrated and angry but unable to say exactly why. Was it because they broke formation and died needlessly, or because they stole his final charge and so prevented him from doing the same? He couldn't say. The emotions and thoughts that had driven him to the charge had faded or fled, so there could be no answer but to accept that more warriors had died, and that he had led the way.

"All units fall back," Ty Wu Non ordered over the general frequencies. "Rendezvous at the village of Chingdasun." Aris noticed the lights on his comm panel change, indicating that the House Master was now speaking with lance leaders and higher only. "I don't want any more warriors seeking their hopeless battle today, so watch the Reserves carefully."

Is it just the Reserves who need watching? Aris wondered. The thought left behind a wave of uncertainty as he continued to wrestle with his own heart. *Is that truly the end I seek?*

=== 7 ===

Hai Fen-ling
Xin Singapore Province, Indicass
Xin Sheng Commonality, Capellan Confederation
10 April 3062

Sang-shao Ni Tehn Dho wearily perched himself up on the foot of his *Victor* while junior officers of the Hustaing Warriors went about the post-combat business of assessing damage to their units and estimating salvage recovery. The eighty-ton assault 'Mech towered over him, its head poking up into the canopy of Indicass' Black Forest. Sunlight filtered down through the roof of thick boughs and wide leaves, a green glow perforated by the occasional pure beam. The green wash of light colored everything. *Very Liao,* the elderly regimental commander thought, easing back to rest against the BattleMech's ankle.

He'd moved off to one side of the earlier battle site, hoping for the shade of a tree left undamaged by the firefight—a promise of better times to come. Out of his cockpit now, he saw that the oak next to which he'd parked his 'Mech had caught some autocannon fire, the slugs having chewed up a few of the lower limbs. Also, the light breeze that blew in from the direction of the battlefield wafted toward him the scent of scorched vegetation. *Not as nice as I'd hoped for, but better than I have any right to expect.* The contraction of cooling metal pinged and rang above him even as his own bones creaked and popped in protest of the last few months' strenuous pace. Doh closed his eyes and sent them empty promises of rest soon enough.

My eternal rest, very likely.

"Sang-shao?" a voice interrupted his repose, young and strong and eager.

Doh fought down irritation, not wanting to begrudge the warrior his youth. Especially one of his better men. He opened one eye to regard *Sao-shao* Daniel Evans. Commander of the Warriors' company known unofficially as the Arcade Rangers, Evans was an overachiever usually one step ahead of other company commanders.

"What is it, *sao-shao*?"

"I've completed my evaluation," Evans said, voice neutral but unable to keep the pride out of his eyes. "The Rangers suffered no loss of BattleMechs, of course, and we're down only sixteen percent, considering armor and heat sinks and a few destroyed weapons."

"So what are your people doing now?" Doh asked, knowing he would object to the answer but also knowing he'd probably let it slide.

At least Evans had the good manners to seem hesitant. "They're painting their latest scores onto their 'Mechs."

Doh stifled a groan, then rubbed his hands briskly over his face. The Arcade Rangers had started off as a lance recruited from a Hustaing college, their main recommendation being regular attendance at a local amusement center that offered simplified BattleMech simulators. Surprisingly, their cavalier attitude of treating combat as a game had worked for them. They even kept "score" of their missions, their points calculated out of some complex set of rules that *Sang-shao* Doh had given up on understanding. He'd set Evans over them in hopes that he could tame them down a little, though the reverse had actually happened.

Don't argue with success, Doh cautioned himself. "How many kills did your warriors account for, Danny?" he asked.

"Six," Evans promptly replied. "Two tanks, scrapped. Four 'Mechs, with good salvage from three."

Not bad, considering. "And how many points did you personally earn?" Doh asked, leaning forward with casual interest.

"Six hundred and seventy-five. I only received—" Evans broke off, reddened, then said with a shrug, "—I only received half credit on the Vedette tank since it was out of ammo."

These kids will have to learn we're not playing a game here. Doh had hoped that the year spent fighting on Denbar might have solved the problem. And if not then, the last few months against the remnants of Indicass Home Guard and the Legers. *But few of them have a solid military grounding to begin with, recruited out of academies and small colleges or called up from the Hustaing Home Guard Reserves. And it doesn't matter how much combat time they see, so long as they keep showing progress.*

At sixty, Doh knew first-hand what it was like to be on the other side of the mirror. The losses in the Fourth Succession War, and a desire to recoup them, still burned within him. *But would I really wish such a time on these kids, just to instill a little more discipline and appreciation for proper Confederation Armed Forces decorum?*

Doh leaned back again, trying to ignore the pain in his lower back. "Thank you, Danny. Pass along my appreciation to"—he'd almost said "your children"—"to your warriors. Dismissed." Then he closed his eyes again. *Would I wish such a time on them?*

Thankfully, that was a question that didn't require an answer. Yet.

Hazlet, Nashuar
St. Ives Compact

With Hazlet's small military hospital overflowing, the Home Guard had moved its more critical cases into the city to Evergreen Memorial. With only an hour to go before

Nevarr's daily briefing, Maurice Fitzgerald had run in to visit the latest admission.

David Sherman looked pale, even against the white sheets of his bed. The astringent scent of cleaners, common to the halls, were especially powerful in the hospital rooms. Fitz rubbed at his nose and caught the ghost of a smile from his old lancemate.

"Hey, Prowler," the bedridden man said, calling Fitzgerald by the nickname he'd worn as a sergeant in the Home Guard Armor Corps.

A nickname the entire lance adopted, Fitzgerald remembered. That had been in the time after his failure to become a MechWarrior, but before then-Captain Nevarr had offered him a new position. He still recalled how nervous he'd been, responsible for three other lives. Especially after his training disaster. Less than a year ago, he marveled. Hard to believe.

"Hello, David," he said, returning the greeting.

"Since you're here, I guess we won, yeah?" The dark-haired man was still a year shy of thirty, but the lines under his eyes and the heaviness to his voice belonged to someone much older. "I bowed out early. Sorry."

Fitz managed a smile, though he didn't feel up to it. Like so many things these days, he was just too tired. "I don't know if I'd call it a win," he said, thinking of the burned-out ruins of Yei Hou, the village north of Hazlet, and hating the Nightriders' armor commander who'd loaded infernos into his Pegasus' short-ranged missile launcher. One missed shot, and a village in flames.

"I heard," his friend said softly, grimacing as if in pain. "Must have been bad. Guess I was already in the rescue chopper by then."

Fitzgerald sat on the edge of the bed, conscious that there was too much room for him to sit. *The war claims its price from soldiers same as it does from the Compact, a piece at a time. David paid with his leg last year. Why did he have to sign back on?*

"Well, we've kept them off the plains again. Maybe that's something," he offered. "We've drawn the line at Hazlet, and the Cavalry seems willing to meet us on it. Sorry it cost you your arm." There it was, the apology he'd come to say and thrown out in the middle of conversation as if trying to hide it.

"What's this, a 'Mech jock feeling sorry for someone who drives tin cans around?" David managed a real smile this time, obviously touched by his old CO's attention. "I'd have taken odds on that happening."

Fitzgerald appreciated David's attempt at humor, but it didn't change the fact that he felt more responsible than usual over this. *I only accepted Nevarr's offer to become a MechWarrior when my armor lance broke apart through attrition. If I'd known how David would come back after the first operation, I'd have . . . what?* What could he have done actually? He'd become a MechWarrior hoping he could make a bigger difference in Hazlet's fight against the Confederation. *No, I wanted to make the difference. Haven't I learned by now that there's no such thing? Not in this war, at any rate.*

Some of Fitz' pain must have showed on his face. "Don't go beating yourself up over this, Fitz," David said. "We all know the score out there. Hell, I could've stayed out of this after the last injury. But I chose not to." He gave his old CO a hard stare. "*I* chose not to," he repeated.

Fitz nodded, knowing but not really understanding. "Why?" he asked.

David exhaled noisily. "Because I wanted to hurt the Confederation." He suddenly sounded small and weak. "Not for Nashuar or for the Compact, but for what they did to me." He laughed, a touch of madness dancing in his eyes. "You know what's really funny? I didn't even mind the return of the Confederation when this first started. But the last six months . . ." He sank back into the bed, looking very frail. "I just didn't care who got in my way."

Fitzgerald didn't know what to say to that. This war had lost its focus. Did anyone remember when they'd lost control? He shook his head, as much in commiseration with David as to answer his own question.

"Doesn't matter," David said. He glanced at the clock.

"Nevarr must be about to give his daily briefing. You better get out of here."

Standing up, Fitzgerald offered his old lancemate a supportive nod. "It does matter," he said, trying to offer his friend some consolation. "You cared more than some. More than the butcher who set fire to Yei Hou."

David flinched, pain etched into his features. Knowing there was more to say, Fitz turned to leave. His hand was on the door when David spoke again.

"Hey, Fitz." David wasn't looking at him, but staring up at the ceiling with a pained look. A few long seconds dragged by, and then he started to weep. "This one isn't so funny. But the truth is, I was carrying infernos yesterday as well." David's gaze flicked to Fitz for brief second, then he turned his head away. "I just never got the chance to use them."

Had he waited there another hour, Fitzgerald doubted he would ever have found anything to say. Without another word, he went out of the room, closing the door quietly behind him.

8

Celestial Palace
Zi-jin Chén, Sian
Sian Commonality, Capellan Confederation
14 April 3062

Isis Marik found her fiancée's throne room a bit Spartan, but in keeping with Sun-Tzu's personality. *Everything with a purpose, nothing simply for ostentation's sake.*

A few simple charcoal sketches decorated the walls, all skillfully rendered by the Chancellor's own hand. Not many people knew that. An ancient suit of Chinese armor stood near the dais, possibly to remind Sun-Tzu of his ancient Asian heritage. From the Nán Bei Cháo Dynasties, he'd told her, speaking of the armor. Though of course he'd told her a lot of things over the years, not all of them true. A plush carpet of red ran from the dais to the bronze-faced doors, the runner shot through with gold thread since his time as First Lord of the Star League. *Gold, the prerogative of ancient Chinese emperors.*

The Celestial Throne itself was a magnificent work of art. Handcarved from mahogany, the brown and red wood grain promised strength and character. *Though, until Sun-Tzu that promise was rather weighted toward character.* The Chinese zodiac wheel formed the upper backrest, another tie to the Liao Chinese heritage and a reminder of the diverse nature of humankind.

And on the Celestial Throne sat Sun-Tzu Liao, Chancellor of the Capellan Confederation.

Isis nodded formally. She knew of the most recent audience he'd had with Ion Rush and Sasha Wanli and was leery of his current temperament. Not that she feared him. Isis saw beyond his parentage, mad Romano and her Maskirovka consort Tsen Shang. But Isis did wish to *help* him, and to do that she would have to make sure he recognized her as his ally today, not as part of the opposition. *He's done so much, and together we can do so much more. If he will listen.*

Interest at her approach flared in Sun-Tzu's jade green eyes, though of course he meant for her to see it. By tradition, the Chancellor would recognize her before conversation was allowed, and one did not break tradition easily in the Celestial Palace. But today there was no verbal sparring as Sun-Tzu came right to the point that was on *her* mind, as if reading her thoughts.

"They want me to pull back from the Chaos March," he said without preamble. "Concentrate my forces against the Compact to bring that conflict to a speedy conclusion."

"I know, beloved. Ion Rush spoke with me earlier." Isis kept her own voice calm and reassuring. "I wish I could help."

Sun-Tzu nodded. "Did he also tell you that the Mask discovered that at least part of the Chaos March resistance is coming out of Word of Blake factions? Some of them competing factions, in fact?"

"Yes. He said they couldn't be sure how much was deliberately set against you, and how much the side effect of a proxy battle for power within Word of Blake."

Sun-Tzu leaned back deeper into his throne. "Then tell me what to do, Isis." He watched her sharply. "What you would have me do?"

Another test, or an actual request for advice? Either way, it didn't change her answer. She shrugged. "Make peace with your aunt Candace, or write off the Chaos March for another few years."

"You can recommend peace with my aunt, after your own ordeal on Hustaing? After the loss of so many Capellan lives since?"

Her time caught in the conflict on Hustaing, nearly captured or killed a few times over, was not something Isis preferred to dwell upon. Especially since that conflict had opened the doors for the invasion of the Compact. *But my endangerment there opened doors for me as well, to become more involved in Confederation politics, and so I must offer sound, unbiased advice.* "It seems that it must be one way or the other," she said.

"Always it must be one way or the other," Sun-Tzu returned, his tone hard and unforgiving. "Always either capitulation or compromise, if you are the Confederation. Give up Chesterton. Give up Tikonov. Give up St. Ives. Vilify the Confederation when it fights for its very survival. Recognize Chaos March realms as legitimate states rather than allow the Confederation to reclaim what only rightfully belongs to it." He raised his right hand from the arm of his throne and clenched his hand into a fist. "No more," he promised.

"But if you were to solve either conflict," Isis persisted, "the entire knot pulls free." She stepped forward, a touch of pleading to her voice now. "Think of how you would then look to the other leaders of the Inner Sphere. To your own people." *To me,* she finished silently

Sun-Tzu blinked a look of puzzlement at her. "How I would look?" He cocked his head to one side, then said again, "How *I* would look," as if testing the phrase. "What about the Confederation?"

"Your Confederation wins when you win." Isis hoped she wasn't counseling acquiescence. "You've been the strong leader your people needed. You gave them someone to follow, in whom they could believe."

"This has never been about me," Sun-Tzu said, jaw set firm. "My people needed to believe in themselves, in the Confederation. Not me. *That* I already had."

He stood and stepped down from the dais to face her. A melancholy look stole over his face, almost pitying. He reached out. The last three fingernails on each hand had been grown out in an affectation his father had worn, carbon-reinforced and razor-sharp. A potentially deadly affectation. He now trailed the backs of the nails on his right hand down Isis' cheek tenderly.

"Goodbye, Isis," he said softly. "Go home."

The abrupt dismissal confused her. She reached up to take his hand, but he withdrew it. "All right," she said. "I'll return to the mansion tonight. But please consider—"

"Not your mansion," Sun-Tzu interrupted, his voice losing its soft edge. "Go home. Back to your League. You will never fit in here. Never know what it means to be a Capellan." He shook his head. "Tell your father that he wins our game."

Isis stepped back in shock at the soft-spoken yet harsh words. "This is not about politics, Sun-Tzu."

He laughed, without any real humor. "If this was not political, I'd have long ago taken issue with your father over the insult of a ten-year engagement."

"Is that what you're angry about? The marriage? All or nothing?" Isis gestured wildly, trying to stave off the icy nausea taking root in her stomach. "Then bring in your priest or Zen monk or whatever and we will marry despite my father's lack of approval. The Confederation is my home."

"If the Confederation was your home," Sun-Tzu said, a harder note of pity in his voice, "you would not have to ask who would marry us."

Isis could hardly breathe for the sudden feeling of desperation that overcame her. *This is not happening. He is angry and confused, but cannot mean what he is saying.* "You would break our engagement because within your realm I would place you first? Because my feelings—"

Again he interrupted. "Nothing comes before the Confederation," he said, nearly shouting.

In all her time on Sian, Isis had never seen Sun-Tzu so close to naked anger.

"Not me or my feelings, and certainly not those of an out-sider," he went on. "If it would leave the Confederation stronger, I would not hesitate to sacrifice my life, or yours, or the lives of every person on Sian if the reward was great enough."

"What do you want of me?" she asked, nearly a whisper, not trusting her voice.

"Haven't I made it clear?" Sun-Tzu asked, calmer but his anger still apparent in the flatness of his tone. "I want you out of the palace, off my world, and out of *my* Confederation." He gestured toward the doors and moved off ahead of her, not bothering to see if she followed. "I'll clear your DropShip through the outbound checkpoints and give your JumpShip a destroyer escort to my borders."

The room spun drunkenly for a few seconds. "But, where do I go?" Isis thought of her father's cold distancing over the last several years. "I can't go back to the Free Worlds League."

Sun-Tzu stopped at the doors and turned, his face blanked of any expression. It was worse than anger, or loathing, or pity. It said that she did not matter at all. "Then go to New Avalon and plague Katrina. Or try the Draconis Combine—Victor certainly found a life there in exile."

Isis felt her world caving in, collapsing over her. Nothing seemed real, least of all the feelings she thought she'd had for this man. *What I have worked toward for ten years, five of those here in Sian. Gone. But the Confederation has become my home, much as I have one.* She had yet to move, and the throne room was not so large, but already Sun-Tzu seemed kilometers distant to her.

Don't send me away, she pleaded silently. "Sun-Tzu, don't do this. I can still be of use to you and your realm."

Sun-Tzu turned away and reached to open the latch on the door.

"Your usefulness to my realm ended," he said, low and cruel, "the day you made it off Hustaing alive."

9

Light Horse Post 6
Layting, St. Loris
St. Ives Compact
22 April 3062

Cassandra Allard-Liao shaded her eyes from the late morning sun, searching the map of Layting that Tamas Rubinsky had spread over a large table outside his tent. Large steel weights forged into horses' heads, like giant knights for the chess board, held down the map edges. The morning's chill was finally burning off, so with a last sip of her tea—provided by Tamas and laced with something a bit stronger—she regretfully placed the cup aside, well away from the map.

"You have decided on eastern route?" Tamas asked, walking back to the table and taking in Cassandra's latest changes.

Small metal miniatures representing the BattleMech forces on both sides of the St. Loris conflict were scattered about the map surface, silver figures representing entire companies while gold ones represented battalions. Cassandra reached down and repositioned the miniature for her Lancers' first battalion, judging the small change to her plan of attack with a critical eye.

She nodded hesitantly. "I think so. It's longer, but it places me firmly in the Confederation rear lines where I can cause the most damage."

Glancing up, she saw that Tamas held two plates with cinnamon pastries on them and smiled her gratitude. He'd inherited from his father his ruggedly handsome features and Slavic accent, both of which she found attractive. Also like his father Marko, commander of the mercenary Cossacks' Light Horse regiment, Tamas owned to a certain warm hospitality off the battlefield. *The Cossacks assail life itself, fighting hard but taking time to remind themselves why they fight at all. They know when to quit and simply enjoy the moment.*

"You read my mind," Cassandra said, knowing Tamas would read the lie and grateful for his attention to such details. She accepted a plate. *Real china,* she noted, *provided in the middle of a war zone.* The cinnamon roll had been warmed, and the heavy spices almost brought tears to the eyes. *I don't want to know how he does it, I only hope he doesn't stop.*

Tamas waited until Cassandra had enjoyed several bites, then reached out and moved all the Confederation forces back toward their own rear lines by several hundred kilometers. He smiled, "Now what does that do to your plan?"

Cassandra frowned, wiped some sugary glaze from her lips, and set her plate aside. "I place more confidence in our intelligence reports." She studied the new challenge Tamas had put before her. *So what if their front-line forces are closer to Pardray than I think?* "I think I'm all right. I left room for maneuvering. At most, this would force me to withdraw only a few hours early."

Tamas nodded. "I think so too," he said, making some more minor adjustments to the map. "Your plan looks very solid."

Tamas had edged the silver *Enforcer,* the piece representing his own company of Rubinsky's Light Horse, closer to the front lines and into the eastern flank of Little Richard's Panzer Brigade. *Where he can possibly punch through to offer support, if the Panzer Brigade doesn't fall on him with a full battalion.* She reached out and tipped the *Enforcer* over with a casual flick. "With any luck, I can sever their supply lines and cause massive reversals."

Frowning at the map, and his overturned piece, Tamas nodded. "Very like what your brother is doing to St. Ives Front," he noted.

"Kai has the right idea," Cassandra said. "We won't win this conflict from the defensive position." She sighed her frustration. "And truth be told, Tamas, I'm tired of reacting instead of acting."

"You hope to do same as Kai Allard-Liao, here along the Teng Front?"

Cassandra shrugged, certain that her noncommittal answer fooled no one. She picked up a new piece, a Confederation DropShip, and rolled it within her hand in an effort to channel her frustration. *Kai is operating in the Confederation itself! Mother has me stalemating the Teng Front.* In her heart Cassandra knew she was being unfair; her brother had proven himself far more the general than she ever had. Yet. *Maybe I'm not in Kai's league—after all, who is?—but I know I can do more.* "I wouldn't mind," she finally admitted, hearing the wistful note in her own voice.

Tamas' laugh, full and throaty, shocked her from her brief touch of melancholy. "You will give Sun-Tzu nightmares enough, Cassandra."

Having served alongside the Cossacks on several worlds, Cassandra knew enough not to be insulted at the rough humor. *And they aren't laughing at you, so long as you laugh with them.* She grinned, and then managed a few short chuckles, though she had to work harder at it than Tamas did. "Come," she said, grossly imitating his accent and so gaining a slight measure of revenge, "we go inspect supplies. Make sure have enough."

She set the Confederation DropShip figure down on the map, took Tamas by the elbow, and guided him away from the table.

Behind her, the Confederation vessel loomed dangerously close to her own Second St. Ives Lancers.

Qining Plateau
Qining Province, Indicass
Xin Sheng Commonality, Capellan Confederation

Standing in the shadow of an *Overlord* Class DropShip, the skyscraper behemoth a lonely monument set down in the middle of Indicass' Qining Plateau, Major Warner Doles barely blinked in acknowledgment when an infantry squad laid the two body bags nearby. He simply continued to supervise the loading of salvage. Two BattleMechs from the Blackwind Lancers wrestled a mostly intact *JagerMech* up the DropShip ramp while a third followed, carrying the remains of the *JagerMech*'s severed leg. A quarter-kilometer distant a team of technicians attacked the ruined frame of a *Cataphract,* while much further afield Doles' sparse infantry assets continued to sweep the plateau for the missing Hustaing Warriors pilot.

If the MechWarrior was found, Doles gave him a fifty-fifty chance of suffering a fatal "accident" before being returned to the base camp. News of Smithson's death and her *possible* compliance with the Confederation—Doles had at least managed to confine it to rumor—had enraged his warriors to the point where his control remained tenuous.

"So why didn't you request marines from the Drop-Ship?" he asked himself out loud, the sound of his own voice strange in his ears. He knew the answer. *Because that would entail dealing with* him.

Doles ran the fingers of one hand back through his brush-cut brown hair. He did not believe that fate had brought him against the Hustaing Warriors here on Indicass. The same unit Sun-Tzu Liao had built with the equipment originally stolen from his Blackwind Lancers. The unit that had helped take Denbar, homeworld to the Lancers second battalion since Denbar had been settled.

No, not fate. Mandrinn Tormano Liao.

So far, the Mandrinn's generosity appeared to know no bounds. General supplies. New warriors and a few new 'Mechs. *Even a DropShip!* Doles glanced up the massive side of the vessel, his feelings mixed to see the blue ax-head insignia of the Blackwind Lancers riding up next to the golden dragon of the Free Capella Movement. *Do I even know how I feel about anything anymore?* Certainly there were benefits to being associated with Tormano Liao. *And he's given us another shot at the Hustaing Warriors, but what will it cost us when the bill comes due?* The question bothered him much less than he thought it should.

But then, most things were bothering him less. He had not forgotten the two body bags lying nearby, though they continued to draw little of his interest. *One of my Lancers, the* Cataphract *pilot, and a Hustaing Warrior. A life for a life.* And where the Warriors lance had scrapped the *Cataphract,* his own had claimed the *JagerMech* and the remains of a gutted *Huron Warrior. So a net gain, right?*

"Major Doles, sir." A young ensign dropped down from the ramp, his ivory and gold shipboard uniform pristine.

The young man was good-looking, with pronounced Asian features, dark almond eyes, and a nice coloring to his skin. All qualities Tormano Liao seemed to look for in members of the Free Capella Movement. Recruiting-poster material, like everyone else with whom the Mandrinn surrounded himself. *Smart,* Doles thought. Though only a small percentage of the Capellan Confederation was Asian by ancestry, Doles knew there was no denying that people associated Asians with the rulership of Capellan space. *And then there are the Blackwind Lancers. Short on Asian blood—but we have our own recommendations.*

The ensign held out a noteputer. "Message came in over open frequencies, sir. From the commander of the Hustaing Warriors, attention to the Blackwind Lancers CO."

"Has the Mandrinn seen this yet?" Doles asked, folding his arms over a wide chest.

The young officer's face remained perfectly neutral. "It is addressed to you, Major."

So Tormano has seen it. So what? Doles shook his head at the offered 'puter. "Just give me the gist of the message, please."

With a light shrug, the ensign dropped the hand holding

the noteputer down to his side. "The Hustaing Warriors welcome the Blackwind Lancers to Indicass, and invite you to accept the legal rule of Chancellor Sun-Tzu Liao. Regardless of your answer, they request the body of their warrior back for its return to Hustaing."

Doles nodded. *The rest of the Hustaing Warrior lance has reported in, and if they are not requesting a prisoner as well, then the third MechWarrior made rendezvous.*

"Call off the search teams," he ordered, knowing the ensign was technically not under his authority but expecting the junior Free Capella officers to be under the Mandrinn's orders to cooperate. "Also, send a message to base. Break camp and prepare to relocate." *If we're so close to the Hustaing Warriors that our routine patrols are running into each other, we should establish a bit more breathing room.*

But not for long, he thought, as much in resignation as in promise to his command. He started to walk away, but paused when the ensign cleared his throat meaningfully.

"Sir, any response on the status of the body?"

"Leave it," Doles said. "They'll trace our flight back here and find it. Then they can ship it back to Hustaing or whatever they want." He looked over at the two bags, searching for a twinge of regret and finding only a numbness. "I'll detail some Lancers to bury our man," he said.

His Blackwind Lancers no longer had a true homeworld. *Wherever they fall defending the Compact will have to be good enough soil for burial.*

It was apparently good enough to die for.

10

Treyhang Liao paused just inside the study's doorway to thank Warren Doles for escorting him. "A pleasure, Major," he lied, offering his hand. So far Indicass had done little to impress him. Treyhang didn't exactly wince at the large man's crushing grip, though afterward he surreptitiously folded his right hand under his left and flexed some life back into it. "If you do make it to Marlette's Riviera in season, be sure to look me up. I can promise you the time of your life."

The major glanced into the study once, a flick of the eyes in an otherwise superb poker face that Treyhang did not fail to catch. "Thank you, sir."

A caution, that glance, or merely a reality check? Treyhang doubted the major knew himself. *Poor man. My father has him tied into knots.* He stepped away, adjusting his Rossini suit jacket and tie as Doles went out and shut the door. Then, still tugging at a cufflink, he turned slowly to face the man seated within the room. He knew exactly how he looked, affecting the correct air of sophisticated nonchalance that would irritate his host.

"Hello, Tormano," he said evenly. A greeting between two equals, nothing more. And not in proper *hàn-yu*.

Tormano hid his agitation well, but not so well that Treyhang could not read it. *"Ni hao,"* he returned more formally, then finished with heavy emphasis, *"son."*

The elder Liao had chosen to dress down for the meeting, eschewing his normal tailored silk suit for a gray cashmere sweater and dark trousers. Vain in the extreme, Tormano usually took great pains to play up his own appearance. But against his son's handsome Asian features and obvious youth, he did not try.

Treyhang slid into a comfortable leather chair across the desk from his father. *Second-best just is not his style.*

"How is your mother?" Tormano asked after a moment's silence.

"You mean your wife?" Treyhang smoothed a crease from the sleeve of his five-thousand-C-bill suit. "She's well. I have her happily ensconced in my villa at New Monaco, where she can live out the rest of her days. Without you."

If the blunt declaration bothered Tormano, it didn't show. Instead, he regarded his estranged son with a sad, almost pitying smile. Treyhang did not seek Tormano's approval of his lifestyle, the parties and games and social agenda, but this casual attitude toward his mother angered him. He fought the urge to get up and walk out, leaving behind him Indicass and whatever mad scheme his father had planned.

Only the barest vestiges of filial loyalty kept him in place. The same that had brought him this far—into a war zone even—to answer his father's rare request to attend him. Treyhang allowed the anger to bleed away, refusing to give Tormano an easy edge in the game they were already playing.

"Nice place," he said calmly, avoiding business and instead looking around, taking in the obvious ostentation of the study. Overstuffed leather furniture. Antique desk and shelving. A full library of classical literature. Based on his brief walk through the house, a mansion almost, this room was not the exception.

His father shrugged lightly as if it were nothing. "Loaned to me by a grateful patriot for the duration of my stay on Indicass. Support for the Movement."

"If it were me, you'd call it taking advantage," Treyhang said, reminding his father of a conversation they had never finished years before. "I think I pay my own way more than you these days."

That score hit home. Tormano possessed the decency to try and look regretful over the harsh words his son would never let him forget. The regret lasted all of six seconds.

"I want you back with Free Capella," Tormano said, not making any bones about why he'd called his son to him.

Treyhang laughed, once, sharp and joyful. His father was a decent gamesman in his own right, but he could be impatient. "You'll have to do better than that," he said, making Tormano pay for his impatience.

Tormano nodded reluctantly. "All right. I *need* you back. Free Capella needs to see a strong heir behind me. There is too much riding on this to overlook any potential problems. Any mistake."

Like when you tried to blackmail Kai into taking over Free Capella, and had it taken from you and turned into a charity organization? How that must have rankled. "Do you know how long it has been since I've been in the cockpit of a BattleMech?" he asked, preparing a polite but adamant refusal.

"I doubt there were many chances along your twenty-two-world tour of seaside resorts and cruise ships." Tormano smiled thinly. "Oh yes, Trey, I've had you followed—and watched very carefully. I probably know your net worth better than you do, and I admit to being impressed. You've done it all with no help from anyone." He smiled with blatant false cheer. "Good for you." Serious again. "But I'm not looking for another attack dog." Automatic flicker of the eyes toward the study door, which Treyhang doubted Tormano even realized he'd done. "Those I have aplenty. I want a standard-bearer. A single person to whom Free Capella can rally. The promise of the future."

Once you have ruled first, Treyhang appended, practiced

at sifting through the pro-Free Capella rhetoric. His father was pushing hard for this, but Treyhang also sensed some desperation behind Tormano's words. "This is your last chance, isn't it?" he said.

It made sense, in a way. Tikonov, the Chaos March realms, Confederation versus Compact—when would the entire Capellan theater be in such conflict again? The playing field lay in shambles, and one lone knight could conceivably sweep the board. *Or at least place a few major pieces in check.*

"I'm offering you the chance to do what you love," Tormano said. "What you do well. Be out front, in the limelight. Lead a few victory parades. Shake hands with royalty. Be *seen.*"

Tempting. Treyhang caught himself rubbing the fingers of his right hand together, one of his worst tells. Yes, tempting, but were the gains worth the price of admission? "How long?"

Tormano didn't waste time with rationales. "Six months," he said flatly.

The young man laughed again. "Be serious. I'd miss *the season* on Marlette, opposite the Solaris Summer Bouts, and then I'm registered in the '62 solar yacht preliminaries."

"Three months." The offer came just as fast and hard. Tormano had obviously been prepared to halve his first offer.

That approached the realm of possibility. *I can't even catch a ride off this rock for two weeks.* But accepting meant three additional months away from the social calendar, not counting travel time. Treyhang settled back into the leather chair to think it over.

It didn't matter whether he really believed in the fight or not. In his honest opinion, Free Capella had done more good under Kai's stewardship. Like it or not, Tormano was back in charge. *That is not to say that he couldn't do some good as well, by accident even, while gathering power for himself.* Someone would rule, and certainly less suitable candidates had sat on thrones in the past. What finally mattered was the wages, and Tormano was offering to pay Treyhang in his coin of choice.

And really, do you wish to bet against him? Despite some personal antagonism between father and son, Treyhang knew Tormano to be a survivor. "Two months," he said, cutting down Tormano's request.

Tormano paused, then nodded an easy acceptance. "Very well, Trey. Two months."

Treyhang smiled. A little time in service never hurt when it came to creditors, and holovid footage would play well in the quick video biography they would run on him during the solar yacht races. *With a little luck, I can even parlay this into some invitations next time I am in Solaris.*

And besides, how much could happen in two months?

11

Chingda-sun Community
Layting, St. Loris
St. Ives Compact
29 April 3062

Aris Sung sat on the polished teak floor of the grand hall, surrounded by members of the Warrior House Hiritsu. He cradled a small bowl of rice in his right hand and held chopsticks in the other. His mantled silk robes bunched up behind him against a massive wooden pillar, one of five such pillars that supported the open-beamed roof. The pace of the last two weeks had settled a weariness over the Mech-Warrior, urging him to lean back and take advantage of the support. He resisted, alternately focusing his attention between the current speaker and wondering how *Shiao-zhang* Ty Wu Non found such perfect settings for House Hiritsu to gather.

The Chingda-sun Community of St. Loris reminded Aris of the T'ao-shui Lakeside Resort back on Nashuar. But where the resort had adopted Chinese architecture and landscaping style only for its commercial aspects, the commune embraced the culture as a whole. Teachings of Master Kung-fu-tzu—never referred to here in the Anglo form of Confucius—helped govern their lives. The philosophy brought them patience, courtesy, and a sense of proportion. The members lived very simply, working the outlying farms and trading some craftwork with local villages. The residences were small but sufficient, their sloping roofs and peaked corners reminiscent of the Sòng period. Less attention had been paid to the grounds, but the community hall was a masterwork of architecture, with an open floor large enough for the entire Warrior House to gather.

The philosophies of Master Kung are also a central part of House Hiritsu's tenets. So why do I feel as if we have lost that focus? He turned his gaze around the room, at the two hundred plus warriors gathered for a formal airing of grievances, suggestions, and advice. A tradition of the House, dealing with problems—personal or military—in *The Family*. Today the talks centered around the conflict on St. Loris, and save for two lances of MechWarriors and a platoon of infantry left patrolling the area, the entire House had assembled. Too many of those faces, Asian features or not, blurred in Aris' mind with the memory of Compact soldiers and civilians.

Is it them, or is it me?

"Why not release a few lances for independent strikes?" Jené Silvers asked of the gathered House, finally coming to her point after several minutes of discussing how the drive to take St. Loris had faltered. Aris leaned forward, surreptitiously taking stock of reactions from those warriors near him. As a lance leader in *Shiao-zhang* Non's BattleMech company, Jené's opinion would carry almost the weight of a company commander such as Aris or even the senior company leader *Lien-zhang* James. He noticed a few approving nods.

"Or Hunter Squads," she continued, gesturing to those infantrymen nearest her. "I'm sure we could find many volunteers among our battlefield cousins." More nods.

Assassination squads. Aris held the frown from his face. In his years as an infantryman, he had once been trained for such tactics. To employ them now, against others of Capellan heritage, seemed wrong. *Or is that the MechWarrior in me talking, preferring the supposed gracefulness of augmented combat?*

Two infantry platoon leaders stood, one of them a veteran House warrior of mediocre accomplishments and the other Li Wynn, who had only recently been promoted to *pai-zhang*. A clear-cut case of seniority existed, but then Ty Wu Non's formal recognition of Li, promoting the adopted warrior, had increased the young man's stock considerably. On Hustaing, Li had saved Isis Marik from capture, and perhaps death. Actions spoke loudly in a Warrior House. If Li Wynn had wished, likely he could have taken the floor. But instead he nodded politely to the senior officer and retook his seat, and Aris allowed himself a small measure of pride for the simple courtesy his charge had shown. *In some areas, he is a model recruit.*

"Speaking for my troops," the veteran began, "we are always ready to forge ahead. At the very least, taking out the St. Ives Lancers CO and possibly Colonel Marko Rubinsky would help to collapse the resistance."

Aris noted that the infantryman refused to name Cassandra Allard-Liao. *The political implications are heavy enough, just implying the idea of having her killed.* Aris had his doubts that her death would demoralize the St. Ives Lancers. It might even turn them more fanatical. Worse, such an act might bring her brother here. He did not fear Kai Allard-Liao, but thought it foolish not to respect a warrior of such proven ability. *We wish to hasten our victory, not increase the turmoil.*

As the infantry officer sat, everyone waited for Li Wynn to take the floor. He rose, pulling at the hem of his dress uniform to straighten the jacket.

"I don't think that *Pai-zhang* Silvers' recommendation is taken far enough," he said, returning to the previous point. He spoke slowly, obviously choosing his words with care in an attempt to hide his usual street-talk rhythm. "It's not only the strength of military resistance that slows the Confederation, but civilian resistance as well. Speaking for a platoon that has garrisoned a lot of towns and cities along our path of advance, I can tell you they are a battlefield as well. I've lost men in riots, to snipers, and to poison. It makes me sick that such dogs are allowed to suppress true Confederation citizens such as those we left behind in Pardray, and those we found here in Chingda-sun."

A mistake, to relate the Pardray government to this community, Aris thought, mentally critiquing Li Wynn's argument. The people of Chingda-sun would be just as hospitable to Compact forces, and it felt wrong to transmute their peaceful neutrality into a pro-Confederation statement. But then most of the Warrior House seemed to be in the grip of a military fervor. *The Warrior Houses are not directly of the Confederation military. We are separate, serving the Chancellor through the will of the House Masters.* If Aris was ever to take issue with that idea, here was his opening.

The bowl of rice was lifted halfway to his mouth before Aris realized that he was stalling. Again.

"And what would your solution be, Li Wynn?" he asked before he could argue himself out of it. He set the bowl aside, rested hands upon his thighs, and stared over at his charge. As Li Wynn's *Sifu*, his Mentor, Aris could interrupt without seeming rude or disrespectful. *So long as I make it into an issue that involves his inculcation of House philosophies.* "Would you suggest to our House Master that we turn our warriors loose against civilians? Those who may be considered Confederation citizens, if misguided? The Lorix Order certainly argues against any more such atrocities."

The Lorix Order, a quasi-religious set of ideals established in the Confederation four hundred years before, could be found within the tenets of all Warrior Houses to a greater or lesser extent. Hiritsu interpretations were loose, but provided Aris with enough justification for the interruption.

And just as Aris had hoped, Li Wynn fell into the trap his Mentor had laid out for him. "Those who resist the return of the Confederation are our enemies. And as enemies of the House—"

"Do not presume to speak for *Shiao-zhang* Ty Wu Non," Aris said abruptly, cutting Li Wynn off mid-sentence. Li opened his mouth to retort, and Aris leaned forward, ready to interrupt again with a harsher reprimand. *I said those "who may be considered" Confederation citizens. Although Li meant to be stating his opinion, he phrased it incorrectly.*

"Please take your seat, Li Wynn." Aris spoke mildly, as if making a suggestion, but it carried the weight of a direct order.

He knew that someone would take up the gauntlet he'd thrown. An infantryman, he predicted, since they dealt more often with the civilian population. Jené Silvers immediately retaking the floor caught him slightly off guard.

"Is it *your* contention then, *Lien* Sung, that *Shiao-zhang* Non should not consider the hostility of the Compact civilians as a threat to our mission?" The lawyerly tone in her voice suggested she was about to catch Aris in a trap of logic or loyalty.

Aris was not so easily caught. He rose to meet her on equal footing, quite aware that his own casual dress against her field uniform would cast them as the civilian and military proponents in the eyes of the other House members.

"So far as I know," he said evenly, "our House Master has set no official word to the matter." *Because no one has forced the issue, until now.* He continued very cautiously, aware of the touchy ground he trod. "I would hope, though, that the will of our House Master would never violate the precepts of his own House."

A dead silence greeted Aris. It was one thing to couch suggestions in the form of opinion, quite another to *ever* suggest that the House Master could be held accountable by anyone but the Chancellor of the Confederation. Technically, if the House Master decided to scrap the formal vows and rewrite them, it was his prerogative. Aris doubted any Warrior House could survive such a reorganization—well, House Imarra perhaps—but the challenge had still been made. *If that doesn't require the personal attention of Ty Wu Non, I don't know what would.*

Ty Wu Non shared Aris' slender build but not the younger warrior's height. However, as he smoothly rose to his feet there was no denying his aura of authority, settled around him after four years as a House Master. He also wore casual attire, his wide-shouldered silk robes of such a dark green as to look almost black in the hall's lighting. Aris hoped the choice of clothing was not coincidence. The growing prevalence of uniforms at social gatherings, while not incorrect for any occasion, was just one of the signs that made Aris believe the House was losing its focus.

The House Master nodded Jené Silvers back to her seat. He stared at Aris calmly for several minutes, as if measuring the younger man's intent. No one spoke. Only the occasional rustle of silk or the creak of a board as someone shifted position interrupted the quiet. Non's dark eyes narrowed slightly into a mask of neutrality when he spoke, as if working to hide anything but his actual words. "Sometimes the situation asks of us a difficult choice, Aris Sung. Sacrifices are demanded."

And sometimes they are not, Aris wanted to reply, but held his tongue. Ty Wu Non was not one to respect bravado couched in insolence. *He is giving me a chance to respond, which validates my concerns, if not my actual conclusions. Now I must prove I am right, or at least force more thought on the matter.* Either left him open for punishment, but he was beyond caring.

Aris nodded, as if having heard great wisdom. "Strong words," he acknowledged. He frowned as if in recollection. "Familiar ones."

The House Master certainly could have ended the conversation right then, taking Aris' comment as a token of submission. Despite Non's attempt to hide his thoughts, Aris read a brief struggle in the tightness around the *Shiaozhang*'s shoulders and face. "Familiar?" Ty Wu Non finally asked, allowing Aris his argument. "I do not recall ever having said them before."

"Hmmm?" Aris feigned innocent confusion for a few moments. "Oh, you wouldn't have, *Shiao-zhang* Non. It's just that I seem to recall a similar argument put forward by a Confederation citizen once, in defense of Romano Liao's purges." Aris shook his head lightly, but never broke eye contact. "Perhaps I am mistaken."

This time, no one even dared move. Many, Aris felt sure, were likely predicting his destruction in the next several minutes. *A veiled insult to both the Master of my House and to the Chancellor himself, all in the same hour. He would certainly be within his right.* But Aris could no longer wander through the conflict blindly, unsure of his own nature. *If the House Master judges me wrong, I will accept that. It may be the end of my life as a warrior, but I will accept . . .*

Ty Wu Non's gaze darkened, showing everyone a hint of his displeasure. Then it cleared, like an avalanche slowly rolling back uphill. "Perhaps you are." His voice was even and full of strength. "Why don't we consider that for a time. Dismissed," he said, his gaze sweeping the room and applying the order to all.

As Aris filed out one of the doors, surrounded by warriors suddenly uncomfortable in his presence, he began to formulate plans. Action, he reminded himself, will carry more weight than mere words. The House Master had granted him a reprieve, and tacit permission to pursue his own thoughts. Some would take convincing, but others he hoped would also recognize the truth behind his challenge. Time would tell. *If we have the time. If I can make the time.*

Aris vowed he would. He would have the answer to his question.

Is it them, or is it me?

12

Celestial Palace
Zi-jin Chéng, Sian
Sian Commonality, Capellan Confederation
2 May 3062

Sun-Tzu Liao studied the Strategic Planning Center's holographic map, the specter of Romano looking over his shoulder while *Sang-jiang-jun* Talon Zahn explained recent troop deployments and Ion Rush rode control over the two junior officers manning the consoles. Sasha Wanli stood quiet attendance nearby, but obviously ready to answer questions as necessary. Sun-Tzu sensed his mother's attentive presence, recalling how she always focused—obsessed?—on matters military.

He had left the traditional silk robes of Chancellorship behind today, opting instead for a black silk shirt and mantled red jacket. Gold-threaded patterns chased *jian* swords and sunbursts up both jacket sleeves. Tradition died hard in any realm, and the times Sun-Tzu would forgo his robes of office while on Sian were few. Today, this hour, he had ordered the underground planning center cleared but for two console stations, his top three advisors, and himself there as a student. He still represented House Liao, but with recent strains in his relationship with Zahn he thought it better to place the formality of his office aside.

"And the Canopian Fusiliers have been relocated to the world of Second Try," Zahn said, wrapping up his presentation of the new garrison posts set along the border the Confederation shared with the Free Worlds League. "This also places them in position to support our 'observation' force on Styk."

The dismissal of Isis Marik was having the expected results—Thomas rattling the saber with troop movements all along the border. "Where is her JumpShip?" Sun-Tzu asked.

"Necromo," Zahn replied instantly, never needing ask to whom "her" referred. "I've ordered the WarShip *Elias Jung* to hold there until her JumpShip recharges. Then as soon as she has cleared Confederation space the *Elias* swings down through the Xin Sheng Commonality on a quick tour."

Ion Rush looked over. "If Thomas Marik has anything planned, it will happen right after she crosses our border into safe space."

Trailing the smooth backside of his left hand's long fingernails down his cheek, Sun-Tzu considered the idea. He imagined his mother's paranoia over massive troop movements along the Confederation border, then dismissed it.

"There is nothing planned," he said decisively, stifling Romano's pending outburst before it distracted him. "Isis did not even try to return to the League. Thomas has no impetus for conflict." He glanced at Sasha Wanli. "Besides, the Maskirovka has assured me that there has been no buildup of the supplies he would need to launch a major offensive."

"I hesitate to point out," Talon Zahn said, voice respectful but showing no real hesitancy, "that shoring up our border with the Free Worlds League has cost us the units we relied on to contain Kai Allard-Liao from deeper strikes into the Confederation."

Sun-Tzu smiled thinly. He rarely involved himself in the direct details of war, leaving them to Zahn and Ion Rush. But the solution to Kai was more political than martial. "Reinforce Sarna with another regiment of observation troops," he ordered. "Pull them down from Styk if you must. In the meantime, *request* that the Sarnese post the Sarna Martial Academy regiment to Capella for garrison assignment."

Ion Rush and Talon Zahn exchanged glances. Zahn spoke for them both. "We have not allowed the SMA off-planet since taking control of the Sarna Supremacy food world of Kaifeng. After their lack of cooperation against Kai's last raid, why do you think they will comply now?" He glanced to the map. "Capella is an important world. Your cousin will find it tempting."

Sun-Tzu nodded his agreement. "But, unfortunately, shipping problems are about to restrict the flow of food-stuffs between Kaifeng and Sarna. About the time the SMA arrives on Capella, their families will be getting very hungry. They will cooperate against Kai, though I'm sure he will be expecting otherwise."

"Do not worry about Kai Allard-Liao," a new voice said from the room's far shadows, deadly sweet. Kali stepped into the diffuse glow that escaped from the spotlights over the computer consoles, her dark red dress looking to Sun-Tzu like the color of clotted blood. She moved around one bank of consoles, but paused before stepping into brighter light. "He will soon have other concerns."

Sun-Tzu remembered Romano's affection for Kali and the almost dog-like, blind devotion his sister had shown their mother. Even now, he sensed the near wraith-like memories of his mother warming to her. *Kali may suffer from madness, but there is no denying her abilities, or resources. Perhaps she does know something.* "What are you talking about, Kali?"

His sister folded her hands together and held them even with her slender waist. Her red-brown hair fell in tangles down her back, wild but not unruly, and her eyes were two dark, narrow slits in an otherwise pale face. "The Confederation has friends, dear brother, apostles who recognize our supreme destiny. The signs promised a reckoning, and through me it now comes to our salvation." Her smile was brilliant. "Within the week, the traitor Liaos will be no more. Within a month, I will have resolved the conflict with St. Ives. The final answer to our prayers."

Has she ordered her Thugee cult of assassins to go after Candace and her offspring? A hollowness gripped at Sun-Tzu's core. Thugees were not known for subtlety or stability. And they worshipped his sister as the death goddess incarnate. If even one such assassin succeeded, their involvement would become known and the repercussions could be catastrophic.

Unless they all *succeed,* Romano's ghost whispered in his ear.

Sun-Tzu's sense of dread grew even stronger. "What is it? What have you done, Kali?" His voice was barely a whisper, but otherwise gave no sign of his trepidation. Then, trying to sound reassuring rather than threatening, he asked, "What is your final solution to our troubles?"

A look of confusion flitted across Kali's stern features for the briefest second, as if she were wondering how her brother could ask, why he did not know. Then her expression cleared, became full of confidence. "The Wei Solution," she said in the easiest manner.

A dread chill ran down Sun-Tzu's spine as Romano's phantom laughter mocked him. "By the gods new and ancient, no!" Though a firm non-believer in matters religious, the oath escaped him before he even realized it. He wrestled a hard mask into place, freezing the expression of shock but allowing nothing more to show. "You obtained the Wei nerve agent, and delivered it into the hands of your religious maniacs?"

Naked anger flashed in Kali's eyes. "My *followers*," she corrected. But next to the appeal of a pogrom, rage against her brother could apparently not last. Already the spike of anger bled from her face, to be replaced by a messianic expression and voice. "*Our* agents of divine retribution."

An old memory surfaced. Romano Liao, calling her family into the throne room and reciting a stylized story version of the Fourth Succession War. Of Candace Liao and Justin Allard. Of the assassin she sent to kill them both. Sun-Tzu remembered the same self-righteous tone, the same madness lighting her eyes, that Kali used now. *She is truly our mother's daughter.* The ghost of Romano smiled and nodded, pleased.

"She has really done this," he said, detached from his surroundings and feeling his protective mask slipping away. He looked over at Talon Zahn and Ion Rush, standing there with horror-struck expressions. Almost as one the two senior warriors turned their eyes toward Sasha Wanli, then quickly averted their gazes. *They know they're looking at a dead woman. And so does Sasha.* The old woman's health, never good to begin with and corrupted by decades of mayhem, seemed ready to give out on her at any moment with the realization of her latest failure. Her skin was ashen, face drawn and reflecting a similar state of shock as the others.

"How much?" Sun-Tzu asked, turning back to his sister. "How much nerve agent?"

"Enough to win the war," she promised, obviously reading her brother's shock as acceptance. "Fourteen canisters," she said proudly, "properly divided."

Sun-Tzu rounded on Sasha Wanli. The elder woman's lips moved, making silent calculations. After a few seconds, she said, "If used for the greatest effect, which would mean breaking it down into small lots. Aerosol disbursement over large population centers." She whispered a few calculations to herself, then swallowed hard. "Enough to kill over five million people."

Five million! Romano was impressed. Sun-Tzu found it hard to believe this was even happening. "Enough to commit the single biggest atrocity since the Kentares Massacre," he said, voice flat with shock. "Enough to make the lazing of Turtle Bay look like a DropShip crash by comparison, and that cost the Smoke Jaguars their Clan." The impact hit him in one blow, and Sun-Tzu's composure nearly broke. He had never truly felt fear as he did at this moment, and he knew that he failed to hide it completely.

"They will tear the Confederation apart," he said, voice trained to a neutral lifelessness. "All of the other Great Houses. Their people will give them no choice. They will demand it."

"That will not happen, Sun-Tzu." Kali stepped forward, though still not fully into the room's best lighting. Her eyes remained dark smudges. "It cannot," she promised.

The Chancellor of the Confederation looked at her calmly, shocked into a numbness of mind. "Why not?"

"The portents are too favorable," she replied with a fanatic's belief. "Why do you think I have waited for so long? It either cannot happen, or another option exists that you will find. The Confederation will endure, stronger than it has ever been."

Stepping over to Ion Rush, Sun-Tzu pulled the Diàn-ya sidearm from the Imarra Master's holster. Rush might have been a statue for all that he moved while the Chancellor disarmed him. Sun-Tzu rounded on Kali, pulse laser pistol held down at his side. He sensed Romano's approval of Kali, conflicting with his own desire to lash out at something, anything. He glimpsed the madness that must have been shared between mother and daughter.

"When?" he asked simply, nearly a whisper, hoping somehow there might be time to prevent the disaster. "When do the attacks begin?"

Kali smiled, obviously blind to her brother's threat. "Do not worry, Sun-Tzu. My people have been in place for weeks now, awaiting the signs. The first wave begins right on time. Today."

Sun-Tzu almost shot her. He brought up the laser pistol, levered at his sister, and the rage he sensed from his mother's spectral presence over the idea nearly drove him to it just to spite her. And then there was Sasha Wanli, standing so close. There Romano agreed, hating Wanli for her other failures.

Kali stared ahead blankly, as if not even seeing the weapon, caught up in her own visions. Sasha paled but did not flinch away, accepting. The laser wavered between them, Kali and Sasha, his finger tightening against the trigger but Sun-Tzu unable to decide whom to kill. *Everyone. No one.* Kali, Sasha, Zahn, Rush, and certainly the two junior officers who sat in frightened silence as witnesses to the scene. Sun-Tzu saw himself emptying the energy clip, pulling back on the trigger until the weapon stopped firing.

And how would that make me any different from Romano? he asked himself, the question pulling him back from the immediate brink. *How often did I skate too close to the edge? How many times did she think to order my father, head of the Mask, to kill me? And how many times did she order it, only to be talked out of it by Tsen Shang?*

Sun-Tzu lowered the gun, his hand trembling. *I am not my mother. Pulling a trigger in rage or frustration would have been her way, it is not mine.* The urge to kill one or both still raged within him, and he clenched his left hand into a fist, feeling the razor-sharp fingernails on that hand slice into his own skin. *I will not be my mother,* he vowed.

He handed the weapon back to Ion Rush.

"Kali," he said, once more in control of his voice and dialing for a serious tone, "we need everything recorded for posterity. Names of the agents, now heroes of the Confederation. Dates, times, and targets of their attacks. Sasha, take Kali up to your offices and try to jog her memory."

Sasha Wanli, clearly surprised that she would escape the room with her own life intact, quickly stepped up to Kali and gestured her back toward the elevator. With a superior smile, Kali followed. Sun-Tzu waited for them to leave, trying to ignore Romano's repeated whispers of *too late, too late, too late.*

"Whatever we have to do, that nerve agent must be stopped," he said. "I will order the information ripped from Kali by any methods, though I believe her too far gone not to believe the 'heroes of the Confederation' line."

He held his hands together, touching them fingertip to fingertip, and bowed his head in thought for a few seconds. A drop of sweat fell from his brow to splash against his fingertips, then ran down to mingle with the blood dripping from his left palm. "Zahn, pull whatever resources you must from the war, but intercept them. Ion, you will liaise with Candace. Tell her everything—everything—Sasha pulls from Kali concerning the Thugee agents and the attacks on any Compact target." Both men nodded soberly.

"We'd all better hope that we can stop this before it is too late." He spun on one heel then and strode off toward the elevator. Romano's mocking laughter chased him from the room.

Gunming, Indicass
Xin Sheng Commonality, Capellan Confederation

Indicass' sun beamed down without a cloud in sight to ob-
scure its warmth or any portion of the sapphire sky. *A good
omen,* Tormano decided, *for those who believe in such.*
Standing in the shade of a wall-less tent pavilion next to
Gunming's governor, Tormano Liao waited patiently for the
troll-like little man to finish his opening speech. He spared
one brief look back at the company formation of Blackwind
Lancer BattleMechs at the eastern edge of the city's fairgrounds and the *Helios* his son piloted at the formation's
head. *I promised you would be seen, Treyhang, but after me.
Always after me.*

The crowds had assembled for Tormano's reception by
Governor Siddara, a minor lord whose landhold included
large amounts of territory currently held by Confederation
forces. Tormano, flanked by the hand-picked best of his
Free Capella followers on Indicass and conscious of the
holovid cameras, smiled his acceptance of the governor's
appreciation for the liberation of Gunming. *During my brief
address, I will gain your direct support for Free Capella.
And after a few more words, I will then call down Treyhang.
My son, descending from a BattleMech to join his victorious father. It will make good drama.*

Warning shouts spoiled the moment, even as Tormano
planned its climax.

A hovercar raced across the open area, trailing pieces of
the cyclone fencing that bordered the fairgrounds. Its fans
made a horrible rattling sound, damaged from plowing
through the fence. A hole in its skirt drifted it left, forcing
constant corrections by the driver who also swerved repeat-

edly to avoid sporadic weapons fire from guards posted back at the fencing.

The crowd began to stir now, the sound of gunfire sending a few fleeing, but the majority pointing and jabbering over the event. *Cattle,* Tormano thought. While Governor Siddara spouted conflicting orders and requests for help, the elder Liao bravely held his position for the cameras. The hovercar's path was currently taking it on a tangent to the pavilion and besides, what was one car against a company of 'Mechs?

"Order Treyhang to bring it down before it hits the crowds," Tormano calmly ordered an aide whose security radio linked into the BattleMech frequencies. But the sight of a tube-like device suddenly thrust up through the hovercar's open sunroof gave him a start. Rocket launcher! Had he waited too long?

The rocket erupted from its launcher on a trailer of fire and smoke, streaking into the sky. More smoke billowed from the hovercar's windows, the backblast from the launcher filling the compartment. Like most of the crowd, Tormano had followed the rocket's short flight, straight up until detonating far above the fairgrounds. He looked back to the car just in time to see sapphire energy from Treyhang's medium lasers slice into it, easily coring through the unarmored vehicle, which erupted into a fireball.

Rockets and BattleMech-scale weaponry. Now people did run, though the danger was past. Too much excitement. Tormano ignored them. He began to think that the interruption might indeed have been good holovid. His eyes watered and he coughed against a sudden stinging in his throat. *Smoke from the burning car.* He stepped out from under the pavilion's shade, intent on waving his son down from the *Helios'* cockpit.

He would never make it.

The pain bit into his lower back first, cutting his legs out from under him. Then he collapsed, his spine on fire and muscles knotting. His eyes burned, vision blurring and then abandoning him altogether. Every breath poured molten steel into his lungs, and his ears filled with the sounds of gurgling screams. Tormano wanted to scream, but couldn't. He gagged, coughed—his throat full of fluids. He couldn't breathe, though the lack of oxygen did not make the pain stop. His heart hammered out of control in his chest, and it was the arrhythmic pain that cleared his mind just long enough for him to realize he was dying.

After me, Treyhang. Always after me. His last coherent thought before chaos engulfed Mandrinn Tormano Liao's mind and mercifully stole his sanity for the last few seconds of his life.

═══ 13 ═══

DropShip Death Blossom
Pirate Jump Point, Taga System
Xin Sheng Commonality, Capellan Confederation
2 May 3062

Petyr Andreyvich finished up his preflight check on the century-old *Lucifer* aerofighter, swimming about in the zero-G environment of the *Union* Class DropShip's well-maintained launch bay. *One final flight,* he silently promised the antiquated fighter, catching a stanchion and anchoring himself to the floor with a hard grip. *A poisoned dagger, into the heart of the St. Ives Compact.*

The first jump warning, relayed from the JumpShip *You-dú Xin-zàng,* had already sounded. One more warning blast and they would jump from the Taga system to a pirate point calculated to put them over Tian-tan, capital of St. Ives. Petyr had won the honor of the flight over longstanding brothers in the Thugee cult. *The goddess favored me; she knows I will not fail her.*

Pushing away from the stanchion, he floated over to the front of the aerofighter and caught a new grip. Gazing into the deceptively simple darkness of its forward missile tubes, he laid a hand against the cool metal skin of the craft.

One missile, touched by the goddess. All it will take to end Candace Liao's unholy reign.

The DropShip *Death Blossom* would detach from the JumpShip and burn for Tian-tan, and at some point along the way his lone fighter would spear outward from her and arrow in toward the Royal Palace itself. *We might never rise again, but that is karma and the goddess will reward me in this life or the next.*

Petyr slid around to the mounting ladder, then levered himself up and into the cockpit. The second warning blasted over the P.A. system even as he strapped in, three blaring notes that presaged the jump to the St. Ives system. He'd chosen to ride out the jump with his aerofighter. Already he thought he could sense the energies being released by the starship to which the *Death Blossom* was currently mated, though he recognized his foolishness.

A JumpShip's Kearny-Fuchida drive released its stored energy in one magnificent burst, piercing through the boundaries of Einsteinian space to propel the JumpShip and its DropShip passengers up to thirty light years. Safety from the effects of a system's gravity well usually demanded that jumps take place far outside the system, at either the zenith or nadir jump points. Pirate points, coordinates within a system where competing gravitational effects neutralized each other, required more accurate calculations but allowed for close insertion. *The chink in St. Ives' armor,* Petyr thought. *We will come as its moon passes almost perfectly over Tian-tan. An eclipsed moon. What better omen for the faithful servants of the dark goddess?*

And then it happened. The *You-dú Xin-zàng* jumped.

To Petyr, jumps rarely seemed to last longer than a few brief seconds, though in fact they could take many minutes of relative time to complete. Effects of a jump on the human mind varied among different people, and even from one jump to another for the same person. Brief or drawn out, sometimes nauseating, at times terrifying; and no one truly understood why. Petyr traditionally paid lip-service to the pilots' superstition that the episodes were brief flashes of insanity as the mind grasped at the concept that it did not truly exist in real spacetime. Once the jump was accomplished, however, he always gave thanks to the goddess for his safe journey and gloried in mankind's power over the laws of the universe.

Only this time it did not end.

The physical universe appeared to stretch into a fourth dimension, everything distorting as it swirled out before him toward an infinite horizon only to swirl back into a nearly perfect vision of reality and begin again. His mind screamed, bright and painful. Never had a jump so thoroughly terrified him. And just when it seemed he had reached his threshold past sanity, the universe stretched in a new direction and pulled him along with it into chaos. Colors possessed scents, and he could see the sound of his own scream as its dark shadow wrapped about him. He fought and clawed at it, felt the stinging sensation as it burned his hands.

The jump must be over, a small kernel of rational thought told him, though nearly lost against the maelstrom that raged in his mind. *It's over because I can reason and move. I'm not caught between seconds.* He tried closing his eyes, but the darkness held more terrors than the warped reality. Petyr wept.

The Lucifer, he remembered. *The goddess.* Nothing he looked at made sense. Biting down into his lower lip, he tried to concentrate through the pain. He identified what might be the wing of the aerofighter, though the scent of oiled metal distorted the view. He clawed for that direction, and found himself unable to move. A dark, bitter aroma held him down, binding him at shoulders and across his lap. *My harness—I'm already strapped in.*

But with that challenge conquered came a new one as he tried to identify his controls. The panel sat before him, a limitless expanse of mountainous terrain, covered with grassy-cold steel. *A test. She tests me.* Atop the mountain, he could just make out the goddess waiting for him.

Chewing hard into his lip, Petyr began the long climb.

DropShip **Death Blossom**
Failed Entry Point, St. Ives System
St. Ives Compact

Petite as she was, General Simone Devon had to twist around to make it through a warped doorway that led into *Death Blossom*'s transship passage. The lack of gravity made it easier than her EVA suit would have allowed under thrust. She noted where the metal bulkhead had buckled, its supports twisted like so much taffy. It was amazing that any part of the ship's hull could still withstand vacuum. She kept the faceplate on her EVA suit helmet securely fastened in between attempting to talk with the wounded.

Devon had just happened to be on the bridge of the *Carthage,* her own DropShip burning for St. Ives, when proximity alarms sounded. With no station to attend, her first glance had been to the primary screen, which until a few seconds ago had been filled with the world of St. Ives. Now a shattered wreck floated in space, a broken-spined corpse floating in a field of debris—barely visible against the dark side of St. Ives.

"JumpShip alert," someone had shouted. "Scramble fighters!"

"Disregard that," Devon ordered, stepping closer to the viewscreen. "My God, look at it. It's smashed." She glanced over at the ship's captain. "Assemble life boats and rescue teams."

She heard someone mutter the name of Kaifeng, the Sarna Supremacy world taken by the Confederation with the ruse of a crippled JumpShip. She shook her head. That JumpShip out there was broken into three pieces, with half its drive section missing. And something she swore right then never to admit to anyone, she also thought she'd seen a large piece of the ship fade back out of existence. *An illusion,* she told herself. *We're looking at it by starlight, after all.*

Simone's rescue boat had taken the *Death Blossom,* whose name was painted on the hull in Chinese ideograms right under the Capellan Confederation insignia. Floating free of the JumpShip, its docking collar ruined, it still looked to be in better shape. If there were survivors, she'd thought, they would be found here.

There were survivors, if one could call them that.

Emergency doors had isolated hull breaches, allowing many to live. Some had obviously killed themselves after the misjump. One crewman had torn his own eyes out and would not stop howling until sedated. Many were simply catatonic, though a few raved insanely or talked calm gibberish. Very few had the presence of mind left to operate in zero gravity, and those who could were in no shape to resist. The marines she'd brought helped carry the wounded back to lifeboats. Simone Devon began to give up hope of finding anyone who could answer questions. *I'd settle for knowing where the ship jumped from, though it would be even better to know what happened to any military equipment a Confederation combat vessel jumping into St. Ives should be carrying.*

She almost bypassed the fighter launch bay, seeing no one floating helpless in the small confines. No screams or crying. Then the image registered, and she poked her head back into the space. There, someone sitting calmly in the open cockpit of an old *Lucifer.* Simone gestured to the troopers following her and led them through the door, over a rent in the deckplates that fell through three levels. Four of them floated up and anchored themselves with grips on the rim of the open cockpit.

In flightsuit but no helmet, the pilot stared without seeing at his instruments. Silent tears streamed down his face, to mix with the bloody mess of his lower lip. One hand was wrapped around the lower half of the joystick, fingers inching up slowly. The other hand remained held out in front of him, hovering over a set of switches as if forgotten.

"Can you understand me?" Simone asked. Her words sounded amplified inside her helmet, but she knew from experience how they could be muffled without. She asked again, speaking louder.

No response. She reached in and took his free hand. At

her touch the pilot's eyes widened and tears fell faster. She opened her faceplate.

"Can you understand me?" she asked again. "We are here to help you." Nothing. "Let's get him out of here," she said, and several hands went in to work at his harness while others pulled at the pilot's arms. The man screamed and thrashed about with his left hand, spasmic, though his right never left the control stick.

In the last few seconds left to her life, General Simone Devon could only wonder what the Confederation could hope to accomplish with one *Union* Class DropShip carrying a single aerospace fighter.

The cockpit filled with colorful sound, then Petyr Andreyvich felt the coldness of the goddess' touch. *Not yet,* he pleaded. *Not when I am so close.* Then half a dozen arms swam through the distortion as his goddess began to take him to her. He thrashed about, begging for another moment. The launch bay doors remained closed, the fighter a sweet-smelling cold, but his reward was promised for firing the blessed missile. He felt an icy ridge through his glove, and he struggled to send the commands down to his traitorous fingers. *Flip up the safety toggle and fire. Flip up the safety toggle. Flip up! Fire!*

A roar of divine approval assailed him, colored tart and orange and washing his face with red warmth. The many arms fell away from him, allowing him to enjoy his victory. Then he felt the dark goddess physically moving into his body, taking away control of his muscles and senses. Darkness closed in, but this time Petyr Andreyvich was not afraid. He had been blessed.

$\equiv$ **14** $\equiv$

Overlake Hospital
Hunan, St. Loris
St. Ives Compact
6 May 3062

Hands clenched into impotent fists, nails digging into her palms, Cassandra Allard-Liao stared through the glass walls that framed Overlake Hospital's critical care unit rooms. A nurse had parted the inside curtains enough for her to observe Tamas Rubinsky, face looking drawn and pale where it was not occluded by the ventilator tubing. Two doctors consulted at the foot of his bed. Though Cassandra would have preferred to see less consulting and more activity, she knew they were doing everything possible for Tamas. Hunan's biggest hospital was among the best on St. Loris when it came to treating industrial accidents involving chemicals. Now it served as one of the primary care centers for the few survivors of the nerve agent attacks.

Where I would be now, if not for Tamas?

Cassandra held herself upright through sheer determination, her strength long since sapped by the pace of the past two weeks and a lack of any sleep over the last twenty-four hours. She still wore the jumpsuit she'd thrown over her cooling vest and shorts during the DropShip flight, but refused to leave until hearing something more definite in Tamas' case than, "We're doing all we can." Coffee no longer helped, not even the bitter, mud-like substance brought to her by an emergency room intern.

She had declined the use of an empty room, and when a concerned doctor tried to force the issue Cassandra had simply traded on her family name. It was one of the few times she had ever tried to gain anything by dint of who she'd been born, but considered it influence well spent.

So when she felt another presence moving up beside her, she did not turn, but merely said, "I'm fine, thank you," in a curt dismissal.

"I would not presume to debate you," came a voice whose Slavic accent was familiar. "But may I join you?"

Cassandra snapped her head around, startled. "Colonel Rubinsky." She paused, at a loss of what to say. "I'm so sorry about what happened, Colonel. And for what it's worth, you have my gratitude for Tamas' bravery."

With all his fifty-nine years of age, Marko Rubinsky held himself with impressive military bearing. Hands clasped behind him, he stood as straight-backed as if his spine were actually a steel girder. Iron-gray hair and close-cropped beard framed the same rugged handsomeness he shared with his son. "When word came through about attacks taking place—St. Ives, Indicass—Tamas took company and went after you. Nothing could have stopped him."

No indication of the colonel's approval, or lack thereof, for his son's heroism. A statement of fact, in the Cossacks' usual straightforward manner. Cassandra chose to read it as acceptance of her gratitude.

"How did it happen?" Rubinsky asked, before she could thank him again for what his son had done.

Where to begin? Cassandra looked back into the room at Tamas, then shifted aside slightly so that his father could also share the view. "The Lancers battalion broke down into companies on day nine to pursue our independent objectives, as planned. On day eleven, the second of May, my command company was hit with heavy radio jamming after sighting a Confederation DropShip. I assumed it to be a

Panzer Brigade company, come looking for us. Since our battle plan called for no heavy engagements, we evaded but could not get out from under its jamming umbrella as it pursued. We caught fragments of messages only, not enough to put anything together.

"Yesterday it caught us."

Rubinsky nodded. "That was after you see Tamas, *da*?"

"Yes. I was catching garbled comms on the private frequency we'd reserved so I knew he was close. Then my scout lance caught sight of him and his company skylining a ridge south of our position. The Confederation DropShip caught us while trying to link up, coming down in between us."

Cassandra shivered at the memory of those next few minutes. She placed her fists against the glass, feeling its cool draw against her knuckles. "We traded fire with the Drop-Ship, Tamas on one side and my company on the other. I saw the rockets go off, four of them, all aerial detonations overhead. I was still waiting for the *Union* to open up its 'Mech bay, but it remained buttoned up tight. Then Tamas ejected. He'd been trying to get through over the commlines, but so close to the DropShip there just wasn't any way. So he punched out of his *Enforcer,* riding the chair up and then sailing his parafoil over the top of the DropShip and into visual. He was wearing a full containment suit, fumbling a bit with the mask." She shook her head. "I can only assume the ejection fouled the mask."

And really what more was there to say. "He must have sailed right through the cloud of nerve agent, and enough got through to put him in there." She nodded toward the CCU bed and then turned to face Tamas' father. No need to mention that she'd understood and ordered her people to seal up their 'Mechs for full containment and retreat. The panic she'd felt, and then the helpless rage when two of her forward-placed warriors were too slow. The rest of it was either implied or could wait. That was Marko Rubinsky's son in there.

For his part, the commander of Rubinsky's Light Horse showed no real emotion. No sorrow or regret. His hard gaze promised retribution, though, and in that Cassandra agreed with him.

"Tamas is strong man," he said simply. "He will pull through." Then he nodded toward his son's CCU room. "It appears they are finished."

Inside the room, the doctors had apparently reached some kind of conclusion. The senior of the two left the room while the other double-checked all equipment. The elder physician closed the door softly behind him, and came over toward Cassandra and Rubinsky.

"Mandrissa Allard-Liao?" he said, more by way of asking for attention than actually confirming her identity. "I'm Doctor Halburren." He glanced at Marko Rubinsky. "You are interested in the status of Tamas Rubinsky?"

Cassandra noted the unkempt dark hair and stubble. The dark rings under bloodshot eyes. *He's probably attended to more serious patients in the last four days, since the attacks began, than in the previous year.*

She nodded. "This is Tamas' father," she said. "Colonel Marko Rubinsky." She looked at the colonel, then asked the question for both of them. "Will he live?"

"Almost certainly," the doctor replied at once, though like most medical personnel Cassandra had ever met he instantly hedged his own opinion. "That is not to say that further complications may not arise."

With Tamas' life out of immediate danger—probably—Cassandra breathed her first sigh of relief in twenty-four hours. Colonel Rubinsky then asked, "Will he pilot a 'Mech again?"

If the physician thought the question cold or callous, he did not show it. Cassandra certainly did not think it inappropriate. She knew it would be on Tamas' lips were he well enough to ask anything. To some MechWarriors, this question could be more important than the first. *Like telling an eagle it may never soar among the clouds again.*

Here the doctor hesitated. "He has lost a significant amount of lung tissue from the agent's blistering effect, and there is no way to judge if the agent will have permanent neural effects."

But he will live—should—*live.* That was something at least. "Thank you," she said for both of them, dismissing the physician. After he left, she said, "I will leave you alone with Tamas, Marko. I need sleep." *But I'll come back later,* she promised Tamas.

And then, a reckoning. *Kali or Sun-Tzu, the Confederation has gone too far this time. I will begin with Confederation forces on St. Loris, and when they have been turned back I will take the war to them. Mother must see the need, or I will convince her. Either way, I will find the hole in the Confederation's armor and I will not stop until my Lancers are dropping on Sian itself.*

However it must happen, I will *see my cousin there.*

Chiang Ho Delta
Xi'an Province, Indicass
Xin Sheng Commonality, Capellan Confederation

Warner Doles waded his *Emporer* out of the Gansu River, at the head of the huge delta that fed into the northwestern arm of Indicass' large inland sea. The last Blackwind Lancer to gain the northern side, he turned around and so fronted the new defensive stand. Brilliantly hued beams of coherent light sniped at his forces from the far shore where two-thirds of the Hustang Warriors regiment formed into a ragged battle line. *Numbers, Ni Tehn Doh. All you have is numbers.*

A *Snake* waded out several meters into the river, followed by several more of the Confederation forces. Its autocannon fired across the reflective expanse of water, ripping a staccato line into the armor of a Lancer *Cossack*. "Target that *Snake*," Doles ordered, determined to make the enemy warrior pay for his bravado.

Energy weapons and streams of autocannon fire converged on the luckless Confederation BattleMech, ravaging its upper half. Doles counted at least one solid blow against its cockpit and hoped for a breach. He didn't get it. The *Snake*'s pilot, realizing his hopeless position and faced with a slow withdrawal from the water, cut in his torso-mounted jump jets and rocketed free of the water's deadly embrace.

With another two companies, Doles thought, *I could retake the southern bank and push the Warriors back into Quining Province.* He had the measure of the Hustaing Warriors now. Enthusiastic and certainly brave, but they had no internal sense of order. *I could break them up into small pieces and destroy them. Where are the rest of the Free Capella Forces?* he wondered, though in truth he knew where. Hiding. Retreating.

Dead.

The attack that had cost Tormano Liao his life and deprived the Free Capella Movement of any effective leadership had not been the last nerve agent attack. A failed attempt had also come against Doles personally. Through a frantic broadcast the Blackwind Lancers learned of a successful use of nerve agent against Brevet-Colonel Emanual and the command lance of his Janissaries, a newer Compact unit recently posted to Indicass to replace the dead Legers. *So Kali did not dredge up a large supply of the nerve agent. Her assassins are going after the Compact's military leadership.*

That did not stop innocents from dying, though. The same attack that took Tormano and Governor Siddara also killed more than three hundred civilians in attendance. ComStar-delivered broadcasts from St. Ives reported that Duchess Liao had survived a second assault against Tiantan, but to expect more of the so-called "Black May" nerve agent attacks. Grudging appreciation had been extended to Sun-Tzu Liao as well, for releasing the information that had no doubt saved thousands, if not millions, of lives. Doles wanted to spit, the taste of that apology bitter even hearing it secondhand.

Doles ordered a tactical retreat from the river bank, falling back north and west. With a bit of luck, the Lancers could lose the Hustaing Warriors in the massive delta. Now was the time for concentrating on their escape. Try as he might, though, he could not stop thinking about the politics of the situation. His white-knuckle grip on his control sticks tightened as he tried to wrap his belief around Sun-Tzu's professed lack of involvement in the nerve agent attacks.

He kept coming up short on belief. *I just can't buy it. Kali's fanatics may be the ones spreading the agent around, but Sun-Tzu still benefits.* Compact units were bogged down by chemical warfare precautions, while Confederation forces with immunity pressed forward.

Of all the attacks to miss, Doles thought, *why did Kali's zealots miss Isis Marik?* He quickly smothered a twinge of conscience over the thought. If they'd even come close, Thomas Marik might have taken the Compact's side and demolished his daughter's ex-fiancée. Instead, by all reports, a Confederation WarShip was ordered to destroy the Thugee JumpShip immediately after it jumped into Necromo, without any chance for surrender.

So Sun-Tzu avoided that possible trap. There would be others. Doles could even hope to set some of them himself. Payback for Hustaing and Denbar. Smithson and Tormano. *The Mandrinn promised me I would get the chance to make a difference, and I intend to hold him to it. Dying doesn't release him from that promise.*

15

Fellfield Plains
Layting, St. Loris
St. Ives Compact
18 May 3062

St. Loris' sun hung low over the Duguan Mountains on the far western horizon, red and orange staining the sky and setting afire a few solitary clouds. Leading the next prisoner escort toward the exchange site, Aris Sung spared the violent sunset only a moment's attention, hoping it portended nothing untoward. *The last place something can afford to go wrong,* Aris thought, *is here.*

On the southern edge of the grassy flatlands, exactly one kilometer distant, *Shiao-zhang* Ty Wu Non held his BattleMech company in reserve against a like number of 'Mechs from the St. Ives Lancers drawn into a battle line one kilometer to the north. Between the two forces, feeling very much like a paper target posted on a shooting range, Aris Sung presided over the prisoner exchange, commanding a single platoon of House Hiritsu infantry. Walking toward the St. Loris Home Guard's position, he knew a moment's regret for allowing them nearly twice as many infantry. *Every one of ours might be worth two of theirs, but it feels a bit different walking into the sights of so many assault rifles.*

Commanding BattleMechs has softened you, Aris told himself. *Taking over in the field today will prove a good reminder.*

Ty Wu Non had originally proposed that Li Wynn handle the exchange of prisoners. Aris, in his capacity as Li's *Sifu,* ordered his charge onto a different operation and personally assumed command of the prisoner exchange. He had been the one to arrange the exchange, following up on his vow to reduce the level of blind violence being demonstrated on both sides of the fighting. If anything went wrong he deserved to be at ground zero. Also, Li Wynn's recent attitude did not exactly recommend him for a diplomatic situation. This prisoner exchange was the next step, Aris hoped, in preventing the conflict on St. Loris from escalating completely out of control. *The nerve agent assaults have strained tensions to the breaking point, no matter that nearly all have been foiled. This has to go well.*

Aris halted the escorting squad at the designated point, waiting for the Compact forces to cover the last ten meters with their next batch of five prisoners. Aris recognized Jasmine Troy, one of his MechWarriors, under Compact Guard. Leg set in a rough cast. Pale and looking a bit gaunt in the face. *Many have shown similar signs of neglect,* Aris noted, *but they are whole and coming home. Now is not the time to make an issue of it.* Preoccupied with finding one of his missing warriors, he nearly missed the female warrior who stepped out of the Compact escort unit just shy of the exchange site.

"You, Captain. Are you Aris Sung?"

He almost ignored the question, sure that the deliberate reversion to pre-Xin Sheng ranking conventions—and regular army at that—was a calculated insult. *The forms that are governing this exchange do not require conversation. They bring over five prisoners at one time and so do we; nothing more.* But a furtive glance at the upstart warrior as he turned away halted him mid-turn. Aris covered his surprise, awarding her a single nod of recognition.

"Major Allard-Liao," he greeted. "I did not think to see you here."

She did not return even the most basic of courtesy. "I wanted to meet the Confederation warrior with enough *qiú* to actually suggest a prisoner exchange on the day of three Black May attacks." Rude and hostile, her tone suggested no forgiveness would be forthcoming.

Aris sensed the increased tension among his infantrymen as they too read Cassandra Allard-Liao's challenging tone. *More than one right now is weighing the risk of taking her out against facing the wrath of Ty Wu Non.* The House Master had guaranteed safe conduct, and at most times that would be enough. But Aris knew from personal experience that some warriors could be pushed too far. "Continue with the operation," Aris said simply, trusting *Ban-zhang* Chess to oversee the current exchange.

To Cassandra, Aris shrugged off her hostile attitude. "We do not coordinate with the rogue Thugee fanatics," he said, voice low and even. Though he doubted she would believe him, he was, in truth, sickened by the nerve agent assaults. He found them appalling. Indicative of the loss of moral center occurring on both sides of this war in which it was Aris' duty to fight. That it placed him at odds with his own nation, *his own House,* was something that could no longer be avoided. The Chancellor's public and furious condemnation of his sister for launching the assaults only slightly restored Aris' faith in the Confederation. *Now it is up to me to restore faith in the House.*

But regardless, he was not about to get drawn into a debate over the situation. *Shiao-zhang Non did not send me out here to argue.* "Shall we continue?" he asked. "The safe conduct is only *officially* in force for another hour."

"I've checked the count," Cassandra said, in no apparent hurry. "We appear to have twelve more captured warriors than you. Home Guard out of Pardray, mostly. Some in need of further medical attention."

"You can deliver them at the end," Aris said easily, though he sensed the attack coming. "Or increase your batches to seven."

Cassandra shook her head, hazel eyes never flinching from Aris. A warm breeze stirred across the grassy plains and tugged at her dark hair. "I see no reason to deliver them without compensation of some sort. That was not in our deal."

Aris folded his arms across his lean chest, trying to affect an air of relaxation that he did not feel. Anything, though, to instill a sense of ease in the surrounding infantry. "We both agreed to bring all prisoners currently held. No provisions were made for anything other than a full exchange."

"Then we can make them," she replied bluntly. "I want a ten-kilometer reversal from your forward lines for every extra prisoner we return." She smiled darkly. "Or would you rather your Pardrayan allies think that their people are not important enough to bargain for?"

"To T'ai Shan, with her," one House infantryman spat, naming a Han god of the underworld.

Aris could not afford to look at his troops. He could only hope their training held out against the major's challenge. "Take them back," he said, gesturing to the Confederation troops Cassandra had escorted over, one of them his own. "All of them if you wish. And we'll take back our prisoners." He shrugged. "Or we can just keep the ones we have, which do include a few more MechWarriors from your St. Ives Lancers." He speared her with an icy gaze, muscles tensing in anticipation of her reaction. "And just maybe we'll begin to treat your warriors with the same *attention* with which you've obviously treated ours."

It was obvious that the last thing Cassandra expected was to hear allegations of misconduct leveled at her. "You arrogant *wang ba dan,*" she yelled, reverting to *hàn-yu* as she cursed him. "I'll set my forces against you right now before I let my warriors suffer another hour in Confederation hands."

Aris waited for a warrior on either side to break the truce, certain Cassandra's outburst would—literally—trigger a response. After two incredibly long and painful heartbeats he said, "You could do that. But before you do, know that the forces behind us are under orders to execute all prisoners remaining before one shot is fired in your direction. They won't have a chance. And with everyone in my squad here gunning for you, Major Allard-Liao, you won't survive the bloodbath either."

"Neither would you, Sung."

"I am certain that House Hiritsu would continue to fight just as well despite my loss," Aris said with due humility and, in his actual opinion, only slightly off from the truth. "Can you say the same for your St. Ives Lancers? Or for what your family would think of the foolish loss of your life?" He let the hard facts sink in. That Cassandra had much more to lose than Aris.

"Bastard," she called him, this time in English.

"Think what you wish," Aris said evenly, feeling the moment's lethal tension beginning to drain away. "I will do whatever is necessary to uphold my oath to House Hiritsu."

"We will begin sending over prisoners in sets of seven," Cassandra ground out through clenched teeth. "But we will be watching the time very closely, I can promise you." She turned and stalked away.

Aris Sung watched her furious retreat. *So much for a gesture of goodwill,* he thought, then immediately buried the idea. *House Warriors do not give up. You will try again.*

It cannot be too late.

Dressed in a full containment suit for chemical warfare, effectively an EVA "spacesuit" for operations under gravity, *Pai-zhang* Li Wynn supervised his platoon's cleanup efforts. Some carried bodies to be cremated on site. Others worked to decontaminate the area with a strong alkaline wash. All the time Li Wynn watched, and nodded his approval.

Ruann's spaceport on St. Loris was the latest site for a Thugee nerve agent attack, a partially successful one, and in the fading light of St. Loris' dusk it looked as much a battlefield as any Li had yet seen. Bodies sprawled everywhere over the tarmac, faces and clothing stained with the blood they had hemorrhaged. Many still clutched small arms of various types, no real organization apparent but their effectiveness showing in two wrecked Líu-yán hover transports that still burned greasy black smoke into the skies tinted red by a slow sunset.

These people died defending Cossacks. They bought time for the mercs to escape the attack and relocate north. Li prodded at a body with his foot. *Serves them right,* he decided. *There is no room in the Confederation for traitorous dogs such as these, who would support mercenaries before answering the call of their own Capellan heritage.* Li prodded at the body, harder, grateful to Aris Sung for the assignment.

On learning that Aris had gotten him reassigned from command of the prisoner exchange to supervising this decontamination, Li had known a moment's anger against his *Sifu. Why send me out here, away from the rest of the House, if not for another punishment?* Ever since the House gathering, and Aris' public chastisement of Li Wynn, the young warrior had gone to great lengths to avoid his Mentor. Better that than have to face the doubts cropping up concerning Aris.

Li was one of the select few who actually knew of Aris' exploits when House Hiritsu had taken Kaifeng away from the Sarna Supremacy. How the young MechWarrior had fallen victim to a subversive movement within House Hiritsu itself, surviving by wits and a touch of audacious luck to finally destroy the cancer within the House. This was the Aris Sung now advocating caution and moderation? The one who blatantly challenged *Shiao-zhang* Non and even implied a rebuke against Chancellor Liao? Li Wynn had suffered his doubts in silence, watching and waiting.

Apparently his worries had been in error. Here, Aris had done him a favor. *Who wants to spend a day under a safe conduct, exchanging prisoners?* Here was where the real war could be found. All about him, a glorious testament to Chancellor Sun-Tzu Liao's absolute power. The Chancellor might shield himself from the political fallout by using his sister, Kali, but Li Wynn doubted anything ever happened on Sian—or in the entire Confederation, for that matter— without Sun-Tzu Liao's direct knowledge.

If Aris sent me here to learn, to understand, then surely this is the reason. Breath loud in his ears, echoing in the sterile confines of the protective suit, Li Wynn gazed out over the field of cold death, watching his men work. A sky of red and orange, blotted by black smoke, hung heavily overhead. *Like the reflection of a world on fire.* Li Wynn found it very appropriate.

Let it burn, he thought, nodding silent approval to the omen. *Let the entire St. Ives Compact burn.*

16

Hondah Spaceport
Hazlet, Nashuar
St. Ives Compact
22 May 3062

Smoke from a dozen fires hung a black shroud over the northern edge of Nashuar's capital, thinning as it reached out toward Hazlet's spaceport but still choking the air with the scent of burning homes and businesses. Orange tinged the sky. The sound of distant alarms promised that firefighters still battled, though radio reports suggested they were finally getting the last few blazes under control.

"It's only property loss," Maurice Fitzgerald muttered, mostly to himself, lowering his end of the stretcher to the ground. "No one left alive to rescue by now."

Holding up the other end of the stretcher, Danielle Singh frowned at the remark. "It could have been much worse, Maurice." She glanced about the triage area, sighed. "And it could've been much better too."

Relief efforts for this latest Black May attack had been set up on the spaceport's southern grounds, proximity and large open spaces secondary recommendations to the arrival of Kuan Yin Allard-Liao and the mandrissa's latest attempt to bring humanitarian aid to besieged planets of the

Compact. Kuan Yin's trio of DropShips, an *Overlord* and two *Union* Class, framed a triangle in which triage and treatment occupied two corners, while an offload of supplies slowly filled the third. Smoke-inhalation victims, such as the one the two MechWarriors had just carried over from the arriving ambulances, dominated the triage area. They came from areas bordering the attack sites. The few survivors from within the burning zones, those who miraculously escaped the nerve agent and arson-set fires, had long since been treated or evacuated to better facilities. Fitzgerald would never forget the open blisters and blinded eyes left by the agent's blistering effect, which he knew were minor compared to the internal damage.

Danielle shivered, possibly recalling the same sight. "Let's be thankful it missed Brevet-Colonel Nevarr."

To that Fitzgerald could only nod, though it was bittersweet consolation. With this latest Thugee attack Major Nevarr, commander of the Nashuar Home Guard, was now the ranking St. Ives Compact officer on planet. Senior Colonel Trahn Soo Lee, Nashuar's military coordinator, had been caught at ground zero with Colonel Leonid Perrin, CO of the Blackwind Lancers regiment and on planet with his first battalion. Hauptmann General Seiser, commander of the Seventh Federated Commonwealth RCT in the city to coordinate with Senior Colonel Lee, was reported killed in one of the several arson-set fires. "If the Nightriders had attacked today, they would've taken the city."

"All indications show that McCarron's Cavalry has pulled back," Danielle said, stepping aside as a nurse moved in to take care of the new patient. "Orders from above, probably. Sun-Tzu Liao trying to distance his forces from the Thugee attacks." Her face visibly tightened, and Fitz noted the grim tone. "Not that it will help him in the end."

Fitzgerald kept his opinions to himself. He knew that the Nightriders had faced the first nerve agent attack on Wei. Perhaps use of the agent in support of the Confederation had them troubled. Something in that thought sat right with him, in the same way it explained the Nightriders' previously yicious persecution of the war on Nashuar. Not that their reluctance to attack now would gain them any amount of empathy. The conflict on Nashuar had reached a self-sustaining level. The larger political picture did not seem to matter as much. So the fighting would continue, Fitz had no doubt. And now it would be worse than ever.

If there was a way to make a difference any more, Fitz couldn't see it.

Royal Palace
Tian-tan, St. Ives

From the third-floor window of her St. Ives' palace complex, Duchess Candace Liao looked out onto the turmoil surrounding the distant main gates. Soldiers in protective suits moved warily around the wrecked Savannah Master that had breached the gates only to be ripped open by a patrolling *Helios* BattleMech. The arrival of a decontamination team confirmed her prediction without need of a messenger sure to be on his way. *Another Thugee attack.*

Candace folded her arms across her midsection, each hand gripping the opposite forearm to hide the trembling she felt building. Not out of fear. At seventy-four she still did not fear death, even by so foul a means as the Wei nerve agent. Her early career as a MechWarrior in service to the Confederation had mostly proofed her against such fears, with a final excising the day she officially broke her St. Ives Compact away from the Confederation. She later survived the assassination attempt that claimed her husband, but avenged him by killing her sister Romano. In the last month she had remained in the palace in the face of five—now six—Thugee assaults, rather than flee to a secret sanctuary.

No, her hands did not threaten to betray fear, but her rage.

Over ten thousand dead to nerve agent attacks. Indicass lost, and the setbacks on Taga and Nashuar threatening to tip the balance there as well. Cassandra, on St. Loris, saved only by the near-fatal sacrifice of Tamas Rubinsky. Simone Devon, an invaluable aide and a friend, not so lucky—paying the price Candace herself would surely have paid if not for a failed pirate-point jump. Tormano dead and his son missing. She still found it hard to believe the last. Her brother had been a survivor, yet was the first to fall to Kali's madness-inspired pogrom. Kali, the death goddess. Truly Romano's daughter.

And a person whose life I held in my hands ten years ago, when I spared both her and Sun-Tzu my vengeance over Justin's death. What was it I told him? "Adversity makes you stronger, and I'd rather you look for adversaries within your own home than outside." Candace remembered her feelings of satisfaction that day. *But Sun-Tzu found an adversary in my Compact regardless. And Kali's madness, with which I had hoped to burden my nephew, has instead returned to haunt me.*

Yes, thousands dead. Only by the grace of Sun-Tzu were the death tolls not pushing upwards of hundreds of thousands. With the information provided by him, through Ion Rush, attacks were prevented or at the least mitigated in severity. But that angered her as well, the injustice that left her in her nephew's debt. His immediate actions and his push for justice against Kali notwithstanding, it would be so easy to blame him. *As my people already do.* But that was an injustice worthy of Romano, or their father before them. It was only her anger speaking.

She knew better than to let rage get the better of her judgment, and certainly not to let it show when her resolve cracked. "The people of St. Ives need stability and strength," she said aloud. And stability she had given them, three decades' worth bought with their defection from the Confederation. *Now I have to be strong, because my nation has no more strength to give.*

Caroline Seng's dire prediction of two months ago, that the Compact had very little time to realize its hope of any viable resistance, became more real with every weekly report. Kai had bought them respite with his drive through Confederation systems. Sun-Tzu's loss of a secure border with the Free Worlds League had helped them even more, bleeding away troops to garrison the Confederation's anti-spinward boundaries. And the Compact forces now fought with a fanatic's zeal, demanding retribution in the form of Confederation lives—*Capellan lives,* she reminded herself. Still, the cracks were telling in the Compact's support and logistics structure, soon to be reflected in front-line performance.

Any remote chance for reconciliation, for any form of peaceful solution, died with Tormano. And with every Compact life lost since to the Thugee attacks. And there could be no sacrificing of worlds, as Seng had suggested, no matter what the benefit to the Compact. Her people could not now accept anything but a victory impossible to attain. Not until their own rage was burned out of them. So the war would continue, the days, weeks, and months paid for by lives that Kali could claim even though they did not fall directly to her Thugee followers. There was no other way.

"Damn you, Sun-Tzu," she said, allowing herself the fleeting release that cursing her nephew brought her. *Damn you for not keeping a rein on Kali, and so forcing me into this decision. Between us, we will grind up the Compact until you sicken over the price we extract, or until nothing remains for you to claim but a shattered realm. Our* hopeless battle. *One final stand.*

Perhaps that is the only solution left to us.

17

Celestial Palace
Zi-jin Chéng, Sian
Sian Commonality, Capellan Confederation
4 June 3062

Sun-Tzu Liao avoided the Celestial Throne, slowly pacing the edge of the dais and feigning deep thought as Talon Zahn and Ion Rush continued to report on the latest situation. His mind swam in a realm of chaos, fighting back memories of Romano Liao as he tried to untangle the various threads that he had begun in the last year and a half. And in truth, he was still upset over Sasha Wanli's disappearance from the palace and, apparently, from Sian. The directed pacing was all he could—all he would—allow himself for release.

He had noticed over the last several weeks, since the day of Kali's announcement, Sasha's mechanical performance of her duties. Her attitude of heavy acceptance when commanded into the presence of her lord, as if expecting the firing squad to be lined up within the throne room. It bothered him, likely more than it should, that one of his closest advisors still thought of him in the same terms as his mother even after so clear an example to the contrary. Romano Liao would've killed Sasha immediately. And though Sun-

Tzu considered ordering her death on any given day, the fact remained that he had made his decision and would not have reversed it. Not for all of the memories of Romano that continued to plague him, hating Sasha for her failures and frailty.

Frailty, or fabrication?

In the space of a single night, Sasha Wanli, head of the Maskirovka, simply vanished. No evidence that she'd even left the palace, though certainly she might have discovered a secret passage unknown to the Chancellor. But then no contact with the Mask, and complete evasion of their search for her? This was not the work of a broken woman. It spoke of preparation, and resolve. And *if Sasha can desert me so easily, how much can I trust my other advisors?*

"Our final reports," Talon Zahn was saying, "place Kai Allard-Liao at only fifty percent material strength, approximately eighty percent in personnel. His losses on Capella were the worst yet."

Sun-Tzu frowned. "Not so bad that he did not fail to escape," he said sharply. The trap set on Capella had closed on his cousin, only to be ripped open as the First St. Ives Lancers fought their way free. "Your estimates place the Sarna regiment at eighty percent material losses, forty percent personnel." The long pause that greeted Sun-Tzu warned him that he had made a mistake.

"Kai went for the 'Mech production sites," Zahn said, tone neutral as he skirted the edge of blatantly correcting his Chancellor, "expecting the same level of resistance the SMA gave him before, and was bloodied for it. His victory there is a hollow one—the Lancers will be forced to withdraw to friendly space for refitting. And the Sarna Supremacy is even more under your control, Chancellor, with their primary regiment shattered." His dark eyes narrowed. "The trap was never designed to capture your cousin."

Kai's military victory versus an even more valuable political gain. That *had been* the plan. Sun-Tzu stopped his pacing and calmly retook his seat on the Celestial Throne. An unforgivable breach of discipline on his part, but certainly Zahn did not need further reason to doubt his lord and master.

"*Sang-jiang-jun* Zhan," Sun-Tzu said softly with an icy stare, "is it so much to ask that occasionally my armed forces perform *above* expectations?"

Reminded of his failure to meet his own predictions with regard to the St. Ives conflict and Chaos March operation, Zahn braced himself to attention. "No, Chancellor," he answered.

Sun-Tzu nodded his acceptance of the formal acquiescence, though inwardly he regretted the unnecessary rebuke. "Do you have anything positive to report?" he asked, giving Zahn any chance to redeem himself.

In this, the senior general was prepared. "We know where Kuan Yin is basing herself," he said with so much calm assurance that Sun-Tzu instantly believed him.

As much as Cassandra's spirited defense of the Teng Front hurt Confederation interests, at times Sun-Tzu thought Kuan Yin's ubiquitous presence even more damaging. She seemed to be everywhere, delivering humanitarian aid and winning the approval of the Compact's people and, more importantly, undercutting Sun-Tzu's efforts to provide the same support for said benefits.

"Where?" he asked, eyes narrowing in anticipation. In his mind he could imagine Romano Liao as eager for the information, and for this one time allowed his own thoughts to mirror hers. If he could shut Kuan Yin down . . .

Zahn nodded to Ion Rush, passing the discussion to the Imarra House Master. "Kittery," he said simply, naming the Federated Commonwealth world that nestled in the fold between the two arms of the St. Ives Compact.

Kittery? A FedCom world? "You are sure?" Sun-Tzu demanded.

"Her travels initially gave it away," Zahn said. "Back and forth between the St. Ives and Teng Fronts, with no sightings of her in transit. That meant she had to be cutting across either FedCom space or through the dead systems. Her speed between worlds argued for the Commonwealth."

"She's using their recharge stations," Sun-Tzu surmised.

Zahn and Rush both nodded. "The Hustaing Warriors captured some supplies she left behind on Indicass," Rush said. "We traced the manufacturer codes on most of the equipment to Kittery."

Where I can't touch her without risking Katrina's wrath. A chill shook Sun-Tzu's core, though he kept it from showing. *A good thing this was not discovered before Kali's killing spree.* A nerve agent attack on the soil of the Federated Commonwealth might have spelled the end of the Confederation. Still, it frustrated him to have another potential handle on the situation placed just out of reach. He tried to ignore his mother's whispers, urging him to hit Kittery regardless.

"What about the nerve agent attacks?" he asked, the reminder of Kali's madness forcing the issue to the front of his mind.

"Only two in the last several days," Zahn answered. "The Thugee cult has about run its course, it seems."

Sun-Tzu nodded. "Damage control?"

The Imarra House Master fielded the question. In the last month, Ion Rush had been working closely with the Maskirovka in anticipation of Sasha's eventual dismissal. With her disappearance, he'd assumed temporary command over Sian operations. "Your swift action in revealing the attacks, and now in turning Kali over for a war crimes trial on Atreus, has distanced you from the atrocities and lessened the impact on the Confederation."

With a shallow nod, Sun-Tzu accepted the report. "Luthien would have been a better choice, in my mind. This gives Thomas a free hand at damaging the Confederation." *I should have expected it. Thomas is positioning himself to become the Star League's next First Lord, so of course he would request to sit in judgment over the trial. Atreus is also much more convenient to the concerned parties.*

Rush held his gaze against Sun-Tzu's without flinching. "Theodore Kurita, acting as First Lord, *has* seconded your request to place Naomi Centrella on the tribunal," he reminded the Chancellor.

"A good indication that the Star League is not about to

condemn the Confederation outright," Sun-Tzu agreed. Though that possibility certainly still existed, should the trial go poorly. "Naomi will safeguard our interests," he said, though he disliked placing so much importance on an event outside his control.

Zahn's uneasy expression showed that the Confederation's senior general was equally dubious about having to depend so heavily on Naomi. Sun-Tzu sensed his mother's displeasure as well, though whether for the trial of her daughter or Sun-Tzu's acceptance of a Periphery proxy representative, he couldn't be sure. *Both,* he decided. "We have to display a motive toward true justice," Sun-Tzu felt forced to explain. "A direct Confederation representative could not be allowed."

Ion Rush merely stared impassively at the Chancellor, accepting the explanation. Talon Zahn's discomfiture appeared to stem from another source, however. "I doubt it would have made the difference if the Federated Commonwealth were not deep in its own difficulties just now. Katrina would have seized upon the opportunity to leverage her entire nation against you."

And, from a detached viewpoint, Sun-Tzu could not have faulted her for it. What perfect timing, to be handed a humanitarian excuse for invasion, with the bulk of the opposing military committed to other areas. Katrina Steiner-Davion's forces would have rolled over his smaller state once and for all, despite their loose alliance. Fortunately for the Confederation, Katrina was not having as easy a time as she'd probably expected, sitting on the thrones of two realms.

"What is our military status?" he asked.

"Misleading," Talon said at once, blunt as ever, "if you consider only our recent advances. The shock of Black May on the Compact's overall ability to defend itself allowed us to make incredible gains, not the least of which is complete control over Indicass. But unit to unit we are taking heavier losses, and the Compact populace is becoming harder to control as well. Insurgent activities are on the increase." He paused for effect. "The deathwatch is down to one minute forty-five seconds."

"Do you know what it is we are lacking?" Sun-Tzu asked aloud, the question obviously rhetorical. "Focus." The answer reflected the turmoil in his own mind as well as that within his realm. "We've lost that over the past year, and our regiments are now caught up in the war for its own sake." He captured the gaze of his two advisors with his own jade stare. "We need to establish our legitimacy."

Zahn frowned his puzzlement. "Didn't we do that?" he asked. "Establishing ourselves in the Compact, and demonstrating a desire on several worlds for the return of the Confederation?"

"Not enough," Sun-Tzu said with a light shake of his head. "We need something more. Something symbolic, that both sides of the St. Ives conflict have to recognize."

Ion Rush leaned forward, a mountain of a man looking for a direction in which to fall. "Do you have a suggestion, Chancellor?"

Sun-Tzu nodded. In his mind's eye, he saw the one thread that might finally pull free the knots. *So many failed attempts,* he reminded himself. *But this could be it.* He trailed the edge of one long fingernail along the arm of the Celestial Throne, its razor edge cutting a thin groove into the dark wood grain. A path, among darker shadows.

When he spoke, it was in a melodic whisper, recalling an old rhyme. "As I was going to St. Ives . . ."

18

Shí-gao Badlands
Henan District, Ambergrist
St. Ives Compact
9 June 3062

Little survived in Ambergrist's Shi-gao Badlands except cactus and hardy scrub brush. Standing rock formations carved up into the horizon. Overhead, in the washed-out blue sky, a solitary fighter belonging to the Hustaing Warriors buzzed low over the battlefield, homing in on the smoke trailed skyward by a burning Drillson hovertank. Twin Vedettes rolled by their luckless comrade, followed by a *Victor* and a *Raven*.

The *Raven* and the Vedettes plunged down into an arroyo, hoping to find a faster path by which to chase the fleeing Free Capella company. *Sang-shao* Ni Tehn Doh walked his *Victor* up to the low end of a hill, taking advantage of what little cover the badlands afforded. Rocks and gravel, the detritus of the high cliffs, were crushed to powder underfoot of the eighty-ton war machine. At the peak of the rise, he surprised a Free Capella *Blackjack* that chose the wrong moment to break cover from behind the edge of a bluff. He pulled his targeting reticule across the main screen, letting it drop onto the fleeing BattleMech. His Gauss rifle spat out a silvery ball that blurred its way across the short distance to take the *Blackjack* high on the right leg. Four short-ranged missiles trailing smoke and fire also arced in on the wounded machine, three of them scattering across its wide torso while the fourth blew large chunks out of a nearby standing rock formation.

The *Blackjack*'s pilot held the medium-weight 'Mech to its feet, and might have escaped into a shallow valley had another Hustaing Warrior not suddenly appeared in its path and blocked the way. The new BattleMech, an older *Griffin* design, was more closely matched to the *Blackjack*'s fire-power. But rather than trade salvos, the *Blackjack* simply spun away from the new arrival and right back under Doh's weapons.

For its part, the *Griffin* turned its back on the *Blackjack* to fire on an enemy machine further up the draw, one that Doh could not see.

"All yours, *Sang-shao*," a voice called over the comm unit built into Doh's neurohelmet. It was *Si-ben-bing* Taho, one of the newest additions to the Arcade Rangers.

Triggering a full spread of weapons, Doh opened up a channel to Taho. "You get an easy backshot like that, you take it," he ordered, watching as his lasers carved more holes into the hapless *Blackjack* and a second Gauss hit snapped the leg right off. A tremor ran through the *Victor* as the *Blackjack*'s light autocannon chewed away armor from the larger 'Mech's left side, but the *Victor*'s gyro was easily up to the task. "You don't turn your back on an enemy and invite the same."

A burst of static in Doh's ear warned him of a broken transmission, which in this maze of arroyos, valleys, and cliffs could happen in under as little as half a kilometer. "I'll take the hit on that one, *Sang-shao*." The voice of *Sao-shao* Evans, Taho's commander. "I pulled his fire my way to help take down a nice new *Cossack*. The FreeCaps don't stick their heads out of their holes long, and I wanted to make sure we brought this one down. Besides"—the transmission could not rob Evans of his humor—"we never expect you to need our help."

Gritting his teeth, the commander of the Hustaing Warriors accepted the implied comment. Battle is not the time for teaching or preaching, he reminded himself, but for harder lessons. But he silently promised Evans a sit-down talk once the area was secure. Not that he expected it to do much good.

It was hard to argue with success.

Disorganized and unsupported, Free Capella forces had been routed off Indicass and now Doh's Hustaing Warriors were contesting Ambergrist. The Warriors were riding high on the elation of victory. Such times were rare in the history of the Confederation Armed Forces, but not completely unknown, and he did not want to begrudge his regiment the moment.

Unfortunately, his children-warriors treated his advice far too casually. They continued to take chances that would normally get a warrior dispossessed, if not killed outright. But did it matter if their approach was still working? If the FreeCaps ever got a moment to see how rash were Doh's Warriors, they could certainly make the victories much more costly. The trick was to prepare for when resistance finally toughened up.

Or at least, that was what the *sang-shao* had discovered over his long career; hard lessons learned during the Confederation's darker times. But for all the unit's bumbling, unorthodox start, the Hustaing Warriors had still to learn true defeat. The hard-hitting, spine-smashing defeat that would rob a new unit of its air of immortality.

Ni Tehn Doh could hope that his warriors would never know such times, both for their own sake and the greater glory of the Confederation, but thought the likelihood remote at best. War, like anything else in life, had its cycles. *When our time is called, nothing can stand in the way of catastrophe.*

I can only hope to be there, to help pick up the pieces.

* * *

Treyhang Liao hated Ambergrist. A stunted social calendar, lack of any good resorts, no major sporting events; the world had nothing to recommend it. He had never, in his tours, heard of anyone saying they'd caught The Season on Ambergrist, and for good reason. He threw back another Gibson with a practiced flick of his wrist, leaving the tiny onion rolling about in the glass as the liquid traced a warm path down toward the emptiness. *Well, at least the planet boasts a flavorful vermouth.*

Trading on the Free Capella Movement, Treyhang had borrowed a rural estate far from any fighting. As he walked a familiar path from lounge chair to the study's wet bar, he passed what he considered to be another semi-permanent fixture of the room. "Sure I can't offer you some refreshment, Major?"

Warner Doles was beginning to qualify as another good object for Treyhang's animosity. Both men had ended up on Ambergrist because the Free Capella Movement listed supporters all over the world, and all JumpShips had headed here after abandoning Indicass. At first, Treyhang welcomed the Blackwind Lancers officer, tired of the way other Free Capella soldiers fawned over him as they had . . . others. Treyhang enjoyed life, and sought admiration in the right circles, but sycophants he did not suffer easily.

The major, though, irritated him in other ways. The big man refused to relax even in the slightest, always staring at Treyhang as if the young Liao owed him some kind of personal favor, and carrying himself around as if nothing could affect him. Even now, with Doles braced up against the wall, Treyhang couldn't be sure which depended on the other for support.

Doles waited for Treyhang to begin pouring, and then said, "I believe your father preferred plum wine."

A violent start splashed gin onto the cuff of Treyhang's suit. He replaced the bottle with a trembling hand. "Bastard." Doles merely shrugged off the curse.

Treyhang tried not to think about Tormano or how he had passed his final moments. That last remark of Doles' irritated him enough that he briefly considered taking a swing at him for it, prevented only by the mere fact that Doles claimed ten centimeters and twenty kilos on him. Treyhang finished making his drink instead. "I know I'm a lot of fun to be around, Doles, but just what is it you want from me?"

"One hundred tons of munitions, twice that in armor, for starters."

Treyhang patted down his suit pockets, pretending to search, shook his head and then fished a new onion from the jar.

The Lancers officer was not about to let it rest. "Free Capella is disintegrating, Trey. Maybe it's not so bad on other worlds, but these people were with Tormano when it happened. They are scattered and being eaten alive piecemeal. Your father's dream is dying out there, man by man."

Taking a sip of his drink, Treyhang broke off with a light shake of his head. "It's not my dream." He cocked his head to one side, studying Doles as if he were some kind of abstract painting. "Not your dream either, really. When I met you, I would have wagered C-bills against Solaris script that you were dragooned into Free Capella. Why are you still around?"

"I made a deal with Tormano," Doles answered quickly. "What's your excuse?"

Treyhang carefully blanked his face and continued to sip at his drink, far too experienced a gamesman to show Doles the hit. The fact remained, though, that he didn't have an excuse. "I've got my own agenda to pursue," he said vaguely.

Doles threw a glance at the Gibson. "I can see that." Then he looked Treyhang up and down as carelessly as someone inspecting a racehorse. "Looks like you're making progress."

Treyhang pulled himself erect with wounded dignity. "What's that supposed to mean?"

"Have you taken a good look at yourself?" Doles asked. He stepped forward and locked a vice-like grip on Treyhang's elbow, guiding him over to a wall-mounted mirror.

Forced to look, Treyhang first noted the rumpled suit, which on some worlds could have been traded for a small car. Sloppily knotted tie, and a dark stain on the sleeve showed where he had recently spilled the alcohol on it. Disheveled hair. Black-ringed eyes. And he needed a shave.

"I've seen worse," he said. "A bit rumpled perhaps." Reaching up, he straightened the tie with practiced fingers and then combed them back through his hair. "With the right barber and a bit of effort, I could turn this into the latest fashion."

"Tormano told me that you'd promised him two months," Doles said bluntly. "You routinely welsh on your debts, Trey?"

Treyhang winced visibly. Now that was hitting below the belt. It occurred to him to wonder how Doles knew of the deal, then figured it was part of Tormano's plans to keep his new heir-apparent around longer. *Well, you failed on your end of the bargain,* he thought with savage fury, not completely sure why he was angry or even to what bargain he referred.

"What do you need me for?" he asked, pulling his arm out of Doles' grip. "You know what you want. Go figure it out yourself."

Doles' eyes burned into him like twin laser bolts. "Having you here makes it impossible. Cooperation is impossible without central authority, and no one is about to trust my leadership when Tormano's son is on planet. They expect the decisions to come from you now."

The other man's words fanned a small ember down inside the emptiness that Treyhang's self-enforced isolation had been nurturing. He quenched it under the memories of an absent father.

"They've made a mistake," he said flatly, turning away but continuing to watch Doles in the mirror.

The look Doles spent on him was not one Treyhang was used to receiving. Pitying. "I guess so. They've mistaken you for a Liao." With a light shrug, the big man turned his back on Treyhang and walked out of the room.

Left to himself, Treyhang Liao spent several minutes studying his own face. He dashed the contents of his glass against the mirror, the splash of liquid blurring his reflection. Watching it drain away, he caught a pale reflection of Tormano staring back at him, the ghost of a smile tugging at drawn lips.

"All right, Father," he whispered. "You win."

19

Fellfield Plateau
Layting, St. Loris
St. Ives Compact
11 June 3062

Cassandra Allard-Liao steadied Tamas Rubinsky with a
hand on his arm, keeping him well back from the edge of the
bluff. From their position they already had a good enough
view of the DropShips of Warrior House Hiritsu. Eight kilometers distant, the four spheroid vessels towered over the
fields of tall, pale-yellow grasses and the occasional stand
of juniper scrub. One could almost imagine them as buildings, the *Overlord* rising more than forty stories high, in-
congruously relocated to the middle of St. Loris' Fellfield
Plateau.

"Think they really are leaving?" she asked, more to break
the tension and draw Tamas out of his heavy silence than a
true need for information. Something deep within Cassandra promised her that the Warrior House was actually quit-
ting St. Loris, though for what darker purpose she was blind
to at the moment.

Tamas drew in a deeper breath, a precursor to speech demanded by his damaged lungs' need for more oxygen.
"Confederation cannot afford to provide WarShip escort for

routine matters," he said, voice weak but still giving off a trace of its former power. "House Daidachi holds at nadir jump point still?"

"As of the latest reports, yes." Cassandra shielded her eyes from the noon sun. "The recharge station has them under surveillance."

The mercenary nodded, what should have been a simple gesture made suddenly unfamiliar in the way his muscles stuttered the motion. "*Da.* They leave, then." With both hands he raised his optics, twin to the set Cassandra wore slung about her own neck, to study the far-off vessels in greater detail. His hands trembled. Beneath her grip on his arm, Cassandra felt the muscles bunching as Tamas fought to hold the optics steady.

Cassandra removed her hand, allowing him some privacy as he fought against the after-effects of the Black May agent. She admired in Tamas his strength of will, though this one time she wondered if the hard-headedness he'd inherited from his father wasn't working against him. Barely recovered from the pneumonia caused by the blistering of his lungs, he still suffered some light neurological damage that evidenced itself in the degeneration of his musculature control.

Cassandra thought he belonged in the hospital, but Tamas had refused further convalescence. He'd told her that "activity would do better for me than wasting away in hospital bed." Certainly he looked better, with some color returning to his skin and wearing his field uniform rather than wrapped in a thin hospital gown. But it was not the field uniform he wanted, Cassandra knew, but the simpler one she wore of cooling vest, shorts, and combat boots.

MechWarrior's gear.

His first stop from the hospital had been to visit the 'Mech yards and his *Enforcer.* The BattleMech responded sluggishly to Tamas' touch, a lack of compatibility with his neurohelmet slowing his movement down and leaving him with the near-blinding headache of Degenerative Feedback Anomaly. Though rare since the advent of better neuro-circuitry technology, the impairment still surfaced in war-

riors with neurological damage. Head trauma was the chief
cause, though the neurotoxic effect of the Wei agent possessed similar effects. "Time," the physician who had diag-
nosed DFA said, "give it time."

His eyes gave him away, however, and Cassandra was
sure Tamas could read the truth in them as well as she. He
might never pilot a 'Mech again. Even in memory of that
moment, Cassandra shuddered involuntarily. *That could
have been me.*

"There they go," Tamas said, lowering his binoculars.
Smoke roiled out from beneath the *Overlord*'s huge
thrusters as plasma scorched the ground and grasses, and
then the skyscraper lifted off St. Loris on a column of fire.
The two smaller *Union*s touched off next, perfectly coordinated, followed by the *Seeker* Class infantry-carrying
DropShip.

The four vessels casually pulled into a loose diamond
formation as they burned their way spaceward. The *Overlord* rolled, bringing its Confederation emblem into view.
Even at this distance Cassandra could make out the raised
darndao sword thrusting out of the inverted triangle,
painted fifty meters high across the *Overlord*'s battleship-
gray side. That would be the *Dainwu,* Ty Wu Non's command vessel. She spared a brief instant wondering which of
the two smaller *Union* Class DropShips would be carrying
Aris Sung, then dismissed him from her mind.

Good riddance, she wished on them. Her only regret was
that the departure of House Hiritsu was not due more to the
efforts of her Lancers and Rubinsky's Light Horse, but at
least they were gone.

"So, House Hiritsu has left St. Loris," Tamas said as if
reading Cassandra's mind. He slowly lowered the binoculars. "Two Warrior Houses with destroyer escort. Spica,
you think," he asked, naming the nearby world that the
Compact actually shared with the Federated Commonwealth, "or maybe Tantara?"

Cassandra had been worrying over the same question.
"The WarShip would make sense if they expected FedCom
opposition trying for Spica." She sighed. "Or for Tantara,

since it's deep within Compact-controlled space and the current logistics center for our resistance along the Teng Front." She chewed on her lower lip in thought, then shook her head. *Trying to second-guess Sun-Tzu is to bring order from chaos. He even managed to set a trap for Kai, which is no mean feat.* "With a double-jump, they can strike at any world in the Compact from here. We'll hear soon enough where they hit."

"Sooner than we like," Tamas said, echoing Cassandra's earlier thoughts. He turned to face her, his expression unreadable. "You will be leaving now?"

After a second's hesitation, Cassandra nodded an affirmative. "Yes. With the Cossacks' first regiment returning to St. Loris you'll be well-matched against the Panzer Brigade, and intel doubts the 151st Air Wing will stray far from Pardray. I've been ordered to Tantara for refit, and then to Ambergrist, where we're taking a beating." She hadn't meant to let that last slip out, with the bitterness it entailed. She was too relaxed around Tamas, she knew. *But by the gods I need someone out here to keep me sane.* And until she admitted to leaving just now, she hadn't realized how much she would miss him.

Tamas smiled thinly, without humor, at her evident frustration. "Still tired of reacting?" he asked.

She nodded. "More than ever," she admitted. "With Kai limping home after the battle on Capella, it's imperative to arrange a new push against the Confederation itself. Kali's reign of death hurt efforts on both sides of this war." She knew a moment of remorse when Tamas flinched, but then pushed on. "And now it's a matter of who can regain the initiative first."

Without either taking any cue from the other, both glanced skyward toward the retreating specks that was House Hiritsu burning toward rendezvous with a Confederation WarShip. Neither put their concerns into words.

"You have done wonders along Teng Front, Cassandra," Tamas said after a deep breath. "In case you forget."

Cassandra could hear the strain of their conversation as his weary tone thickened his Slavic accent. She tried to demur, give him a chance to recover, but Tamas shook off her concern. "Without you, many Light House warriors would have died on Indicass. We not forget that. Neither will others you help." He paused for a few more deep breaths, a slight wheeze betraying the effort it required. "You build up much good"—he paused, obviously in search of the right word—"much good *karma*. I believe you will get your wish."

Cassandra appreciated Tamas' effort, though it really did little to loosen up the concern tying her into knots. "Then I wish to drop on Sian," she said, then sighed as she added, "someday. For now, though, it's Tantara and then Ambergrist."

Tamas nodded. "When you do take offensive, you will come back for me first," he said.

She blinked her surprise. "For you?" she asked.

"Me and my company. You need watching over sometimes." Tamas' tone was light, but his expression deadly serious. "We have deal, Cassandra Allard-Liao?"

A year ago—a month ago—Cassandra might have taken offense at the suggestion that she could not take care of herself. At the very least she would have deflected the conversation to a lighter subject. But Tamas had earned several times over the right to question her limitations, and she wasn't about to make light of his concern for her well-being.

"We have a deal, Tamas Rubinsky," she said formally, with a slight bow.

Tamas' serious mask fell away slightly at her words. "Good. Now, we go back to your 'Mech. I have bottle and glasses stashed."

Wading through his accent, and her own weariness, it took Cassandra a few moments to make sense of the statement. "You what?"

"Vodka," Tamas said. "And two glasses. Hidden in your *Cestus*. We toast deals in the Light Horse, you remember."

Why should she feel surprised at his preparations, Cassandra couldn't be sure. It was the same level of attention she had come to know from Tamas Rubinsky. "Reminded," she said, "and gratefully." She gestured back toward the treeline and offered him her arm to lean on. *If nothing else,* Cassandra told herself, *take a lesson from the Cossacks and learn to enjoy a moment with a friend. Leave tomorrow's troubles for tomorrow.*

Sound advice, if only she could displace the nagging doubts that continued to plague her.

A final skyward glance couldn't find House Hiritsu.

Riding The Tempest

Your aim must be to take All-under-Heaven intact. Thus your troops are not worn out and your gains will be complete. This is the art of offensive strategy.

—Sun-Tzu, *The Art of War*

When it appears impossible to gain the military advantages once so easily apparent, a ruler must ask two hard questions of himself or forever be ill at ease. What is the goal? Is it worth the price that will be paid?

For myself, I sleep well at nights, able to answer both.

—Sun-Tzu Liao, journal entry,
8 October 3062, Sian

20

Matawan Flats
Jersey District, Nashuar
Xin Sheng Commonality, Capellan Confederation
19 June 3062

The air shimmered as Nashuar's sun beat mercilessly down on the battlefield, raising outside temperatures to a scorching forty degrees Celsius while inside the cockpits of BattleMechs and armored vehicles the MechWarriors and tank crewmen sweated out temperatures even higher. Azure whips of particle projection cannon fire arced out between 'Mechs and just as often between a 'Mech and the ground, these errant shots alone raining more energy onto Nashuar than the worst electrical storm in the planet's history.

Bursts of autocannon fire ripped through the air and the smoke trailing missiles slowly dispersed downwind. Gem-colored laser fire washed pale in the brightness of the day. Several areas blazed out of control, trees and brush baked tinder-dry in Nashuar's recent heat wave and easily set afire by energy weapons that otherwise failed to hit their mark. Blankets of smoke screened off large portions of the battlefield.

It was the largest battle in which Subcommander Maurice Fitzgerald had ever participated. And just as he'd predicted several weeks ago, the fighting was no less brutal for Black May having run its course. Fitz recalled the confidence with which Brevet-Colonel Nevarr had explained the day's battle plan involving Nashuar's Home Guard battalion, the remnants of the Blackwind Lancers on planet, and two battalions left from the Seventh Regimental Combat Team. All told, better than a full regiment of 'Mechs supported by half that strength in armor and infantry. Certainly enough to sweep the two remaining battalions of Nightriders from the field, if the opposing commander had not hit upon a similar plan and fielded two additional 'Mech battalions from a recently arrived Canopian regiment. Over twenty thousand tons of war machines. Over one thousand warriors. Nashuar would claim its price in the blood and resources of four different nations today.

Fitzgerald triggered a full salvo from his *Men Shen,* a new Confederation OmniMech captured this last week from the Nightriders and an impressive trade-up from his old *Blackjack.* Three of four medium pulse lasers stitched emerald darts down the entire left side of a Canopian *Marshal* while the LRM rack mounted over his forward-thrust cockpit drilled nearly a full flight of fifteen missiles across the *Marshal*'s broad torso. The Canopian MechWarrior staggered under the blows but did not fall. His heat levels pushing well into the red zone, Fitz raced the *Men Shen* for the relative safety of a nearby stand of trees not yet ablaze. The *Marshal*'s return fire chased him the entire way, its large laser slicing deep into his right arm and two missiles clipping his rear torso just as he made the treeline.

"Fitz, you're pushing too far east." Though flat and tinny, the transmission failed to completely rob Danielle Singh's voice of concern. "Rein your lance back in."

Sweat stung Fitz' eyes and burned salty on his lips. Gasping a few quick breaths of the cockpit's stifling air, he opened a channel back to Danielle. "Talk to the Blackwind Lancers," he said. The Lancers were supposed to be holding the eastern flank, with Fitz' lance bridging the gap between them and the Home Guard at the center of the battleline. "They pushed northeast, past that burning stand of alder. My flank's open."

As if to underscore his concerns, an aerospace fighter trailing plasma fire and smoke slammed into the ground two hundred meters downrange, nearly burying a Home Guard Galleon tank and blossoming fully into an inferno that rained debris over a wide area. A victim of the battle for air superiority taking place high above.

"I need to know if we're safe to leave that side open." He rushed the last few words, hyperventilating to pull more oxygen from the scorching atmosphere of his cockpit. *And the* Men Shen *runs fairly cool,* he thought, feeling sorry for Danielle in her new FedCom-designed *JagerMech III.*

"Roger. Checking that," was all she said.

Meanwhile the Canopian MechWarrior had made the mistake of trying to follow Fitzgerald toward the treeline, but his 'Mech's standard engine was no match for the power of the *Men Shen*'s extralight fusion plant and myomer accelerator signal circuitry. As the two remaining warriors in Fitz' lance swept in to help cover the spread of ground his maneuver had opened, all three grabbed line of sight on the Periphery 'Mech, caught in the open, and lit it up.

A BattleMech brought down by overwhelming fire rarely died quietly. The *Marshal* lost its left leg to a PPC and several medium lasers. More laser fire cored into its left side, penetrating armor and touching off the machine gun ammunition, which erupted in a violent explosion that tore through the 'Mech's chest cavity. A death sentence for a BattleMech, but still survivable if one third of Fitz' missiles and a final laser beam had not carved into the *Marshal's* head, decapitating it.

Fitzgerald turned his *Men Shen* away from the *Marshal's* death throes. *That was an execution,* he thought, *and nothing else. The warrior never stood a chance.* That the Canopian pilot was an enemy did not enter into his thinking. He recalled a thought from several months before, prior to Black May, that it was a MechWarrior's responsibility to limit the horror of warfare, not build on it. But damn it, someone had to meet him halfway.

"Fitz." Danielle's disembodied voice interrupted his brief mourning. "We're only getting fragmented comms from the Lancers," she said, her voice frantic with concern. "Nevarr's worried they may have been shattered. He's pulling the entire battle east. You recon with your lance. See if there's anything left out there to save."

Concern over the fallen Canopian vanished with the possibility of a rout taking place on his immediate flank. "Strikers Two and Four," he said, calling in his remaining lancemates, "with me. Best speed." Cutting in the *Men Shen*'s MASC system he bounded off at better than one hundred-twenty kilometers per hour, swinging wide around the fired woods and leading his lance straight through the curtain of smoke.

Not that he could maintain such speeds. Designed for short-term applications, a MASC system could lock up if overused and leave him paralyzed. Fitzgerald feathered its operation, varying his speed down as low as ninety-five kph in order not to burn out the system. He crested the final ridge not half a kilometer ahead of his lancemates, and so bought only an extra few seconds to survey the devastation spread out over the shallow valley. The *Men Shen*'s Beagle Probe detailed the scene in brutal clarity.

Better than two dozen 'Mechs lay scattered about like some giant child's discarded toys. He spotted insignias for the Blackwind Lancers and the Nightriders regiment of McCarron's Armored Cavalry. Although he'd seen other such killing fields during the fighting on Nashuar, this one was exceptionally brutal. In some places BattleMechs were piled atop each other, later casualties brought down as they worked their way over the tops of their fallen comrades.

Two machines still operated on the field, a Nightrider assault 'Mech trying to help a medium-weight *Wolverine* hobble along without its left leg. With Fitz' arrival, the *Yu Huang* assault 'Mech moved around to place itself between its wounded comrade and Fitz' *Men Shen*. Considering the savaged armor of the Cavalry machine, the fight would be well-matched. Then Fitz' lancemates also crested the hill, and the odds shifted dramatically in favor of the Compact.

Or would have, if memory of the shattered *Marshal* were not still plaguing Fitzgerald.

He opened his lance's private channel, well-imagining what Danielle or Nevarr would say to his plans. "This one's mine," he barked. "No one interferes." With that, he ran the *Men Shen* forward at its best speed.

The *Yu Huang,* possibly surprised by the *Men Shen's* speed or at the idea of single combat with a 'Mech nearly half its weight, held its position for several important seconds while Fitzgerald closed. The mechanics of the fight would be simple. At range, the *Yu Huang* would tear Fitz apart. Close-in the odds were better, though not much. The *Men Shen's* advantage would be speed, including liberal use of its MASC system. The *Yu Huang* only need hope for a few solid connections.

Fitz danced the *Men Shen* around the larger *Yu Huang,* pushing his new 'Mech to its limits and learning things about it he had not thought to try before. Based on the successful *Raven* design, the *Men Shen* was extraordinarily balanced and could turn inside the main arc of the *Yu Huang* almost every time to prevent the other 'Mech from bringing its large-bore autocannon into play.

He also learned something about the *Yu Huang* in that it was nearly impossible to find a blind spot on it, and he paid dearly for the lesson. While his medium pulse lasers whittled away at the assault machine's remaining armor, the *Yu Huang's* right arm-mounted PPC and medium lasers returned the damage with interest. Armor rained onto the ground in chips and shards and molten dribbling, and inside the cockpit of the *Men Shen* sweat wrung out of Fitz' body by escalating heat levels ran as freely.

He had known the opposing MechWarrior would be no easy mark. The warrior had survived the devastation of the valley already, and the Confederation would not trust one of its newest and toughest designs to a green warrior. Fitz was betting on his opponent being a company commander at the least, maybe even a battalion CO. But how good the other pilot was he learned a moment later when the *Yu Huang* managed a leaning torso twist that far exceeded the normal range. The Nightrider MechWarrior brought all weapons to bear, its twelve-centimeter LB-X autocannon belching out a spray of cluster rounds that sanded armor off the *Men Shen's* right body profile.

Several fragments rang off the side of the BattleMech's head, throwing Fitz repeatedly against his harness. At least one located a breach in his armor, cracking the engine's shielding and flooding the *Men Shen* with excess heat. Shaking off the rough treatment, Fitzgerald edged in closer and concentrated his return fire against the *Yu Huang's* severely damaged right side. His lasers scattered emerald pulses into the Nightrider's arm and leg. Then, feeling the worse for the exchange, Fitz cut in his MASC system and sprinted for one of the few stands of trees not already smashed into kindling by the earlier fighting.

Only from the safety of the woods did Fitzgerald first note the *Yu Huang's* difficulty in moving. Whether a result of the *Men Shen's* laser fire or the assault 'Mech's leaning twist or both, the *Yu Huang* now hobbled on a frozen hip joint. Its already-limited speed now halved, the Nightrider 'Mech showed no enthusiasm for following up on its devastating assault of a few seconds before.

Panting in the stale, stiflingly hot air, his shoulders and chest bruised where his restraining straps crossed his body, Fitzgerald watched his heat levels fall as he waited out his opponent's next move.

It didn't come from the *Yu Huang*.

Fitz' sensors screamed a warning as four new threat icons popped on his HUD. A heavy Nightrider lance crested the northern ridge and dropped down into the valley, moving to immediately flank the *Yu Huang*. While he had the chance, Fitzgerald selected his private channel to Danielle Singh. "Fitzgerald to Commander Singh," he almost whispered, as if the Nightriders would overhear.

"Got you, Maurice." Danielle sounded winded, probably fighting her *JagerMech's* heat levels. "Find the Lancers?"

"Got 'em," Fitz said, voice finding strength as his heat levels fell into the yellow band. His atmospheric system pulling the scorching air from outside his own 'Mech might not sound refreshing, but it made a big difference when dropping down from forty-three Celsius or better. "Looks like the core of the Blackwind Lancers has been smashed. No idea about the warriors. Keeping their heads down." He stared at the impressive array of BattleMechs coming together. "If they're smart."

"Why?" Danielle asked, possibly reading the implied threat in Fitz' words. "What's your situation?"

The five Nightriders pulled into a line of battle, keeping between Fitzgerald and their wounded comrade.

"Situation *extremely* hostile," Fitzgerald said. "Stand by."

He closed communications, taking stock of his situation and preparing for fight or flight. His path of retreat wasn't good, allowing the Nightriders with their long-range weaponry too much time to bring him down. Committing his lancemates couldn't buy much time either, their lighter machines a poor response to so much armor and armament. *I gave you a fighting chance,* Fitz silently called out to the *Yu Huang* pilot. *Don't suppose you'll return the favor?*

The Nightriders did him one better. Obviously on a transmitted cue, two of the new machines peeled back away to assist the *Wolverine* with the missing left leg. The other three backed away carefully, slowed by the *Yu Huang*'s damaged hip. The officer in charge either did not like risking two severely damaged machines or, if it was the *Yu Huang* pilot, maybe he was returning the battlefield mercy Fitzgerald himself had shown.

And just *maybe* Fitz had glimpsed a promising sign that the Nightriders could be reasonable as well as deadly.

A betting man, Maurice Fitzgerald did not normally call upon religion to back him. Today, however, he found himself offering a quick prayer that he had witnessed a favorable omen. *If so, now we just need to build on it,* he thought.

He could not have realized exactly how that prayer would come back to haunt him.

21

Bào-feng Spaceport
Wuhan, Ambergrist
St. Ives Compact
24 June 3062

Free Capella members busied themselves about the large room, shifting desks and consoles around into concentric circles and papering the walls with large maps of Ambergrist's various districts. Some worked to remove the old air traffic control equipment, mothballed in this auxiliary wing of Bào-feng Spaceport's administrative building. In the room's center, working inside an area cordoned off by ivory ropes, two women labored meticulously over painting the Free Capella insignia on the floor—a gold and ivory serpentine dragon with starburst eyes coiled protectively around a world. The buzz of a dozen different conversations filled the room, all charged with an air of expectancy for the recent pace of organized effort.

Standing well to the side of the room's main doors, leaning back against a wall already papered, Major Warner Doles nodded his cautious approval of Treyhang Liao's command center. Wuhan's spaceport made good strategic sense. The largest on Ambergrist, it made for a fine logistics center as well as a staging grounds for troops. An easy

DropShip flight to the forward lines being established by Confederation forces, Doles noted, certain that was more accident than planned. And an hour by fast hovercar to Ambergrist's capital, where the few royalty this world possessed would certainly be found.

That, Doles knew, was a fact not lost on Treyhang Liao.

And speak of the Liao . . . Treyhang entered the room with a confident stride Doles could not remember seeing since Indicass. Since before Tormano's death. His soft blue eyes flicked about as he took in the room, their color and Asian tilt reminding Doles of nothing so much as the unfathomable gaze of a Siamese cat. Warner Doles braced himself for the encounter, pulling himself up into strict attention and clasping his hands tightly behind his back. He meant to have something from Treyhang Liao, but he doubted that trying to physically wring it from the smaller man would get him anywhere.

Treyhang quickly picked Doles out for his size and the colors of the uniform he wore. The silk cape of his own immaculate dress uniform billowed slightly as he strode over. "Looking for me, Major?"

"I wanted to see how things were coming along," Doles said with feigned casualness, wary of rushing the conversation. Heavy into drink and depression, Treyhang had been an easy target. But Warner did not forget that Trey had held his own against Tormano Liao.

"Very orderly," he noted, glancing about the room. "Strategic maps along the walls for instant reference." He gestured to the three-level arrangement of concentric circles being created with the desks and consoles. "Keeps everyone focused on the center of the room, where I imagine you will be."

Treyhang smiled. "Also gives me an informal method of promotion and punishment. Shifting people more toward the center as a reward for service."

Doles nodded. "In the Blackwind Lancers we shift warriors into more prestigious units, usually the command lances, for exceptional duty." It was a not-so-subtle move to turn the conversation toward the status of his battalion.

A tactic Treyhang deftly parried. "Same principle," he agreed, blue eyes giving nothing away. He nodded toward one of the radial aisles and gestured for Doles to join him as he began to walk. "I needed something to help me organize the upper echelon of Free Capella," he said, voice dropping to keep the conversation more private. "There are some good people in here, and the movement can't afford to waste resources."

They stepped aside while two men wrestled a bulky radar console onto a cart and wheeled it toward the doors. "Looks to me like you're wasting some good equipment, though," Doles said. *And some good warriors, who are sitting around waiting on material.* That he didn't say, though certainly Treyhang must be picking up on his implied rebuke by now.

"Everything in its time, Major," Treyhang said, a vague platitude that could be interpreted several ways. "Everything in its place." Warner Doles did not care for the implication of *that,* and he doubted Treyhang missed the meaning of his frown.

But the Liao shrugged as if nothing seemed amiss to him. "A local mandrinn, hereditary title, not very well known but with some influence on Ambergrist, has helped me procure new equipment for my command center."

"Did that include the new uniforms?" Doles asked, a touch of pique edging the question. That his Lancers were sitting around waiting for armor and munitions while Treyhang bothered with new clothing for the Free Capella Movement upset him immensely. The more so since Doles' own efforts now seemed actively blocked rather than simply ignored.

"The old uniforms were inappropriate," Treyhang said, "the ivory and gold colors a calculated insult by Tormano toward Sun-Tzu."

Doles scoffed. "So now you have tan with ivory," he said. "So?" He hated to admit feeling the slightest bit of interest. Doles was as proud of his Capellan heritage as the next man, as any Asian, but he admitted to being slightly ignorant when it came to the more subtle nuances of *Han* politics. He had the feeling that Treyhang somehow sensed his curiosity. Pausing near the roped-off area to study the insignia being painted, he was obviously letting the moment draw itself out.

"Gold was the prerogative of the emperor in ancient China," Treyhang finally said. "Adopting it for Free Capella was Tormano symbolically laying claim to the throne of the Capellan Confederation."

"But you've kept the coloring on Free Capella's insignia," Doles said, pointing down at the nearly complete painting. "It's the same as before."

"Two differences. The first, which you would have no way of knowing by looking," Treyhang explained, "is that I've renamed the insignia. Tormano referred to it as *The Challenge*. It has now been dubbed *The Promise*. And the world, in the dragon's coils, used to be Sian."

A quick glance down and Doles recognized the shape of the land masses. "Indicass," he said.

"Indicass," Treyhang echoed softly. "Where Tormano," he paused, "where *my father* fell. *The Promise* is a message to Sun-Tzu that the Free Capella Movement is no longer about claiming the Celestial Throne but about protecting the Capellan people. The gold in the dragon is a reminder that *The Promise* should be his as well."

Inventive, Doles decided. *Impressive, even, if Sun-Tzu understands the message.* But he dismissed the idea just as quickly. "Seems like a lot of wasted time and effort. Symbolism will not win this war. Soldiers will, *if* they are allowed to fight."

Treyhang cupped his left elbow in his right hand, supporting the arm as he reached up to slowly tap a slender forefinger against the point of his chin. The look of appraisal he awarded Warner Doles reminded the major of a master chess player he'd seen once. Studying his next move. Judging the value of a piece.

"Direction comes in many forms," Treyhang said, voice neutral, giving away nothing. "My father ran Free Capella for years from his estates on Solaris. I see no need to get any closer to combat than I am right now. And when I'm ready, I have people like you."

"So when do I get to fight?"

"When *I* am ready," Treyhang reiterated. "Until then, you'll have no luck with supplies, I promise, so spend your time in another fashion."

Behind his back, Doles clenched his hands into tight fists. To suspect interference was one thing, to have it confirmed to his face was quite another. "You don't wish to see justice for your father's death, do you?" he asked, simply trying to hurt Treyhang.

That Siamese cat gaze never flinched. "The Hustaing Warriors did not kill Tormano. And if I'm going to see justice for his death, it will likely be through the war crimes trial convening on Atreus next month." His eyes narrowed as he peered up into Doles' face. "I know why I'm fighting, Major Doles. Do you?"

Yes, Doles answered at once, but silently. Then it was *I think I do* as the doubts crept in, raised by Treyhang's calm yet persistent attack on Doles' anger. *He's playing me,* he realized. *Just like Tormano did with Smithson.* Again Doles struck out, not with logic or plan, but simply in an attempt to hurt. "If it were my father, I'd want to avenge him personally in some way."

Treyhang grinned humorlessly, eyes fierce. Warner could almost hear the chess call of "check" sound off in the other man's mind. "It's reactionary thinking like that which allowed you to be manipulated by Sun-Tzu's agent," he said, voice hard. "Which got your Lancers battalion disgraced on Hustaing."

With a sharp cry Doles struck out in blind fury, one large fist looping out from behind his back and arcing in toward Treyhang Liao's proud visage. Only Treyhang was no longer there, having easily ducked under the wild swing. Doles could not remember ever being so easily evaded, and that more than anything helped him immediately recognize the blind rage that claimed him. He reined himself in with effort, conscious that the entire room was now scope-locked on Treyhang Liao and himself.

"It's what got the Blackwind Lancers' first battalion destroyed on Nashuar," Treyhang said quietly, his calm assurance hitting Doles harder than any punch the smaller man could have thrown.

Doles forgot the rest of the room. Suddenly at a loss for words or actions, he stood there in mute shock.

"Colonel Leo Perrin was killed in a nerve agent attack," Treyhang continued. "The Lancers broke battle line during a fight, trying to take it out against McCarron's Armored Cavalry." He paused, obviously allowing Doles to process the information and come to his own conclusions about the result. "I got the report today."

"I'm sorry to hear that," Doles said mechanically, the shock holding distant any emotion.

"Why?" Treyhang asked, picking up on the lack of feeling. "Sorry he's dead, or that you didn't get to sword him down yourself, like you did Smithson?"

Rage flared again inside Doles, the same rage he had felt on Indicass during the rout and on Ambergrist ever since. Now, though, he recognized it and refused to let it rule him. If nothing else, he wouldn't give Trey the satisfaction.

Treyhang nodded approval at Doles' regaining his self-control. "I've looked into your history, Warner, since our last little conversation. Talked with some of your friends. Requested your complete personnel file from St. Ives. Imagine my pleasure to discover that I can return the *favor* you did for me."

Doles' anger urged him to storm out of the room, his pride refused to let him go. He wanted to hear more. He wanted to twist Treyhang's head from his neck. "What favor?" he finally asked.

Treyhang simply shook his head at the request. "No," he said. "I better not make it too easy for you. I'll let you answer that question." He shrugged indifference at the situation.

"But don't take too long," he said, turning his back on Doles and heading for the door. "Because until you do, to *my* satisfaction, there will be no room for you in Free Capella."

22

Celestial Palace
Zi-jin Chéng, Sian
Sian Commonality, Capellan Confederation
2 July 3062

Sun-Tzu nodded to Talon Zahn as he dropped the disk into a concealed slot and started the playback unit built into the desk of his private office. They both studied the video image of Katrina Steiner-Davion as she began the message with her usual false pleasantries. The screen, built into the glass surface of his desk, compacted the holovid into two dimensions and robbed Katrina of the detail her holo-camera had certainly recorded. Pale skin, golden hair pulled severely back, icy blue eyes; Sun-Tzu found her beauty too cold and Spartan under the best of circumstances. He would have listened to the message with video off if not for the slim chance that by an expression or offhand gesture she would let something slip.

That also might have quieted Romano's anger. He remembered too well his mother's near-violent aversion to anything Davion-tainted. And Katrina was one of *the spawn of Davion*, as Romano had referred to the children of Hanse and Melissa in her better moods. He took a final sip of his wine, wishing it could drown the memories of Romano that continued to plague him, and then set the glass aside to concentrate on the message.

"What George Hasek does in the Capellan March," Katrina said, "does not concern me at this time. If he wishes to squander his family's private resources on an internal Capellan matter, that is his business. And as I have offered Candace Liao sanctuary on New Avalon should she wish to abdicate her realm, I certainly cannot and will not censure Duke Hasek for providing Kuan Yin with a staging ground for humanitarian aid." Katrina paused, obviously for effect to lend her next words greater strength. "Nor will you!" she said.

Sun-Tzu tapped the three longer fingernails on his left hand hard against the desktop. He wanted Zahn to see a measure of his agitation. *Next she'll threaten the use of force if I should try to cross the pre-3025 border as per our arrangement, and then bring up the fighting in Tikonov.*

"That I have allowed the trouble in the old Tikonov Reaches area to continue for so long should not be taken as a lack of my resolve," Katrina continued calmly. A kind reference to the fact that she had used the unrest there to unseat Victor's regent and steal her brother's realm while he was away from the Inner Sphere, Sun-Tzu thought, though he could hardly begrudge anything that so sabotaged Victor Steiner-Davion. "If I felt less confidence in Treyhang Liao's revised Free Capella Movement to end the fighting caused by your *Zhanzheng de guang*-sponsored Free Tikonov, I might be forced to take issue with it myself.

"But I certainly *will* take issue if you so much as threaten Duke Hasek with retaliation on, around, or against Kittery." Katrina's blue eyes flashed dangerously, for the briefest instant showing the predator that lurked beneath the usually calm facade.

All right, so I had the order reversed. The memory of Romano deep within Sun-Tzu's mind railed against the fates that kept her hands from around Katrina's neck.

Katrina settled back, calmer now and voice chillingly sweet. "Black May could still serve as a rallying cry to topple your Confederation, Sun-Tzu Liao."

She bid him farewell with a formal nod Sun-Tzu found more petulant than regal, then her image winked out to be replaced by the sunburst-and-gauntlet of the Federated Commonwealth. Her use of that insignia made Sun-Tzu laugh softly. *She only wishes her two realms could unite under that emblem.* The sunburst-and-gauntlet faded to black, a symbolic ending to it, he thought.

Sun-Tzu leaned back into his leather chair, closing his eyes as he mentally reviewed the video. The sweet scent of sandalwood incense drifted to him from the brazier, and he could hear the light shuffling as Talon Zahn shifted position in his chair. "Comments?" he asked, forcing a calm into his voice that he did not feel.

"Not quite Katrina's usual style," Zahn said, speaking his mind immediately. "Very little in the way of vague promises or guarded threats. A fairly blunt ultimatum, actually."

Sun-Tzu agreed. "Resulting from?"

Here Zahn hedged only slightly. Only fair, since his expertise usually lay in strategy and tactics and not in the political arena. "I'd say that the unrest we're hearing of on FedCom and Lyran worlds is more serious than we've been led to believe. What with the distractions Arthur and Victor pose."

Arthur Steiner-Davion was an upstart child, in Sun-Tzu's opinion, looking to impress people. Victor, though . . . "Victor distracts Katrina just by being alive." For that, Sun-Tzu could almost forgive Victor his existence. It surprised him to realize that he had not truly thought of Victor Steiner-Davion in months. *I could get used to that.*

"Unfortunately," the Chancellor continued, allowing a measure of frustration to touch his voice as he opened his eyes to directly acknowledge Zahn, "Katrina plans to allow George Hasek to serve much the same function against my efforts in the Xin Sheng Commonality. Private aid," he scoffed. "He's funneling Commonwealth state resources to Candace, including military hardware." *And I had hoped my major difficulties with the Haseks died with George's father, Morgan.* "Katrina needs the St. Ives conflict to continue, to keep the Capellan March focused on something other than her and to tie up my state indefinitely." It would have been easier for Sun-Tzu to appreciate the tactic if it hadn't directly worked against his efforts.

"Not indefinitely, Chancellor." Zahn leaned forward, his dark eyes hungry for a final solution to the St. Ives conflict. Sun-Tzu could read the eagerness in his senior general, and the firm resolve as well. "I've already reassigned units for the first wave," the *Sang-jiang-jun* informed his master. "This can work."

It has to work, Sun-Tzu finished for him, reading the implied caveat, whether Zahn intended it or not. "Taking the world of St. Ives itself will bolster the drive behind our own forces and reestablish our legitimacy in the eyes of the Capellan people. Of *all* the Capellan people." He felt Romano's influence, so sure of the Confederation's superiority over her sister's realm and predicting a complete collapse of the Compact. "It *may* even tear the fight out of the St. Ives Compact Armed Forces," he said.

Talon Zahn nodded. "The fall of St. Ives could certainly be our rallying point."

"Except?" Sun-Tzu asked, hearing the hesitancy. He had seen the latest loss reports from the Chaos March, as well as evaluations of Cassandra Liao's actions on the Teng Front. He had been expecting this moment. "You have a request?"

Zahn rose from his chair, bringing himself to strict attention before his Chancellor. He tugged once at the hem of his dress jacket, presenting the best military image he could, and nodded. "Six more regiments," he said.

Sun-Tzu contained his fury, the words he wanted to say burning like acid on his tongue. In his mother's day, the Strategic Military Director would have nodded a simple acceptance of the Chancellor's order. *As it should be,* Romano whispered up from the depths of his mind. Sun-Tzu ruthlessly throttled the voice. *Sasha Wanli is lost to me, whatever hole she has decided to crawl into. Ion Rush hasn't been the same since the explosion, and the surgery after. I can't afford to alienate Zahn.* The situation called for both patience and reason. Sun-Tzu tapped his reserves. "Use the regiments we had trying to contain Kai," he said calmly.

"We only need to hold our current lines while St. Ives is won."

"I *am* using those regiments, Chancellor," Zahn said. "They are reposted to the Sarna Supremacy, the Styk Commonality, the Chaos March. One of them is fighting to hold a world in the Disputed Territories. In order to honor our commitment to the Magistracy of Canopus I've had to shift troops toward the Periphery." His voice grew harder. "So, which area do I gamble in order to take St. Ives?"

Romano's whispers distracted him again, counseling Zahn's censure for his brashness. "You can do it without them," Sun-Tzu said.

Zahn bowed his head in respectful disagreement. "You are telling me what you want, Chancellor. I'm letting you know what I need. The Confederation has not launched an assault of the magnitude of the St. Ives conflict since Ilsa Liao's offensive of 2828 during the Second Succession War, and here we're suffering under restrictions imposed on the Confederation by outside forces. Word of Blake in the Choas March. The renewed safeguarding of the Marik border. SLDF and Com Star interference—including Nova Cat forces flying Star League colors.

"The first wave against St. Ives proper is running far lighter than I would like against estimations of what the Compact may throw back at us, but it will be enough to claim a solid foothold."

"A foothold?" Sun-Tzu could see that Zahn was deliberately trying to provoke him, stretching the liberties the Chancellor allowed his military director. "You will do better than that," he said evenly, reining in his anger and channeling it to provide an intense focus of thought.

Zahn wasn't finished. "Hanse Davion taught us in the Fourth Succession War. Three to one odds promotes the best margin for victory."

Taking lessons from the Davions? That was enough to send the specter of Romano Liao into screaming apoplexy. "Are you trying to see how far you can push me, Zahn?"

The *Sang-jian-jun* flinched at the coldness in Sun-Tzu's voice. "No, Chancellor. But my aim *is* to take All-under-

Heaven intact," he said, quoting directly from the *Art of War*.

Where further argument might have risked the Chancellor's immediate wrath, the historical reference allowed Sun-Tzu to put everything in context. *St. Ives must fall. Nothing else matters so much right now.* Through clenched teeth, he asked, "Six regiments?"

Zahn nodded, then hesitated. "Seven, if I am to deal with the problems developing on Milos."

The Eridani Light Horse, on the first world to openly embrace the return of Confederation. Somehow, that has to be Victor's doing. "Take our garrisons on Menke and Rollis," he ground out, each word bitter. "Half the new regiment on Victoria." *There* was a dangerous gamble, inviting a raid against the site of the Confederation's newest BattleMech production site. "Begin moving them into place for a second wave."

Talon Zahn nodded, but not without a frown. "I'll take them. But that leaves our Periphery border with the Commonwealth and Taurian Concordat extremely vulnerable," he pointed out. "Grover Shraplen of the Concordat isn't due here until next month. Are you that confident of his support?"

"No," Sun-Tzu admitted, seeing no reason to keep that worry from his senior general. Better they both be considering the possibility of treachery on that front. The spectral Romano agreed. "So I had better be convincing. *Na duì ma?*" *Isn't that so?* "I also allowed him an escort of two regiments, to accompany him as far as Castrovla. You will have those as well," he promised.

"And the Eridani?" Zahn asked hesitantly.

"Lord Colonel Baxter can send one of the regiments guarding the Cavalry's new warren," Sun-Tzu decided. "They are Confederation citizens now. They can share the risk." He nodded a dismissal to Zahn, and settled back into his chair, steepling his fingers over his chest. *So be it*, he thought. There was nothing else to be done.

Not quite true, a ghostly voice reminded him. There *was*

one more thing. *Armies might march at the direction of the general, but always on the direct order of their liege lord.*

"Zahn," Sun-Tzu called out as the *Sang-jiang-jun* made the doorway. "You said the first wave is in place?"

The Confederation's senior officer drew himself back to attention, anticipating the order. "Yes, Chancellor."

Sun-Tzu closed his eyes, trying to search out any final flaws to his plans. He risked far more than he cared to, but at this late stage of the game the only other option seemed to be nothing short of abandonment of the entire movement. And that was completely unacceptable.

"Send them in," he ordered.

23

Scottsdale Wash
'Zona Province, St. Ives
St. Ives Compact
4 July 3062

Lien-zhang Aris Sung landed his *Wraith* among a patch of scrub, drawn toward the vegetation more by habit than anything since he doubted the stunted trees and brush of the Scottsdale Wash offered much in the way of cover. Leveling his large pulse laser at a St. Ives Home Guard *Blackjack* maneuvering at the edge of his effective range, Aris cut loose with a burst of ruby pulses. The brilliantly colored swarm stung into the *Blackjack*'s right shoulder, reddish-orange drops of molten composite spattering against the desert floor.

   The flatlands southeast of St. Ives' desert metropolis of Scottsdale showed the usual signs of a desert flood plains. Brush and twisted excuses for juniper trees all bent southwest, warped over years of winter and spring flooding that swept down from the Bai-se-shan Plateau to the northeast. The land was uniformly flat, with the occasional low-lying rocky outcropping and narrow, flood-cut arroyos that might hide some infantry but little else. A targeting-range battlefield. The land's open nature favored House Hiritsu's attempt to establish a foothold on St. Ives. It demanded simplified tactics relying on skill rather than luck, and it allowed for easy tracking of the enemy.

Of the opposition, Aris corrected himself with due contrition. If care in defining the conflict was to be taken anywhere, Aris suspected the world of St. Ives demanded it most.

Without aid from any sensor, Aris saw the *Blackjack* and two other Home Guard BattleMechs track on his landing. He knew the blued-steel finish on his *Wraith*'s armor stood out as a prime target against the pale desert and low horizon line. Trying to follow the *Wraith* over a two-hundred meter jump, though, proved too difficult for the Home Guard MechWarriors. A single brace of five long-ranged missiles pockmarked the armor over his left side. A Galleon tank that had moved in from the right scored better, cutting into the *Wraith*'s chest with two medium lasers. The tank paid for its exposed position, though, as two *Transit* aerofighters from the supporting Thirty-third Air Wing strafed its position on a high-speed pass. They left behind a smoking ruin, the armored vehicle split wide open and gutted.

"Movement," *Lien-zhang* Jason James called out over the battle frequency reserved for company commanders. "Their line of battle may be turning."

With Ty Wu Non's incapacitation following a cockpit breach, James now commanded the battle. Aris visually picked out the senior company leader's *Jinggau* Battle-Mech, its squat, broad-shouldered silhouette easy to spot. A bad omen, to lose *Shiao-zhang* Non so early in the St. Ives drop, but the medics promised him out of surgery and conscious within a few hours.

Aris exchanged fire with the *Blackjack,* trading another hit with his large pulse laser for a PPC that sliced into the *Wraith*'s right leg. *In the meantime, we still have this battle to win.*

"*Ma de dan,*" James cursed. "They're swinging north again."

Of course they are, Aris Sung returned silently. On his HUD the Home Guard battalion continued to shift its line of retreat. Right up toward Scottsdale. He throttled the *Wraith* into a run, moving laterally along the Hiritsu front while a *Ti Ts'ang* moved past his old position to threaten the *Blackjack* with a hand-held hatchet. The Home Guard warrior wisely chose to give ground.

Li Wynn, where are you? Aris sniped pulse laser fire at a Home Guard *Griffin* straying too far from the protection of its comrades. "If they get inside the city fortifications, we'll lose them," he reminded James. And that would undermine Ty Wu Non's strategic plans, which called for House Hiritsu and a battalion of Ishara's Grenadiers to stage out of Scottsdale, the key to 'Zona Province. Worse than that, in Aris' opinion. If the Home Guard battalion buttoned up inside Scottsdale, House Hiritsu would eventually go in after them. That would demand a high price from both sides, and from the Capellan civilians of Scottsdale, who simply lived in the wrong city when the Confederation returned. *We can't let that happen. I won't let it happen.*

The personal conflict that had reared up on Hustaing and finally came to a head on St. Loris still burned within Aris Sung. And in others, he knew, from the changes he'd seen in various House members since the recall from St. Loris. Here, on St. Ives, Aris fought a final battle for acceptance—over his own warrior nature and the lately conflicting interpretations of Hiritsu philosophies.

But with Ty Wu Non sidelined, tradition now demanded strict adherence to the *Shiao-zhang*'s battle plan at a time when innovation was clearly necessary. Most Warrior Houses fought under very formal rules of engagement, and one dared not break—or even bend—them lightly. Not even victory guaranteed mitigation for the disrespect inherent in such action. But it is possible, Aris knew from experience. As always, interpretation is everything.

Lien-zhang James must have been of a similar mind. "Can we get the Grenadiers down here in time before the Home Guard forces make Scottsdale?" he asked, searching for an alternative.

Aris shook his head, too busy engaging the *Griffin* for a

transmitted response but answering the question to himself. Cutting the armor away over its left-side ammo bins sent a suddenly concerned *Griffin* pilot bounding for the Home Guard lines and safety in numbers. He never made it. Raven Clearwater led her lance forward, pummeling the fifty-five-ton 'Mech with long-ranged energy weapons until her lancemate's PPC cored through the rent in the armor and cooked off the ammunition stores. An older design, Aris noted with pity for the opposing warrior, the lack of CASE protection allowing the explosion to rip through the *Griffin*'s entire torso.

"Impossible," Aris finally answered, glad to be distracted from the Home Guard BattleMech's death throes. "Their last reports have them heavily engaged up near the plateau, holding off elements of the Fusiliers." He faded back as a lance of Vedettes probed out from the Home Guard line. "And it's too far anyway."

Frustration evident in his voice, James asked, "Any ideas?"

Checking his company's position off the *Wraith*'s HUD, Aris almost missed the explosion that showed only as a sudden geyser of dirt and brush around the feet of a distant Home Guard *JagerMech*. That looked like—the thought was interrupted by a second, silent spray of earth that cloaked the lower half of a newer *Cossack*—a minefield detonation.

As the Home Guard retreat staggered to a confused halt, Aris opened up the comm to *Lien-zhang* James, "I think you just received your answer," he said.

From the narrow arroyos at the feet of the Home Guard, two squads of infantry slid out of concealment and attacked nearby BattleMechs, one using grapple rods and satchel charges and another of anti-Mech jump infantry. So complete was the surprise factor, only a single Home Guard 'Mech fired off a shot before the warriors dove back into hiding, and it missed wide.

"Infantry?" James' confusion did not last long, realizing the nearest position from which infantry could have been summoned. "*Shiao-zhang* Non placed Li Wynn on our northern flank," he said, tone flat with sudden disquiet. "Those two platoons are supposed to be guarding the borders of Scottsdale."

Aris pulled back, allowing his company to move slightly ahead while he dealt with the senior company leader whose *Jinggau* also drifted to the backfield. "They still are, Jason," he said cautiously, hoping the familiar use of the other man's name would buy him a moment's consideration. "They're guarding Scottsdale from the Home Guard. And they are north of our position. It's just that our line has swung to place a flanking unit directly in front of us." *Work with me, Jason. We needed this.* "Are you going to hold up the battle to complain now?"

James' flat, "No," promised little concession and certainly no support, but it left the situation open. For now.

It's a start, Aris thought. *And this early in the battle for St. Ives, I'll take what I can get.*

Pai-zhang Li Wynn had reveled in the authority of his new command, if not its assignment. Being given sole charge of the two platoons of Hiritsu infantry demonstrated Ty Wu Non's confidence and, Li felt sure, primed him for his next promotion to *lien-zhang*—company leader. Removed from the chance of combat—the chance to strike down the Chancellor's enemies—reduced the honor only slightly. On this glorious day of the Confederation's return to the traitorous world of St. Ives, Li Wynn felt he could afford to be generous.

Until Aris' call to battle, that is.

"*Shiao-zhang* Non's BattleMech is down and he is injured," Aris had said over the secure link to his charge. "He will be fine, though, and we still fight on under his original tactical plan."

Rage burning at his core, Li Wynn immediately swore vengeance against the St. Ives Home Guard. They dared touch the Master of House Hiritsu? There would be no compromise on the St. Ives battlefields. Li Wynn hungered for battle, and the glory he would bring himself and his House.

Aris obliged. "Li, we need your forces to establish a forward flanking position. I am estimating grid twenty-one slash eleven."

Was that a note of hesitancy, of doubt, in Aris' voice? Li couldn't be sure through the flattening effect of transmission.

"You will continue to monitor and report any activity coming out of Scottsdale," Aris went on, "and you will also prevent any Home Guard forces from retreating toward the city. I am relaying to you a limited tactical freedom to establish yourself as necessary." A short pause, and then, "Li, we depend on you not to let them through."

Vanished was any twinge of doubt. Nothing more need be said; Li Wynn would not fail his House. He only hoped the Home Guard did attempt a run for Scottsdale. It never occurred to Li to verify the orders. Of course Aris Sung had spoken with Ty Wu Non, and the orders came from the House Master—Aris had said as much.

Setting up in the path of the Home Guard retreat had been easy, planting a dozen vibrabombs nearly at the last moment. Li gambled on typical MechWarrior blindness, which often ignored anything under ten meters tall or not weighing out in tonnage.

The first two squads slipped from cover to attack the 'Mechs wounded by the minefield detonations, leaving the *Cossack* sprawled over the desert floor, minus a leg. The slightly more robust *JagerMech* limped away, but the fight had obviously gone out of its pilot. Li grinned in triumph and readied one last surprise for the St. Ives dogs.

The tactic was really a lesson learned under the direction of his *Sifu,* Aris Sung. Escalating threat levels. First the mines, which were very few but the Home Guard had no way of knowing that. Then the anti-Mech infantry attacks. Next . . . Li Wynn tapped his throat mike to activate it.

"Fa Shih, target the *Cataphract*. It's pushing too far north." The *Cataphract* was an old trademark design of the Capellan state, and Li Wynn planned to remove it from Compact rosters. They didn't deserve it.

"Attack," he said casually.

Ready hands pulled back the camouflage netting covering a dry gully specially widened to hide the battle-armored infantry, and four warriors suited up in the new Confederation battlesuits leaped out to swarm the heavy BattleMech. *Fa Shih,* the Taoist *Masters of Methods,* now brought forth in a new incarnation to show people *The Way.*

Li laughed as the *Cataphract* nearly stumbled, its pilot obviously shocked by the sudden appearance of armored infantry. Those four were all he had at his command, but again, could the Home Guard chance that?

The *Cataphract* tried to brush away its attackers, but the agile suits evaded its clumsy attempts. They tore at its armor, ripping large holes into it and then pumping energy from their right-arm-mounted small lasers into the rents. When the heavy 'Mech attempted to flee, Li Wynn popped two more anti-Mech squads, one of which made a successful knee-capping attempt. The unarmored infantry melted back into the desert floor, while the battlesuits rode the toppled *Cataphract* to the ground. Seventy tons of BattleMech impacting the earth sent a tremor through the ground that Li found extremely satisfying.

He tapped his throat mike again. "Finish him," he said with calm pleasantness. The Fa Shih clustered around the *Cataphract* cockpit, ripping past the ferroglass viewscreen to get at the pilot. Then they, too, faded back into one of their specially dug hiding places.

That turned the Home Guard, who wanted nothing more to do with Hiritsu infantry. They shifted westward, and as the House Hiritsu BattleMech forces swung up to take advantage of their infantry–held territory, the Home Guard drifted more southerly until their path of retreat had shifted ninety degrees from its original course.

Li Wynn moved out of his own place of concealment, walking over to inspect the Fa Shih's work against the *Cataphract*'s cockpit. Impressive, if a bit bloody. Li shrugged indifference.

However it must happen, the Confederation would know

victory on St. Ives. And Li Wynn would be a part of that, assuring his place in House Hiritsu and the Confederation. *To be what I am,* he thought, paraphrasing a House adage, *and to become all I am capable of becoming.*

What more was there in his life?

=== 24 ===

Royal Palace
Tian-tan, St. Ives
St. Ives Compact
12 July 3062

Duchess Candace Liao stood in the middle of her Tian-tan palace war room, pretending to study one of the large, wall-mounted flatscreen video units that framed the room. Unmoving, hands clasped in front of her in a studied picture of strength and poise, she might have been sculpted from marble if not for the fierceness that still backlit her gray eyes even at seventy-four. She wore an ivory silk dress, cut *Han*-style with wide sleeves and slightly uneven hem, trimmed in blue and red to match the thin silk scarf wrapped loosely about her throat. Those were the colors of Kai's Cenotaph Stables on Solaris, a fact she knew would not be lost on her "guest."

The last time Candace had gathered with two other women in the war room to discuss the fate of her small nation, one of them had been her Federated Commonwealth liaison, General Simone Devon. An early casualty of the Black May attacks, Simone had died from the nerve agent intended for Candace. Candace recalled the petite, fair-haired warrior with melancholy fondness, remembering her devotion as well as an uncanny memory for details that the Duchess had come to trust as much as any computer. A valued aide to the Compact, and a friend.

Sasha Wanli seemed a poor substitute.

"Your information has been remarkably unhelpful in preventing Confederation gains on St. Ives." Senior Colonel Caroline Seng, the third woman present for this latest interview, began on the offensive as earlier directed. If Wanli grew hostile or too defensive, Candace could step in on her advisor's side and quickly bring the renegade Maskirovka Director to heal.

Sasha, however, merely shrugged a light indifference. "I have provided you with all information at my disposal that *might* apply to the push for St. Ives proper," she said, voice toneless to the point of being bland. "I was not privileged with the strategic or tactical plans, only the information gathered by the time I"—she paused, choosing her words with care—"took leave of Sian. If you cannot figure it out for yourself, Caroline Seng, I suggest you arrange for the defection of *Sang-jiang-jun* Zahn."

The barb left Seng speechless, while Candace frowned a light warning to the defector. Sasha Wanli looked the frail, old woman her age suggested, but her eyes gave her away as something more. *Windows to the soul, and Sasha's diamond-cutter eyes are warning enough to never underestimate her.*

"We are not arranging any defections," Candace said, heading off Seng's hot reply and turning the conversation back toward the extraction of further useful information. "You came to us, you recall." *And I have to admit, with your story you had reason to fear for your life. Not that I will make it easy on you, now or ever.* "My protection extends only so far as your usefulness to the Compact."

"Wo dong le," Sasha said with grave politeness. *I understand.* "Would the names of deep-cover operatives within your military be helpful?" she asked. Then, holding up one hand in a gesture of mitigation, she added, "Those I have had access to, that is. Of course, some are only code names

and units, but it would be a start for your own intelligence agents."

Candace nodded regally, the barest hint of a bow. "That would be a wonderful start," she said, automatically reducing the significance of such an intelligence coup. "Please prepare a list. Today."

Her tone suggested a dismissal, and Sasha left after a single bow. Her two escorts gathered her at the door, neither armed but both accomplished in various fields of martial arts. Candace would take no chances of Wanli picking up a weapon. *My assassination might win her back into my nephew's good graces, though I doubt it. Not now. Sun-Tzu may have forgiven her a mistake, but never a betrayal.*

"Well?" she asked, once the door had slid shut behind Sasha Wanli.

Seng took a few seconds to collect herself. "I let her get to me," she said. "I apologize."

Candace had known Caroline Seng long enough to hear the half-truth for what it was. "She was getting to you before the interview even commenced," Candace said, though kindly.

The Compact's senior colonel nodded. "I find her presence on St. Ives offensive, Candace." It was rare for Caroline to exercise the privilege of familiarity, and that she did so now was a measure of her agitation. "To shelter the Maskirovka Director. . ." She rubbed her hands together, as if trying to clean away filth. "Frankly, I find the idea more in keeping with Sun-Tzu's nature than yours."

"Sun-Tzu is not so desperate as to need such help," Candace Liao said simply. "We are." Every day evidence to support Caroline's dire predictions of the imminent collapse of the Compact's military continued to manifest. Trying to stand up to a more powerful adversary, and to support a two-front war on top of it, was slowly killing the smaller Capellan nation. Only the fanatic spirit with which her military fought on the face of overwhelming odds and the resistance of Compact citizens had delayed the fate Caroline had envisioned a few months back, but it did not solve the problem.

The resistance of *some* Compact citizens.

"Wanli was right about that," Candace said aloud. "We should have looked more closely at the data. We knew Maskirovka agents were priming areas of the Compact for the return of the Confederation. Especially after Milos, the defections on Denbar, and the Pardray continent on St. Loris." She shook her head. "Right in front of us the entire time."

She pointed to one of the screens, displaying Confederation gains. "Xi'an, Scottsdale, Petreyvisk." Candace recited the names of the three province capitals her nephew's forces had targeted. "All vocal now in welcoming back the Confederation. Sun-Tzu has won a solid base of operations and a legitimate claim to the world of St. Ives."

Seng shifted uneasily. The failure to predict Talon Zahn's plan of battle was mostly hers. "St. Ives was once a key world in the Confederation's 'elastic defense strategy.' The world remains heavily garrisoned and every important city fortified." She shook her head, obviously angry at herself. "I *assumed* that an invasion would try to cripple St. Ives by taking Tian-tan."

Fault also rested with Candace, and she accepted her due share. "That had been my assumption as well. But Tian-tan is not crucial to the military survival of St. Ives." Just as St. Ives was really no longer the military lynchpin of the Compact. It now shared responsibility with Indicass, Texlos, Warlock, and Teng, worlds with the production capacity to directly support military units. St. Ives proper was a symbol, yes, but symbolic victories did not win wars of themselves. Candace resolved to keep that in mind, as the next few months would force on her incredibly difficult choices.

"Sun-Tzu will have more surprises planned," she said, sure of *that* at least. "Go back over Wanli's reports, and make sure you keep a healthy guard over her, Caroline." Her next words came hard. "Much as I hate to admit it, we need her."

"Then we fight this out to the end?" Seng asked. "Our *hopeless battle,* yours and mine?"

Candace slowly shook her head. "This was never really

our battle. It was a decision the Compact made over thirty years ago when we severed ties to the Confederation."

"But do we fight it out to the end," Seng asked, pressing her sovereign.

Turning to fully face her friend and advisor, Candace Liao hedged, wanting Seng to consider all possible approaches, just as she did.

"We will do what needs doing, here and elsewhere," she said gravely. That was not intended as confirmation of the question put to her, and by Seng's expression she knew it. "Here, today, that means we fight. Symbolic victories may not win wars, but they are still worth fighting for. My people deserve and demand nothing less than our best effort."

"And later?" Seng asked, almost a whisper.

"Later does not exist," Candace said firmly. "Later is karma." Then, her voice becoming more subdued, "Later we hope there is enough left of the Compact to save.

"It is the final solution left to us, to weather the tempest no matter what price it demands."

25

Three *Union* Class DropShips and one very-old *Intruder* framed a square on the tarmac of Wuhan's Bào-feng Spaceport, outlining a parade grounds for the Blackwind Lancers' third battalion. Two platoons of infantry and one of tank crewmen formed up the bulk of the assembly, with sixteen MechWarriors set in a single line across the front. A single company of BattleMechs backed the assembled battalion, four brand-new *Helios* 'Mechs comprising the center lance flanked by mixed lances to either side. Heat rolling up off the tarmac shimmered the air around the 'Mechs and Drop-Ships, but not one person broke parade-rest to wipe the sweat from his or her face.

Warner Doles stepped up onto the temporary reviewing stage to meet with Major Jahna Castillian, who stood at stiff parade-rest as she faced out toward her troops. As Doles' first bootstep came down on the steel platform, Major Castillian snapped to attention and called out, "Third Battalion, *ju*-yi!" One hundred boots came down against the tarmac with a sharp, rifle-shot crack as the battalion was called to attention just as Doles mounted the stage.

Three long strides brought him up to Castillian, who turned and rendered a crisp salute. Doles stood at a height with the major, staring directly into her eyes—blue, flecked with small dots of turquoise, and regarding him with a calm appraisal.

Returning her salute he said, "Welcome to Ambergrist, Major."

"Thank you, Brevet-Colonel Doles."

Doles blinked his unease at the new title. Treyhang Liao had personally delivered the paperwork to him this afternoon, not forty minutes ago. No supplies, no orders for combat, Doles had noted at the time. A worthless promotion meant to buy his patience.

He still had not forgiven Trey their meeting of three weeks prior, no matter that for the incident to have struck so deeply it must contain some truths to it. Following the promotion came Treyhang's casual announcement that Third Battalion had just made planetfall and awaited Doles' inspection, and he'd had no more time to think about his anger or the full meaning of his new rank. All he cared about was that here would be troops ready for combat and possibly with supplies enough to equip and field both battalions.

Now, standing on the stage, reviewing and certainly being reviewed, the full weight of his new position came down fully on Doles' broad shoulders. *The Blackwind Lancers are my responsibility now. Every piece of equipment. Every life!* Not just the warriors with whom he'd suffered through the disgrace of Hustaing, the ones who might have followed him willingly into the teeth of the enemy if it meant taking Confederation warriors with them, but other members of the Blackwind Lancers regiment who now depended on him for leadership. It forced him to consider the near-reckless attitude he'd fostered since Tormano Liao's death, and he found himself lacking. *This is not who I am, is it?*

He doubted the answer to that question would be soon in coming.

Castillian nodded to her warriors and then gestured to the four *Helios* 'Mechs towering over the assembly. "All fresh from Warlock," she said. "And we have two of the brand-new *Catapult* variants being fielded by the Confederation, courtesy of Cassandra Allard-Liao." She shook her pale blonde hair back over one shoulder and looked a question to Doles. "We just need to know when we're taking to the field."

Now, Doles wanted to say. *This hour.* But he could not trust that inner voice until he knew better whose it was.

"Billet your warriors, Major," he said. "And then stop by the Free Capella command post and I'll bring you up to date on the situation." He turned to leave, but stopped himself just short of doing so. If he was going to recognize Trey-hang Liao's authority, vested by Duchess Candace Liao herself, it had to be now.

"We march," he said, though the words almost stuck in his throat, "when we get orders."

Home Guard Staging Grounds
Hazlet, Nashuar
St. Ives Compact

Nashuar's sun had long set when Subcommander Maurice Fitzgerald received a summons to the colonel's office. Colonel Nevarr stood leaning against the front edge of his desk, arms folded over his chest in a study of patience. Tall and muscular without running to bulk, and with his tousled white-blonde hair and washed-out blue eyes, Nevarr might more easily have stepped out of some Norse legend than a Compact recruiting poster.

Fitz' first thought was to wonder how, after assuming direct command of Nashuar's defense, Nevarr still got away with not wearing a traditional uniform. His simple cut of heavy black cloth chased in silver fit him well, though, and after two years the young MechWarrior really couldn't imagine Nevarr in anything else.

"A bit late for a staff meeting, Colonel," Fitz said by way of greeting.

Nevarr regarded him with cool regard for a long minute, then nodded. "This will be just you and I," he said. Soft-spoken and a bit hoarse, Nevarr habitually spoke in short, easy speech. It reminded Fitz of battlefield comm practice, where warriors kept all communication clipped and to the point. "Some things are better discussed in the silent hours."

Fitzgerald worried for the briefest second that he was about to receive a reprimand for his recent conduct. Ever since his unresolved duel with the *Yu Huang,* he had worked to bring back a moral focus to battles in which he was involved. The day before, Fitzgerald's lance had surrendered territory to a Canopian unit rather than fight near a cluster of farmhouses. The concern passed quickly, though. *When the Canopians pushed past the farming community, we tore them apart. And besides, Nevarr has never been one to put off a reprimand any longer than necessary. This is something else.*

"What kind of things?" he asked, curiosity peaked.

"The survival of Nashuar," Nevarr said with just a trace of gravity. His wintry gaze never flinched.

That could be a prelude to several different discussions, not all of them safe ones. Cold fingers traced chills over the back of Fitzgerald's neck and scalp. "You're, uh . . ." He hated to guess, but Nevarr obviously wanted to sound him out on something and was waiting for Fitz to make some tentative stab. "You're not talking surrender to the Confederation, are you?"

Nevarr's expression never changed. "And if I am?"

Fitzgerald exhaled heavily, almost a strong sigh, feeling trapped by Nevarr's command of the conversation. After a moment's thought he said, "If you're looking for my recommendation, Colonel, I would advise against it. Not the least argument against it is that Duchess Liao specifically gave orders to deny Nashuar to the Confederation."

"That was before Confederation forces fell on St. Ives." Nevarr levered himself away from the desk, grabbed one of the chairs set out for visitors to his office and seated himself backward, straddling the chair, his arms folded across the backrest. "Sit down, Maurice." Fitz took the other chair, sitting carefully at attention to avoid feeling too relaxed at the subject. "Nashuar was important only to keep the Confederation engaged away from St. Ives. We have no other intrinsic strategic value. And that position is no longer necessary."

Fitz nodded cautiously. "But if that were put to the Duchess . . ."

The colonel picked up where Fitz trailed off. "Duchess Liao has her own concerns—political concerns. She could never be seen giving away any territory to the Confederation. Not and maintain any strength behind the Compact's defense."

"Are you saying that she—"

"All I'm saying," Nevarr interrupted, obviously predicting the question and not wanting to discuss it, "is that somewhere, someone has got to become responsible for the *people* of Nashuar."

Fitzgerald couldn't have agreed more. *But this is not a decision to be made lightly, on the personal preferences of two soldiers, even if one of them is Nashuar's military coordinator.* And there were still major stumbling blocks in the way. Fitz wrestled with the worst of them, before admitting defeat.

"It won't work. The Compact military command would declare you—us—traitors and simply place someone else in charge." He shook his head. "No matter the cost to Nashuar, we've stalemated the Confederation for too long now to justify surrender."

Nevarr nodded his agreement, smiling grimly. His eyes appeared frightfully fierce. "Yes, but what about a truce?"

A truce? Fitzgerald rocked back on his heels as he considered it. "A coup of neutrality?" he asked, testing out the concept verbally.

"Exactly." Nevarr levered himself to his feet, went behind his desk and removed a holographic still from a drawer, then scaled it across to Fitzgerald. "Recognize that?"

Fitzgerald glanced down. He recognized it all right. In fact, he was willing to bet the still was created out of footage from his *Men Shen*'s battleroom. "It's the *Yu Huang* I fought last month," he said. "Part of the force that gutted the Blackwind Lancers."

"Part of the Nightriders' command company," Nevarr added. "That"—he leaned across and tapped a finger over the *Yu Huang*—"was Colonel Amanda Gahn-Skeeng, the regimental CO." He paused, allowing Fitzgerald to digest that information. "She let you walk off that field, Maurice. And she didn't have to. That tells us something about her we can use."

"You really think she'll agree to a cease-fire?" Fitz asked, wanting to believe Nevarr.

Nevarr nodded. "If it's put to her the right way, by the right person." He stared meaningfully at Fitzgerald.

Fitz swallowed against a suddenly dry mouth. "You mean me?" Nevarr nodded again. "You want me to take my *Men Shen* out alone—"

"Not the *Men Shen*," Nevarr interrupted. "And before you ask, not your old *Blackjack* either. Too confrontational, and I can't risk losing a BattleMech should they decide to attack before hearing you out, or hold you prisoner after."

Fitzgerald couldn't hold the shock off his face. "Not going to sugar-coat this, are you, Colonel? I'm not going in walking, am I?"

Nevarr moved back around his desk and half-sat on the forward edge again. "I've had your J. Edgar hovertank prepped and fully serviced. If you have to cut and run, it gives you the best chance to make it back."

Driving a twenty-five-ton hovercraft into the face of a regiment of BattleMechs. No support possible. No guarantee of his reception. And Fitz hadn't touched the controls of the J. Edgar in better than a year. *Talk about your long odds.*

"I'll do it," he said, before he could talk himself out of it. *Nevarr is right,* he thought, taking the colonel's hand on the deal. *Someone has to be responsible.* And like most long shots, the payoff justified the risk.

26

Celestial Palace
Zi-jin Chéng, Sian
Sian Commonality, Capellan Confederation
25 July 3062

Sun-Tzu allowed Ion Rush to help him onto the dais that
supported the Celestial Throne. His legs barely supported
his own weight, and Sun-Tzu knew the Imarra *Shiao-zhang*
felt the trembling that occasionally rose against his best
efforts to contain it. *Adrenaline, not fear.* Sun-Tzu sensed
Romano's influence in the rationale. *How could the
Chancellor of the mighty Confederation ever show fear?*

*Because this is the second assassination attempt against
his life in less than four years,* Sun-Tzu allowed, forgiving
himself a few moments' weakness even if his mother's
memory would not. And if his shock must be displayed before anyone, certainly Ion Rush had proved his worthiness
this day. The Chancellor knew he'd never forget how the
blood dripping heavily from Rush's arm nearly blended into
the dark red carpet that trailed back to the throne room
doors. At a time when the Chancellor's trust was hard to
come by, he let Rush's actions speak loudly.

Easing back into the Celestial Throne, hands locking
tight on the heavy wooden arms, Sun-Tzu noted the two

people still standing at the throne room's open door. The Maskirovka agent who'd also been in the antechamber when the attack came, scheduled to give a report, and the Death Commando first on the scene after the initial shots shattered the Celestial Palace's morning stillness.

The Death Commando finally shut the door against the rising commotion in the outer hall, guarding it from the outside. That still left the Mask agent, and so Sun-Tzu kept his back straight and head up in a show of strength he currently did not feel. The door opened again, briefly, to admit Talon Zahn and almost immediately thereafter *Sang-shao* Michael Hyung-Tsei, commander of the Death Commando battalion.

With the arrival of Hyung-Tsei, Sun-Tzu felt safe enough to dismiss Rush for medical attention. The Imarra Master had taken at least two bullets in the right arm, and the claw of the assassin's light exoskeleton had ripped through the flesh covering his chest. Sun-Tzu saw the gray, ropy myomere musculature that covered Rush's chest knotting and relaxing beneath a thin layer of blood. It reminded him of the way Rush had punched through the assassin's thin breastplate armor, crushing the man's chest, and suddenly Ion Rush's proximity did not feel so comfortable after all.

"Thank you, Ion," he said, almost a whisper. "Please retire and have yourself attended to."

Rush nodded, though he seemed unconcerned about his injuries. "At once, Chancellor."

Michael Hyung-Tsei bowed to Ion Rush as the *shiao-zhang* passed, his own shoulder muscles bunching up impressively. The commander of the Chancellor's bodyguards then borrowed Talon Zahn's sidearm and frisked the Mask agent remaining in the room. She submitted with an air of indifference—almost amusement. Sun-Tzu ignored the brief flash of offense Zahn failed to hid. *If Sasha could betray me so easily, running to Candace, how can I trust anyone?*

"I will remain inside, Chancellor," Hyung-Tsei said, keeping Zahn's Diàn-ya laser pistol for himself. He positioned himself at the throne room door, gun held against his massive chest and ready for instant use.

Sun-Tzu knew that in his mother's day, Hyung-Tsei would have answered for such a failure in security with his life; no matter that he had not been present. *Just as Sasha should have answered for her failures,* Romano reminded him, her spectral presence within his mind urging him not to make the same mistake again. But Sun-Tzu needed these people, and could not afford his mother's blind rage, however much it might satisfy a personal desire for vengeance.

That is not *who I am,* he thought, though wondered just whom he was trying to convince anymore. Given the straight choice of Sasha's death or her defection to the Compact, he found it harder to argue against Romano's point.

Finding his voice again, Sun-Tzu fed it a strength of purpose that would camouflage any remaining unsteadiness. "I want to know how this happened," he informed the Death Commando officer. "Sian is supposed to be a secure world and Zi-jin Chéng my personal fortress. To say nothing of the sanctity of the Celestial Palace itself."

Hyung-Tsei nodded his understanding, and whispered briefly into a lapel-mounted microphone he'd clipped into place. Another thin wire trailed from his collar up to an ear plug. He was obviously in contact with his men, and just as obviously not about to trust the Chancellor's safety to anyone else at the moment.

"Candace?" Talon Zahn asked, breaking with tradition that demanded he be recognized before addressing the Chancellor. He strode forward, but stopped at a respectful distance from the dais.

The concern in Zahn's voice, real or affected, bought him enough leeway to avoid Sun-Tzu's wrath. The Chancellor was equally impatient for answers. He didn't think his aunt had condoned the attack, though the timing with the Confederation's assault against St. Ives was suggestive.

"What do you say?" he asked the Maskirovka agent present. He recognized her as the deep-cover operative he'd once placed in his uncle Tormano's organization and who'd

been reassigned to the Maskirovka's Bin-xin-zàng Special
Services Branch after her discovery, now in charge of monitoring and enforcing the loyalty of the Confederation to its
Chancellor. Nancy Bao Lee. She was also on the list of potential replacements for Sasha Wanli, an endorsement that
helped her not at all just now.

"I wouldn't think so," she replied, with just the right
amount of hesitation when speaking directly to her Chancellor. Her soft brown eyes belied the strength that backed
them. "He shouted 'Liao!' right before the attack, and to me
that suggests an agency with no ties to the Compact."

Sun-Tzu recalled the loathing and hatred the would-be
assassin had poured into his family name. The only warning given, and even then barely enough time for Ion Rush to
physically pick Sun-Tzu up and throw him behind a heavy
mahogany credenza. More accrued karma burned. *No, not
Candace's direct agent. Nor likely a rogue officer of the
Compact.*

He rewarded Lee with a shallow nod of agreement. Not
bad, considering her lack of time in any analysis branch of
the Mask.

"You have something for me?" he asked, remembering
the entry on his calendar.

"My division is one of the three monitoring your sister's
war crimes trial on Atreus. Counsel delivered opening statements before the tribunal yesterday. I was asked to bring
you the report." She held up a small disk.

The Chancellor did not miss Hyung-Tsei's flinch, before
the Death Commando assured himself she held no weapon
he might have missed. It made Sun-Tzu slightly suspicious
about her overt reasons for being present when the attack
came. "I will review it later," he said slowly, "but give me
the gist of the openings."

She did not hesitate at all, a point in her favor. "The
prosecution made vague promises to show premeditation
on the part of the Confederation, mostly in your lack of control over an obvious cat's paw. The defense is claiming not
guilty by reason of insanity, though more politically put
than that, Chancellor."

"Anything else?" Sun-Tzu asked, sensing a slight hesitancy on Lee's part as to whether she should proceed.

"Kali had to be removed from the courtroom," she said. " 'Failure to recognize the authority of the court,' was the official reasoning. In truth, she refused to be silent and kept threatening a final reckoning as the portents promised."

That can only strengthen our case, Sun-Tzu noted. "Which raises another good point. Candace might still hope to capitalize on the atrocities of Black May, either in court or at a Star League session, should I ever attend another. If her Compact was found backing an assassination attempt, it would undercut her credibility."

"Who then?" Zahn said, glancing furtively at Lee. "Resistance in the Chaos March proper has gained more momentum."

Sun-Tzu knew that was a subtle way of asking whether or not Word of Blake might be behind this attempt as they were the last one. "The Toyama's attempt on my life cost them severely in resources," he said, allowing Nancy Bao Lee into the select group who knew of the earlier attack during his visit to the Periphery world of Canopus. He planned to assign her to the investigation of this recent attempt, and so she required the information. "The Shengli Arms Factory on Victoria was fully reconditioned through their generous reparations. I doubt Cameron St. Jamais would risk his recent rise in power just yet for so little gain."

Still, there could be advantage even if it were only *rumored* to be true. Same for dealings with the Compact. He looked over at Nancy Bao Lee. "No matter what is discovered by the Maskirovka, I want a number of credible reports detailing how this attempt was backed by the Compact or Word of Blake." *Why stop there?* It was his mother's question, but Sun-Tzu found no complaint with it. "Detail a third report for Katrina Steiner and mention George Hasek as well. Leak the reports into unofficial channels."

Zahn grimly nodded his approval over the political capital so easy an operation could win for the Confederation. Nancy Bao Lee smiled her open admiration. "Brilliant, Chancellor Liao. I will personally oversee their creation, and will include one to show how Sasha Wanli arranged for the attempt as part of Candace's blood price for her protection."

Sun-Tzu had been about to brush off the compliment as an obvious ploy by Lee to gain favor as the next Maskirovka Director. But her closing remark snared his immediate and intense interest. "You think Sasha *might* have had something to do with this?" he asked. How Sasha Wanli had managed to escape the Confederation for St. Ives was still under investigation, and it could prove that the assassin and his equipment were smuggled onto Sian by a similar method.

Again, Lee demonstrated just the slightest caution in her reply. Enough to keep the line of investigation open, and certainly headed by her. "No, not really," she said. "It lacks Sasha Wanli's style. Too brute-force. But I will certainly look into the possibility."

This time Sun-Tzu allowed her the assumption of further responsibility. "Do so," he commanded. "For the time being, forward your reports through Ion Rush." That distanced her from his circle of advisors, one step further from Director. It also raised a natural level of distrust in Nancy Bao Lee for the Imarra House Master, who would now proxy the Chancellor's direct approval of her work. *Good,* he thought. *I want you at odds with each other. Conspiracies require cooperation, and if I cannot trust you, then at least I can be assured that you will not collaborate against me. Against my Confederation.* For one thing was certain. Sun-Tzu would never again allow someone to hurt his nation as had Sasha Wanli.

"One more thing," he said, directing his attention to the Mask agent. "I want to know how Sasha made her way off Sian." He paused for a moment, but decided almost instantly to proceed with what he'd resolved to do. "And I want her silenced." He noted Nancy Bao Lee's easy acceptance of the order, and Zahn's initial start followed by grim purpose.

Perhaps Romano's whispers were right, and I never should have allowed Sasha to leave the room alive that day.

No matter now. *On St. Ives, she will continue to hurt the Confederation, and that I cannot allow.*

His mother may not always have been totally sane, but that did not mean she was always wrong, either.

══ 27 ══

House Hiritsu Field Camp
Liaoning Province, St. Ives
St. Ives Compact
31 July 3062

Aris Sung met his protegée as Li Wynn disembarked from the Maultier infantry carrier. The accompanying squad looked weary to Aris' trained eye; dark circles from lack of sleep and the bedraggled appearance of uniforms slept in over too many nights straight. A few were bandaged, hits by small-arms fire. But they carried themselves with the pride of victorious troops. Aris had no need to ask if the extended raid against the First St. Ives Lancers' supply train had been successful.

Still, courtesy suggested that conversation be opened with an innocuous topic, so Aris glanced over at the Maultier and asked, "How did it perform?"

A product of the Taurian Concordat, the Maultier was a recent gift to House Hiritsu from the Pleiades Hussars, one of the few Concordat units loaned to the Confederation the year prior and now assigned to oppose the Fourteenth Donegal Guards on St. Ives. Part of the deal arranged with Chancellor Liao, Aris had heard, that Concordat forces were always to be stationed opposite a Federated Commonwealth unit. Retribution for some supposed meddling in Periphery affairs.

Li Wynn glanced at Aris with a careful mask of neutrality set into place. It cracked briefly, showing a small measure of pride in the Maultier, and with fair reason. The gift had come about as a result of Li Wynn's platoon's reconnaissance of the Liaoning Province, in which they had discovered and foiled a massive counterassault about to be launched by the Donegal Guards against the Hussars.

"It's fast," he said, sounding almost surly. "But it is under-armored and under-armed just like the Blizzard we were shot out of on Nashuar last year."

A few of the infantry had lingered, waiting on Li Wynn. Hearing the note of hostility in their commander's voice, they edged in closer in support. Aris fixed the nearest of them, *Ban-zhang* Mikhail Chess, with an icy glare and backed him off without a word. With a final glance at Li Wynn they faded, leaving student and *Sifu* alone.

Aris nodded in the direction Li's squadmates had taken, toward debriefing. Li fell in beside his Mentor. "I will excuse your rudeness," Aris said, "given the success of your latest mission. Congratulations, Li Wynn, on its completion."

The young warrior looked mollified, but not completely. "Given the mission's success," he asked, "or the fact that I aided you in defying our House Master?"

Aris steeled himself against a sharp retort. If they had been within hearing of anyone, he would have taken issue with Li's serious breach of courtesy. As it was, he decided to partially accept the rebuke. After all, it was not wholly undeserved.

"What happened near Scottsdale was on my authority, not yours. I accepted full responsibility for the new *interpretation* of *Shiao-zhang* Non's orders, but credited you with the success of your strike. I was in position to accept the blame, but instead *Shiao-zhang* Non chose to reward you for salvaging the operation. Where is your complaint?"

Li looked away, obviously trying to regain full control of his own emotions, failing. "You deliberately tricked me into a violation of my orders. I don't care that it was a success." He glanced back, his face a study in anger, confusion, and sorrow. "You were wrong, Aris Sung."

Aris shook his head. "That was for Ty Wu Non to decide. Not me and certainly not you, Li Wynn. I did what was necessary for the greater good of our House. Can't you understand that?" *You would have, once upon a time. Before the false glory of warfare blinded you.*

Aris wanted to get through to Li Wynn—as to no other member of House Hiritsu—the reminder that a Warrior House was devoted to more than just the conduct of war. More than strict adherence to tradition, for tradition's sake. *The killing fields have grown worse as we have forgotten or ignored that the Compact is Capellan in heritage. As we have drifted from a few of our founding precepts.* Warriors were responsible to the Capellan citizenry—past, present, and future—as prescribed by the Lorix Creed. The teachings of Master Kung, even more central to Hiritsu philosophy, called for respecting all stations in life above and below one's own. That House Hiritsu members were responding to Aris' call gave him some amount of vindication. *But if I fail here, with Li, how can I hope to revise the thinking of an entire Warrior House?* Again the question surfaced. *Is it them, or is it me?*

And he was failing.

"All I understand," Li Wynn said, "is that I have been made to question the orders of my House Mentor—my *Sifu.*" He stopped, stared Aris Sung straight in the face. Behind his eyes, Aris saw the confusion that ate away at the younger man. "If I cannot trust his orders, how do I trust his vision?"

Because you listen to your own conscience, Aris wanted to say. A Warrior House did not demand of a member that he sacrifice his individuality, only temper it with the House precepts and formal teachings. But Aris remained silent, too many doubts surging against his resolve to argue further with Li Wynn. This was the man Aris had once thought to understand as he understood himself, their origins so similar and both of them for the same thing. A place to belong.

Now, as Li Wynn turned his back on Aris and walked off, Aris could only wonder if he'd ever understood either of them.

Aris heard the careful approach of someone behind him. The dry crack of a twig snapping underfoot. The rustling of branches as someone pushed his way cautiously past them. Someone trying not to be silent, which would have alarmed the House warrior, but simply trying not to interrupt another's meditation. Aris did not turn, though he was sure he knew who approached.

"You certainly know how to pick your places for"—and here the House Master paused, reminding Aris of a conversation they'd had a year ago—"*reflection.*"

Aris felt Ty Wun Non kneel next to him, and the House Master's green and black uniform registered in Aris' peripheral vision as the elder man leaned forward to admire the view. From under the high branches of a pine, the two of them stared out through a few sword-leafed ferns into a field of wildflowers. A riot of summer colors and fragrant scents assailed the senses.

"I remember," Aris said slowly. "I said then that I didn't believe House Hiritsu could ever turn on another Capellan, even Compact citizens, with the ferocity we'd witnessed in other units."

Ty Wu Non nodded. "Which may well be the reason Chancellor Liao selected us for such an operation."

"I was wrong," Aris said simply.

Shiao-zhang Non disagreed. "No, not wrong. Overly optimistic, perhaps." A pause, while the Hiritsu Master gathered his thoughts. "You did not take into consideration the House's ability to *approach* such a level of common disregard. Or the Chancellor's possible disposition toward forcing on us a change in our House philosophies."

Aris gaped at the House Master, his tranquillity shattered by the suggestion. "Chancellor Liao has ordered us—"

Ty Wu Non laughed, full and hearty. "You fall for one of your own traps, Aris Sung. I said *possible* disposition." The mirth evaporated quickly, though. "Who can guess Chancellor Liao's thoughts?"

Shaking his head, Aris said, "I've given up attempting to read minds."

"Yes, I'd heard that you traded words with *Pai-zhang* Li Wynn." Was that a touch of humor in the House Master's voice? "Not what was said, of course, but reports suggested a rather inconclusive ending. Reminiscent of some words I once had with another warrior, I believe." A pregnant pause, and then Non's voice took on a pleasant, fatherly tone Aris had never heard in it before.

"Aris Sung, you once helped me save our House from collapse. I have not forgotten, and neither should you. Last year you alerted me to the philosophical dangers of fighting the Compact, and still I was blind to the changes occurring until your actions pointed them out."

Aris breathed a tentative sigh of relief. Perhaps not all was yet lost. "Your endorsement, *Shiao-zhang* Non, would go a long way toward helping me correct those changes."

"Yes, the will of the House Master being the will of the House. But you and I both know how tenuous that can be. Which is why I must refuse you."

Ty Wu Non shook his head as Aris stared at him in confusion. "Think about it, Aris Sung. You know, as I do, how far we have slipped away from our original course. Li Wynn, for all his confused state, possesses a following among the younger infantry, and he is not the only one to have drifted so far from the purer light. Entire MechWarrior companies have embraced their hostility in a way I'm not sure can be repaired. If I were to force the issue now, I risk irreparably fracturing the House, as nearly happened on Kaifeng. We must wait. In the meantime, I can only hope that your own efforts will turn House Hiritsu from its present course."

Feeling the exhaustion of all his previous efforts warring with the frustration of how far he had left to travel, alone, Aris shook his head slightly. "But if I cannot even affect Li Wynn, how can I hope to affect the others?"

"You already have. I've seen the difference, even if you have not." Ty Wu Non's dark eyes sought out Aris' gaze. "Li

Wynn is a special case, though. You forget that he is not truly of House Hiritsu. And he never will be."

The House Master forestalled a protest on Aris' part with a raised hand. "He has been an asset, Aris, that I will no longer deny. But when I agreed to adopt him, I knew then that the benefits could be short-lived. He needed years of conditioning, but we were not allowed that and now he has the fanatic's zeal of one come lately to a purpose in life. Old enough to adopt some of our ways, but already too set in his own to truly understand it all and adapt to changes as you did. And as the House must now."

"Then why keep him?" Aris asked. *Why keep any of them if they risk the foundations of our House?*

Ty Wu Non rose fluidly to his feet, eerily answering Aris' silent question over his first. "Because we need them, and the fight for St. Ives may yet require of us that I embrace their vision and not yours. The Chancellor requires of me assistance in the conquest of St. Ives, and that I will do, though it cost me the soul of our House."

He smiled, a bit sad but obviously resolved. "Nothing is more important than the Confederation, Aris Sung. Not for us. Not unless the Chancellor deems it so."

Aris nodded a reluctant agreement. "Is there nothing left to be done?" he asked in a whisper.

Shiao-zhang Ty Wu Non, Master of House Hiritsu, gripped Aris' shoulder with his right hand and nodded. "Watch. Listen. And pray that when the time finally arrives, we are in the right position to guide House Hiritsu back toward the light."

=== 28 ===

The battle entered its third hour, raging on in isolated pockets of Ambergrist's Yè Huar Rain Forest. Beneath the thick canopy that washed both 'Mechs in green light, Major Cassandra Allard-Liao dropped her *Cestus'* sighting reticule over a *Thunder,* spearing the sun-in-hand insignia of the Third Confederation Reserves painted over her target's right side. Her lasers flared, one medium-sized weapon taking the *Thunder* in the right torso while the rest of the jeweled energy scattered over its arm and leg of the same side.

Fall, she mentally commanded it. The silvery blur of her nickel-ferrous Gauss slug, only a fraction of a second behind the coherent-light show, slammed into the Confederation machine dead center, crushing the barrel of one medium pulse laser and raining shattered armor onto the ferns and creeping vines that covered the forest floor. *Fall! Go down!*

Of all the places Cassandra believed might have merited her attention, Ambergrist fell way down the list. No large-scale production facilities requiring defense. No major strategic value in its position. No high-profile Confederation regiment on-planet. Already well-garrisoned by Treyhang's Free Capella forces and a battalion of the Illician Lancers mercenary regiment still "on-loan" from the Commonwealth. Better that she return to St. Loris and assist the Cossacks, or stage a forward raid against Indicass. *Better still, why am I not on St. Ives with mother and Kai, fighting for the very survival of our capital? What am I doing here?*

Simple questions, both with the same simple answer. *Mother ordered my Lancers here from Tantara.* In her—debatable—wisdom, Candace saw something of value in keeping Confederation forces heavily engaged on Ambergrist rather than pull units in for the defense of St. Ives.

The *Thunder* had staggered back several paces under Cassandra's heavy onslaught. The seventy-ton 'Mech rocked onto one foot—just to taunt her, it seemed—then the enemy MechWarrior regained control and returned the off-balance 'Mech to a stable, wide-spread stance. The way the *Thunder*'s lower-leg armor flared down into large, wedge-shaped feet left the impression that the machine might have grown up from the surrounding vegetation, drawing its strength directly from the earth. With almost insulting slowness the heavy machine began walking backward.

Power demand from her lasers spiked the *Cestus*' fusion reactor, and the heat in Cassandra's cockpit jumped by several degrees. Sweat beaded on her forehead and bare arms, but the coolant flowing through her vest kept the distraction to a minimum while the *Cestus*' double-capacity heat sinks bled the excess heat away within a matter of seconds. She ran the *Cestus* forward, shouldering aside smaller trees as she pursued the fleeing *Thunder* into thicker woods.

What began hours ago as a battalion-scale engagement had deteriorated quickly into occasional single combat, where opponents faded in and out and often changed while lost from sight among the thick vegetation. But Cassandra would be damned before giving up the *Thunder,* scope-locked on its destruction as if the opposing pilot were directly to blame that she remained on Ambergrist and wasn't allowed to go where most needed.

From the dark shadows within a cluster of sequoia, the *Thunder* spat out a steady stream of depleted-uranium slugs that tore into the left side of the *Cestus*. Splinters and shards of armor sprayed about—some ricocheting off the side of the ferroglass fronting her cockpit and others ripping through leaves or sticking into the bark of trees like small darts. Tracers flared briefly in the forest gloom, red-yellow pieces of fire that clashed with the emerald darts from the *Thunder*'s pulse lasers.

To maintain balance, sixty-five tons of upright metal depended heavily on the massive gyro located within its torso cavity and the neural feedback from the pilot's own sense of equilibrium for normal operation. Cassandra wrestled against her control sticks, fighting the damage to her machine. Then, feeling the hopelessness of her cause, she cursed and abandoned the 'Mech to gravity and worked to lessen the impact of her fall.

The *Cestus* fell hard against its left side, an internal support beam snapping off and piercing the shielding of its extralight engine. Cassandra's heat levels jumped again. She rolled the *Cestus* to its front and propped up on one arm, wary should the *Thunder* attempt to take advantage of her fall and rush her.

But it was gone, vanished back into the forest, no longer registering on her sensors.

Ma de dan! she cursed again, slamming one fist down against the arm of her seat. Working her controls, she hauled the *Cestus* back to its feet.

The path the *Thunder* had taken stood before her, a tunnel through the greenery. Bleeding heat, her armor more memory than fact, and feeling bruised from the rough landing against the forest floor, Cassandra stared into its depths for a few long seconds. Then, more cautious than before, she followed the Confederation 'Mech deeper into the forest. *You do not get away so easily,* she promised.

She would trade Ambergrist in an instant if it meant being able to help save St. Ives, but that was not her choice to make. So she would continue here on Ambergrist, and she would make the Confederation pay dearly for ever threatening her home. Then, maybe, her mother would listen to her. Allow her to come home, or take the fight to the Confederation. *Either way, I know I can make a difference.*

She couldn't see how her cousin's forces could hope to stand against her rage.

Ganxia Foothills
Shaanxi District, Ambergrist

The Blackwind Lancers drove forward, two battalions crossing the rural highway and bursting through the thin belt of woods bordering it. Scattered weapons fire fell on the Lancers from 'Mechs holding position behind a set of low-lying hills barring their path, which they returned with interest. The azure whips of PPCs flayed armor, dropping large sheets to the ground. Laserfire cut as deeply, rivulets of molten composite dripping off the 'Mechs and starting several small brush fires while autocannon hammered away at both sides. Missiles arced out on columns of smoke, but where the Lancers ran beneath the umbrella, the Hustaing Warriors abandoned their position to escape further into Ambergrist's Ganxia Foothills.

And the chase was on again.

Colonel Warner Doles tried once more to summon the anger, the rage, he had known at the start of today's battle but had slowly lost to time and a bone-aching weariness. With it he hoped to reestablish an impetus to his tactics, bringing the fury to bear against the Hustaing Warriors and turning their fighting retreat through Ambergrist's Shaanxi District into a total rout of the Confederation regiment. He didn't just want them beaten, but crushed. Battered beyond reformation and sent back to Hustaing in humiliation.

Or at least he had.

Now, doubts assailed him—reminding him too much of the confusion he'd known right after his recruitment by Tormano Liao. Doles had worried that such might be the case during this, his first engagement on Ambergrist finally authorized by Treyhang Liao. For the last few weeks his ambiguous feelings over promotion, over his command of the Blackwind Lancers, and certainly over Treyhang Liao's leadership left him in a repeating cycle of anger, depression, and confusion. He'd hoped for combat to solve the dilemma. Certainly it seemed to, early on, giving him a purpose and a target toward which to focus his anger. But it didn't last, and its unstable nature made him overly cautious. *Even so,* he noticed, *they cannot stand against us.*

His two battalions of Blackwind Lancers continued to drive the Warriors' full regiment ahead of them, trading fire over the open spaces that separated the low hills and sparse woods. Just as Doles predicted on Indicass, the Hustaing Warriors traded on enthusiasm over discipline. Using hard-hitting striker companies, his Lancers split the enemy ranks time and again and forced them into costly efforts to regroup. The path behind them was littered with BattleMech corpses and burning vehicles, the majority belonging to the Hustaing Warriors. 'Mech by 'Mech, lance by lance, Warner Doles recouped many of his earlier losses to the Warriors.

An enemy *Cataphract* crossed his sights at long range, slugs from its light- and medium-bore autocannon pitting the armor of Doles' *Emperor* as they tracked up his left leg and out over his 'Mech's broad chest. The rage sparked within him, briefly—long enough to bring his own autocannon to bear. Cluster munitions sanded armor off the *Cataphract*'s upper torso and head. Warner Doles struggled to retain that spark, to fan it into the flames that had burned within him not so long ago, but the spark died and left behind what had become an all-too-familiar void of uncertainty.

"Here they come again," an unfamiliar voice warned Doles over the general battle frequency. Someone in Major Castillian's command.

Doles backed off his *Emperor* from the forward lines, trying to find the latest rearguard action being staged by the Warriors. His sensors located it on his far right flank—Castillian's command all right—and displayed portions on an auxiliary screen. Twelve BattleMechs, medium to heavy weight, and all painted slightly different as if to reinforce the lack of cohesion that was the Hustaing Warriors' greatest weakness. Only a series of numbers, painted across their torsos and each different from the others, left any clue that these were 'Mechs of a similar unit. This time a lance of heavy armor supported them, Drillsons and Vedettes.

"Bravo Company, swing east," Doles ordered, trying to threaten the rearguard attempt with a flanking maneuver. The anger was there, to be sure, but competing with it was something akin to . . . admiration? Doles shook the thought from his mind. *You do not admire the enemy, you destroy him.*

The new company set up a skirmish line, daring the Blackwind Lancers forward. Two companies challenged them, the one Doles sent swinging in on their flank. Weapons fire exchanged, and then again. The line wavered, broke. But not in full retreat. Half the company, those in jump-capable 'Mechs, bounded south and west while the rest, including the armor, formed a new line of battle that charged the previously flanking Lancers company.

Now Doles' warriors were caught heading into a crossfire, which they immediately backed away from. It cost the Blackwind Lancers their momentum, as the entire line staggered to a halt rather than lose its cohesion. Then a final PPC caught one Hustaing Warrior *Hunchback* in the rear as it retreated, coring through and slicing deep into support structure.

Metal spat out the back of the *Hunchback* at high velocities, a gyroscope tearing itself to pieces. The pilot ejected, parafoil spreading out at the top of the arc and sending him gliding after his fleeing unit. A Warriors' *Snake* held out its left arm, clotheslining the parafoil and tangling its cords within its fingers. With his comrade swinging along, the *Snake* throttled up into a run that quickly caught it up to the retreating regiment.

A witness to the spectacular rescue, Doles caught himself wishing both pilots luck for their lives, if not their 'Mechs, and the duality bothered him. *They are one and the same,* he first thought, then quickly corrected himself. *No, they're not. But do you really have any business making such distinctions?* That he could not answer so easily.

Doesn't matter, he decided, shoving aside the arguments for later examination. *We have them on the run, for the first time ever. Not just a raid, or a battle, but the beginnings of a campaign to push the Hustaing Warriors off Ambergrist for good. That will please both Duchess Liao and Treyhang.*

It wasn't until several moments later, during another lull, that Warner Doles first noticed that he hadn't spared a thought for pleasing the Blackwind Lancers, or himself.

Celestial Palace
Zi-jin Chéng, Sian
Sian Commonality, Capellan Confederation
15 August 3062

On the third day of Protector Grover Shraplen's state visit to Sian, Sun-Tzu decided to meet him in one of the more elegant receiving rooms of the Celestial Palace. It would be the first real chance for the two rulers to talk since the initial audience and the formal reception in the Protector's honor given on his arrival. *Three days, giving him time to inspect factories, attend some prepared briefings and tour Sian—properly accompanied, of course.*

Nancy Bao Lee escorted the ruler of the Taurian Concordat into the room, her hand curled under his arm. She wore a turquoise evening dress, open to mid-thigh and with daring necklines that plunged in both the front and back. It said *Canopian* as nothing else could. *And hopefully suggests that the Confederation is open to influence from its allies, rather than the reverse.*

And placing a beautiful woman in Shraplen's company no doubt kept him distracted. A whisper from the darker shadows within his mind.

Sun-Tzu tried not to credit the memories of his mother

with the idea of using Nancy, though certainly for Romano sexuality had been as much a weapon as any other. It had proved devastatingly effective in her control of Tsen Shang. Then he decided it did not matter where the idea had come from.

Only the results.

Shraplen walked stiffly, obviously aware of Nancy's attention and doing his best to put on a proper military bearing. She led him up to Sun-Tzu Liao, as previously directed, approaching the Chancellor rather than allow Shraplen to pause and force Sun-Tzu to go to him as a host would be obliged to do. There she broke away as the two rulers first bowed to each other in Asian fashion and then shook hands with the double-clasp common to the Concordat.

"An honor, Chancellor Liao." Shraplen's deep voice gave off the proper amount of courtesy. "You have a beautiful capital," he said, and seemed to mean it. Just a touch of wistful regret to suggest envy. Easy enough to feign, though since his gaze followed Nancy as she excused herself from the room. Sun-Tzu hoped that losing his lovely escort would throw him off balance, but Shraplen's voice never lost its edge. "A most beautiful capital."

That voice was Shraplen's saving feature, in Sun-Tzu's opinion, eloquent to the point of being nearly hypnotic. The Chancellor certainly did not think much of the other man's physical stature. Median height and thickening about the waist. Dark hair fading to an iron gray, in tactical retreat over both temples. Hazel eyes, but no real fire to them. His one physical claim to character a scruffy goatee, kept dyed an immaculate black. Not a man one would associate with the leadership of a strong Periphery realm, and certainly not a man to put a person on his guard.

Except that Sun-Tzu Liao stayed forever on his guard.

The Chancellor took no one lightly, regardless of his outward attitude toward them. He also did not concur with the typical Inner Sphere view that Periphery leaders were a cut below the rulers of the Inner Sphere's five Great Houses. Four years before he had taken audience with Emma Centrella of the Magistracy of Canopus, as much a ruler as

Thomas Marik or Katrina Steiner-Davion and certainly more impressive than Haakon Magnusson, former Prince of the Free Rasalhague Republic. Emma Centrella's only disadvantage was in being the head of a realm weaker than most Great Houses, and Sun-Tzu understood that position well. So no, he would not underestimate Shraplen.

Besides which, the man assumed control of the Taurian Concordat too smoothly after Jeffrey Calderon's untimely death last year.

"You are very kind, Protector Shraplen." Sun-Tzu gestured toward two high-backed chairs drawn up to a large picture window that overlooked gardens four stories below and the city of Zi-jin Chéng over the palace walls. They moved toward them. "I have often heard similar claims made for your home colony of MacLeod's Land, with its"—he paused, as if searching his memory for the word—"*innocent* charm."

Sun-Tzu tugged at the hem of his Han jacket, gold with red dragons chasing up the sleeves and across the back, straightening it before seating himself with precise care. Let Shraplen be reminded of his homeworld's precarious position, set near the borders of both the Confederation and the Federated Commonwealth. Having been duly informed by the Maskirovka of the other man's great concern for its safety, Sun-Tzu felt sure that it would become the opening gambit of the game they were about to play.

Shraplen did not disappoint. "I have noticed that such innocent charm is often targeted by Inner Sphere realms," he said, trying to subtly turn the conversation toward business. "Mistaken for weakness, or simply out of envy for what they do not already possess."

Sun-Tzu nodded agreement, content to play the *sensitive* role against Shraplen's *subtle strength* if it would help make the Chancellor—and by extension the Confederation—seem less threatening. "Such as that horrible business on Detroit," he said, widening his eyes with feigned scandal. "Maltin's coup on the eve of a winter holiday, taking both Emma Centrella and Jeffrey Calderon hostage. Calderon . . ." He trailed off, frowning his distaste for such methods. "And the Federated Commonwealth sponsoring the event."

"Yes," Shraplen said, but instantly recanted. "That is, we're fairly certain of Davion involvement. Sherman Maltin's immediate application to the Commonwealth for recognition and protection of his 'colony nation' is certainly suggestive." He sighed, relaxing slightly into his chair, which Sun-Tzu knew was far more comfortable than his own. "I doubt we'll ever uncover hard evidence."

You won't, the Chancellor promised. *Hard evidence can be proven false, but implications endure forever.*

"You should consider yourself fortunate," Sun-Tzu said, sympathizing with Shraplen, "that you did not lose a large piece of the Concordat." He pretended to relax, to reminisce. Not an easy task, since the spectral presence of Romano Liao railed against the topic. But Sun-Tzu had to bring up the war with the Compact before Shraplen did, and present it correctly.

"The Confederation knows what it is to surrender worlds and people to the Federated Commonwealth. It has taken us thirty years to attempt to reclaim what is rightfully ours, and even now we may fail." The memory of his mother cursed him for suggesting the thought. Sun-Tzu ignored her best he could, sitting suddenly forward with face apologetic as if worried he had offered insult. "Not to imply that your troops have not helped," he said quickly. "They were of great service in neutralizing Commonwealth forces already stationed in the Compact." A touch of a sullen tone. "Except that Victor Davion simply assigned more regiments after your forces successfully stalemated his." *Actually, by request of Candace, better to play up the* Davion intrusion *angle.*

Control over his voice Shraplen might have, but not over his face. Sun-Tzu read the flash of pride that briefly shone in the other man's eyes at hearing his forces praised. "It seemed the best for all concerned," Shraplen said. "Concordat forces demanded vengeance for Calderon's assassination, but I could hardly risk war with the Commonwealth." He regarded Sun-Tzu coolly. "And, of course, the Magistracy of Canopus has shown that there are indeed benefits to treating with some Inner Sphere Lords."

Ah, now that we all know what we are . . . Sun-Tzu bit down on his lower lip in thought and pretended uncertainty. "Yes, I had hoped to offer you a similar relationship. We both have alliances with Canopus, why not with each other?"

The Concordat Protector frowned his seemingly honest reluctance, then said, "I'm not sure that is possible."

The first bargaining chip, Sun-Tzu translated. "But why?" he asked.

"Your troops in the New Colony Region between the Concordat and the Magistracy unsettle me and my people." He tried to look abashed, failed. "My Defense Ministry points out that though Maltin's coup *may* have been Davion-sponsored, it is Capellan troops now occupying Detroit." He paused, coughed apologetically. "And with the recent terror your sister unleashed, the Confederation is not exactly seen in the best light."

Sun-Tzu winced over that remark, with no need to play-act. His mother's memory urged him to Kali's defense. Instead, he colored it with melancholy resignation. "My sister is mad," he said with bitterness, working to remain focused on task, "and I hope she never returns from Atreus." Of course she would return; Thomas Marik certainly wouldn't want to keep her in his realm and Sun-Tzu would never allow that regardless. *Kali belongs here, in the Confederation, much as I might wish otherwise.* "I just don't know what to do with her." And that *was* true. *But if you think to trade a reference to Black May for possession of Detroit, you can forget it. The Confederation has poured too much into those factories to release a claim on them.*

"But surely," he said, cloaking his thoughts and looking hopeful, "Concordat citizens can recognize the difference between a rational military campaign and actions brought on by mental instability." It was as close as Sun-Tzu dared come to bringing up the paranoia for which Jeffrey Calderon's father had been known. Placing the Concordat on military alert for *eight years* over a freighter's misjump constituted *some* measure of insanity.

The Protector of the Taurian Concordat likely drew the same conclusion, though he managed to hide it. "Perhaps," was all he said.

Shraplen wanted what Sun-Tzu's realm had to offer, or he would have killed the discussion. But just as obviously he was not about to bargain from the weaker position. Or at least, what he *perceived* the weaker position to be. And he did make a good argument. Sun-Tzu tried another tentative stab.

"Confederation troops on Detroit are part of an agreement with the Magistracy," he reminded the Protector. "Technically, they are under the command of Naomi Centrella." He sighed, lightly, as if in partial surrender. "But I take your point."

He thought in silence for a moment, to draw out Shraplen's sense of victory. *Let him enjoy the moment.* "Would it ease your mind if I allowed Concordat troops into the Confederation, as the sole garrison on the worlds of Rollis, Larsha, and Zanzibar?" He named three worlds from which Zahn had recently been forced to shift troops, now in need of garrisons against possible Commonwealth incursion. Romano's spectral presence cursed for having to give up any of *her* worlds. "That establishes a neutral buffer between our realms," Sun-Tzu continued. "And I would allow you the resource rights to those worlds, similar to the bargain offered to the Magistracy." Actually, the Magistracy had been deeded resource rights over two worlds, but both of much higher quality.

Shraplen was cautious now, seeking to confirm the concessions won. "You will begin bringing our military up to the level of your own?" His tone remained wary, almost disinterested, but there was no disguising the avarice in his eyes.

Sun-Tzu nodded agreement. "I will order the refitting of your troops fighting in the Compact first," he promised. *A move that benefits me more than you.* "And your garrison troops inside my realm next. Spare parts can be routed out from the Shengli facility on Victoria."

"You promised the Magistracy a great deal more than that," Grover Shraplen noted. "You have sent them teachers and instructors. Technicians, engineers, military advisors."

Scavenging, back-biting, treacherous mongrels. Romano's vitriol, finally unleashed, flung scathing indictments at Shraplen, in particular, and the Periphery, in general.

Sun-Tzu reigned in the memories with a steel hand. From dealings with Canopus, he understood how great a store Periphery realms put on education. *They learned long before the Inner Sphere that knowledge is even more valuable than technology, for technology can be too easily lost.*

"I would promise you the same," Sun-Tzu said. "To be delivered as soon as they are available." *As soon as I decide to make them available.* Here he allowed a touch of desperation to show. "You understand that much of our resources is currently dedicated to ending the conflict in the St. Ives Compact. I cannot hurt the efforts of my own nation in reclaiming our rightful territory." The last word almost stuck in Sun-Tzu's throat. *Territory. A concept that the Periphery considers important. It's not the worlds, but the people, who make a nation.*

His own demands satisfied, Shraplen made the obvious move toward setting a better timetable. "I have two regiments on Castrovla," he said as if reminding Sun-Tzu of their agreement. "If I allowed them to join the others currently in the Compact, perhaps bring in more from the Concordat . . ." He trailed off suggestively.

As if I needed to be reminded, Sun-Tzu thought, but outwardly he perked up and jumped in where Shraplen left off. "I would begin upgrading them at once," he promised. "And I'm sure that would allow the Confederation to send an immediate shipment for the Concordat." *A small shipment. I expect several delays.* "You could accompany it back on your return trip."

Shraplen smiled, the first sign of his agreement to the

bargain being struck. "We will be stationed opposite the Davion units," he demanded. "The same conditions as before. Concordat troops will fight the Compact only in self defense. I would want no lasting bad relations with your future subjects."

Better for you than I, Sun-Tzu thought, nodding to the concession. *Fortunately, self defense can be liberally construed.*

"Think of it," he said, settling back into his own chair. "Our forces fighting side by side as the Concordat"—he was careful to place Shraplen's realm first—"Magistracy, and Confederation work together toward a new era, as equals." *But some more equal than others.* A memory of Romano Liao and her whispered comment regarding the other Great Houses during the Outreach conference of 3050.

Sun-Tzu suppressed the thought, not wanting his mother to spoil this moment. *I have what I want, what Talon Zahn needs, and now all that remains is to make sure that the Concordat shows some advancement. But not as fast as they would like, never as fast as they would like. What are two regiments? I can make it cost them so much more.*

In the back of his mind, the ghost of Romano Liao laughed at Grover Shraplen even as Sun-Tzu turned to give the Protector a beatific smile.

"Welcome to the alliance," he said.

30

Shen Pass
Liaoning Province, St. Ives
St. Ives Compact
15 August 3062

Vision blurred and head throbbing, Aris Sung attempted to shake off the dizziness and paid with a sharp pain shooting along his neck and left shoulder. Restraining straps cut against his chest, suspending him over his 'Mech's instrument panel and a viewscreen half-buried into overturned earth. Grabbing at his control sticks, he worked the Battle-Mech's arms and legs to help pull the *Wraith* back up into the fight.

House Hiritsu battled against Raymond's Armored Infantry, trying to force the Shen Pass, which opened up the route to Tian-tan, St. Ives' capital. It was a well-matched fight, two battalions to a side, the Warrior House edging out their opposition in raw BattleMech strength but Colonel Raymond's armor regaining that against Hiritsu infantry. Well-matched, until Aris ran up against a *JagerMech* flanked by a full lance of Vedette armored vehicles, their autocannon fire concentrating against his 'Mech and driving him to the ground. A quick glance at the *Wraith*'s wire-frame damage schematic showed a loss of armor all over his 'Mech, but no internal damage. Yet.

The *JagerMech* and Vedettes stood roughly two hundred meters off Aris' location—now engaged against Raven Clearwater, one of Aris' lance leaders piloting a *Huron Warrior*. There were hardly any changes in position, reaffirming that Aris hadn't been knocked unconscious. *Just a brief brush against the darkness.* Two Galleon light tanks raced in from the far left flank, having skirted the edge of the nearby town—likely hoping to finish off the *Wraith* while it remained prone. They instantly peeled off as the fifty-five-ton 'Mech regained its feet and turned in their direction.

"You all right, *Lien-zhang* Sung?" Raven's voice came whispering from the communications set built into his neurohelmet.

Aris nodded, more to himself than her. A twinge in his left shoulder promised a pulled muscle. "All systems go," he said, triggering off a large pulse laser at one fleeing Galleon. The ruby darts stung at its rear, melting away half its armor and adding impetus to the tank crew's retreat.

With Aris' company moving up, the *JagerMech* and its armored escorts surrendered ground. "Slowly but surely," Aris said over his company's frequency. "No one get anxious, now." *No one else, at least.* He'd pushed his *Wraith* too far forward, trusting his speed too much for defense. But he wanted to make sure they gave Naqiuo a wide berth, still concerned with the small town sitting just outside Shen Pass. *Once we push the Armored Infantry well past its northern reaches, we claim the town peacefully, and Colonel Raymond loses any logistics support. The pass falls to us by default.*

Checking his head's up display, Aris noted the other Hiritsu companies holding even, guiding off his company as per *Shiao-zhang* Non's order. Unofficial support, which Aris gladly accepted. Infantry ranged out slightly wider, vehicle-supported squads and Fa Shih battle armor under far more tactical freedom, but still they kept to a ragged line of battle as set by Aris' warriors. He began to feel optimistic.

It didn't last.

The same distance that Aris hoped would provide a safe region between Hiritsu forces and Naqiuo proved a tempting opening for the Armored Infantry. A lance of two *Clint* BattleMechs backed by a pair of new *Helios* designs separated from their lines and tried to slip into that gap, supported by a mixed lance of armor.

Recognizing the danger, Aris engaged jump jets and rocketed his *Wraith* skyward on fiery jets of plasma. "Shift left," he ordered. "Push them back toward the pass." The faster machines in Aris' company leapt or ran forward with him, those with long-range weapons firing. Having no trouble with target selection, the Hiritsu warriors concentrated against the two *Helios* designs with their threatening Gauss rifles.

"Moving up," a new voice called over the comm system, tinny and flat from transmission but still edged with a trace of excitement.

Busy holding his 'Mech to its feet as PPCs from both *Clint*s blasted the *Wraith* with man-made lightning, Aris at first thought the transmission came from one of his own warriors. It wasn't until his own pulse lasers bit deep into a *Helios* that he realized the frequency flashed onto his head's up display had been an infantry channel. And then the voice sparked recognition.

First reading the bad news off his HUD, Aris then confirmed it with a quick glance to an auxiliary monitor. Two of Li's squads, those equipped with Fa Shih battle armor or vehicle transport, slipped into Naqiuo's southern reaches.

"Li Wynn, you remain outside of that town," Aris ordered, though his direct authority over the infantry was tenuous at best. "Repeat, do not enter Naqiuo."

"Too late, *Lien Sung*." That was *Zhang-si* Smith, his *Thunder* guarding the far left flank. "They're already inside."

Aris stifled a curse, his hands gripping the control sticks with knuckle-whitening strength. By pulling his company out of line to meet the Armored Infantry threat, he'd given tacit permission for the rest to reposition as necessary. *But I* know *Li Wynn. This was no coincidence; he waited for this chance.* Aris cut laterally across the fire zone, stitching more ruby pulses into the same *Helios* as he tried to deflect the Armored Infantry drive from reaching the town.

The quick action by Aris' company almost prevented the disaster.

The *Helios* 'Mechs were too slow, unable to anchor against Naqiuo before House Hiritsu pushed them back. Losing their fire support might have convinced the *Clints* to retreat as well, except for the spread of long-ranged missiles that arced out from the eastern edge of the town to rain down over one of them. Both medium-weight BattleMechs pivoted and broke for the town, followed by a Vedette and a Blizzard hovertank.

Raven Clearwater's *Huron Warrior* accounted for one *Clint,* a long-distance Gauss slug catching it square in the back and nearly blowing out the front armor, in the meantime shoving the gyro straight through engine shielding and into the fusion plant. A fireball consumed the forty-ton machine, but the other BattleMech and two armored tanks gained the protection of Naqiuo's streets.

"Break off," Aris ordered as *Zhang-si* Sainz in his new *Ti Ts'ang* cut in toward the town. It pulled up short and veered away just as Li Wynn's first call for assistance carried over the air waves.

"Echo and Foxtrot squads requesting immediate support," Li said, voice calm. "Heavily engaged against four—repeat four—armored vehicles and *Clint* BattleMech."

Li pushed for this, Aris had no doubt. *His infantry are well-rehearsed in city fighting, and he resented my steering the House around Naqiuo.* An explosion near the outskirts of the town told of one enemy destroyed.

"Engaged against BattleMech and *three* armored vehicles. Casualty rate mounting." Still no panic, but Aris caught traces of concern breaking through the cracks in Li Wynn's calm front. "Single 'Mech requested for support."

Smoke drifted lazily into the clear St. Ives sky. *That fire will spread.* Li Wynn cared nothing for the people of St. Ives. He respected the House—he worshipped it—but Ty

Wu Non was correct in that he would never understand the most basic tents. *He cannot understand the problem, let alone my efforts to* alleviate it. Aris felt sorry for Li Wynn, for the first time wishing he'd never brought the younger man away from Kaifeng.

The *Ti Ts'ang* held position, hovering between rejoining the main drive to push Raymond's Armored Infantry back into the mountains and waiting for the order to support Li's overmatched infantry. *My flank, my decision.* "Continue on original mission," Aris ordered, choosing the all-hands frequency so that Li Wynn would at least know he was on his own. "Drive forward. Watch for reappearance of *opposing* forces."

We all have our paths, Li Wynn. Aris throttled his *Wraith* into a walk, swinging behind Clearwater's lance and rejoining his own. *I'm sorry ours did not travel together.*

Li Wynn cracked the seals on his Fa Shih battle armor, levering off the helmet and then working his way free of the damaged suit. A heavy pressure sat in his lower chest, and pain shot up his left side when he moved. He examined the blisters and charred flesh showing through the hole burned into his mesh undersuit, tailings of the laser that had finally put his suit out of commission.

I'll live, he decided, but then coughed up blood. Not a good sign.

The enemy *Clint* stomped away from Li's position, past several collapsed buildings, blind to the single warrior left behind or simply deciding Li was no longer worth its time. *It will keep to Naqiuo's streets until hitting the northeast edge of town, coming out behind House Hiritsu.* It's what Li himself would've done in a similar situation. With luck it could rejoin its regiment, or else sell itself dearly. *As dearly as my warriors sold themselves here,* he thought, surveying the destruction.

The Maultier transport was more scrap than serviceable; nose half-buried into the street, engine burning and rolling black smoke skyward, where it joined that of three other tanks and a nearby office building set ablaze during the battle. The Blizzard hovered in the mouth of an alleyway where his battlesuit squad had ripped it open to get at the tank crew. Li tried not to look at the mangled bodies thrown to the street. Instead he set about searching for survivors.

Li had known that Aris would not come, even as he made the request. From the top of a nearby building, the one currently in flames, his battlesuit's amplified vision had shown the *Ti Ts'ang* pull up short of entering Naqiuo. He'd also noticed the *Wraith,* its blued-steel finish nearly black against the horizon, standing mute as Aris weighed his choices. At that moment Li Wynn knew that Aris Sung would abandon the infantry unit to its own fortune.

The way I abandoned him.

There, in the middle of battle, he understood something of what Aris had been trying to teach him. *Aris Sung was never responsible to me, but* for *me. My* Sifu. Li Wynn had declined to listen, to learn. He had refused to trust his Mentor, and took exception against what he—in his short time with House Hiritsu—thought inappropriate. Those were Li Wynn's failings. Even during today's battle, Li had been waiting, watching, for the chance to enter Naqiuo. Not because the St. Ives' people deserved to have war brought into their streets or because his platoon specialized in city fighting, although those were both in his mind. He'd done so simply because Aris Sung hoped to spare the town. He hadn't really cared about anything else. Not the citizens of Naqiuo. Not himself.

Not his squad.

Li rolled over bodies, checking for vitals and finding none. *Dead, everyone dead.* His warriors, a few belonging to Raymond's Armored Infantry, civilians who had been caught in the streets-become-battlefield. *I brought this to them. To all of them.* And in the grief for his own warriors—his family, members of the same House—he also knew a twinge of guilt over the other Capellan lives he'd destroyed. This wasn't the glory he'd sought. This was carnage.

Fire shot through his chest and Li coughed again. Body wracked with pain, thoughts muddled, he barely tasted the blood's salty residue. A groan echoed in his ears, and it took several long heartbeats for Li Wynn to realize that the groan had not come from him.

Near the wreckage of the Maultier a body twitched and groaned again. Li stumbled to the warrior's side. Mikhail Chess, a compound fracture poking through his uniform sleeve, but alive. Chess' eyes fluttered open at Li's touch. "The *Clint*?" he asked. His first question not for himself or Li, but about a possible danger to his House.

Li shook his head. Coughed. "Got away," he said.

Unable to meet Mikhail's gaze, Li cast about for anything else to occupy his attention. He noticed the Maultier, its nose buried into the street, having pushed up a pile of earth and broken asphalt. He noticed the Blizzard, still alive and ready for a hand at its controls.

"Listen to me," Li said, coughing up blood to one side and then bending over Mikhail. "You're going to be all right. The House will be back soon. When you see Aris Sung, give him a message for me. Tell him—"

Tell him what? I'm sorry *wasn't about to explain anything.* "Tell him I do not understand. *Exactly* that." Li stood, swayed on his feet but kept himself upright by strength of will. *I do not understand. The declaration for the beginning of wisdom,* as he recalled from the teachings of Lao-tzu. Li certainly did not know if he understood his Mentor or not, and suspected he had no time left to do so, but it might give Aris peace of mind to know that his charge had at least acknowledged such.

"Where?" Infantryman Chess asked, then grimaced as a wave of pain washed over him. "Where are you going, Li?"

Li did not glance back, his gaze locked on the Blizzard. "One last *glorious* charge," he said, the sarcasm alone draining strength from him. "One last service to our House," he whispered.

Aris' first notice of the *Clint*'s return was a symbol flashing and then disappearing on his HUD, followed barely a second later by *Zhang-si* Smith's transmission. "We've lost *Pai* McDaniels."

Aris had dropped *Pai-zhang* Jill McDaniels and *Zhang-si*

Smith from his order of battle, their 'Mechs severely damaged and better placed guarding the northeast edge of Naqiuo should the *Clint* or a tank try to surprise House Hiritsu. The *Clint* had shown but against their flank, having slowly worked its way to the northern edge of the city before springing out at a full run and slicing deep into McDaniels' *Blackjack* from long range. Through bad fortune more than design the *Clint*'s PPC caught her SRM ammunition bay, touching off the remaining missiles in an explosion that gutted the *Blackjack*.

The *Thunder*, relying mainly on short-ranged weaponry, let fly its small flight of long-ranged missiles, which detonated against the *Clint*'s right arm with little effect. And then the faster *Clint* sped out of range and hurled itself against the Hiritsu backfield, obviously intent on breaking through to its regiment.

Aris' decision had to come quickly. Drop two 'Mechs back to deal with the *Clint*, thinning his forward line, or wait for it to approach and risk letting it probe at the weaker rear armor of his warriors. Neither appealed to him. A second transmission by Smith nearly deprived him of choice.

"Blizzard," Smith said, calling attention to the hovertank flying out from city borders further south at an impressive one hundred-fifty kilometers per hour. At that speed it would easily rendezvous with the *Clint*, the two of them then able to work together. Aris nearly ordered Raven Clearwater to drop back with one of her lancemates, but was interrupted by Smith's, *"Na Shen-me?"* What is that? "It's firing on the *Clint*."

Li Wynn. Aris pulled his *Wraith* from the battle line, rounding on the exchange forming behind him and zooming in on an auxiliary monitor. The Blizzard had opened up at long range with its LRMs, and continued to close on the *Clint* with each passing second. The front of the hovertank looked ripped open. And likely it was, by Fa Shih claws.

The *Clint*, realizing it could not flee, suddenly spun to bring its particle projection cannon to bear. Azure lightning arced out, scoring ground just off the Blizzard's left side. The next attempt drew a jagged scar across the front of the hovercraft, energy flooding through the hole already ripped into the armor. The hovercraft began to veer away, but at the last moment cut straight back in catching the *Clint* in the right leg and wrenching the limb out at the hip joint. Both machines tumbled, the 'Mech slamming to the earth and the hovertank flipping end over end, tearing itself apart against the ground. Its engine blossomed into a fireball long before it stopped rolling.

"*Lien-zhang* Sung?" Ty Wu Non's voice filtered through the radio waves strong and curious. "Can you explain that occurrence?"

Unsure where to even begin, Aris turned his *Wraith* back to the battle and opened the comm. "No, *Shiao-zhang*."

He rejoined his company, and pushed them forward again against the Armored Infantry.

"Call it a warrior's *hopeless battle*," he said. "And certainly a glorious death."

After all, that was what Li Wynn had really sought.

31

Backed against the rough plaster wall to the right of the open door and held in place by the business end of a Nakjama pulse laser rifle leveled at his head, Subcommander Fitzgerald couldn't see into the office and made no effort to do so. Instead he slouched back and stared at the floor, attempting to project the most non-threatening attitude possible. His hope was to win some charity from the Nightriders' infantryman, who seemed just a bit overzealous in keeping Fitz under guard. He finally closed his eyes, trying not to think about the security manacles cutting into his wrists or the fun barrel hovering centimeters in front of his face.

Not an easy task.

What else should he expect? Nothing about Nevarr's assignment had been easy. He'd had to follow his daily routine without a word spoken to anyone about the plans for Nashuar, waiting for intelligence to report a position on the Nightriders' CO. Locating what Fitzgerald *hoped* would be her command post, and then a midnight departure in his lightly armored J. Edgar hovertank. No goodbyes. No final words with Danielle Singh or any of his own lancemates. Through the gates and then on his own. Trying to sneak through enemy pickets and hoping the large white cloth he'd tied to his radio whip—after leaving Hazlet, of course— would buy him a chance to talk before drawing fire.

And then, the command post had been moved! Fitzgerald wasn't about to leave *that* off his list should he ever get the chance to speak with Nevarr again.

The *sao-wei* who had led Fitzgerald in from the transport came out of the office. "The prisoner will follow me," he said with a sidelong nod toward the open office door. The Nakjama barrel followed Fitz' every movement as he slowly levered himself away from the wall and followed.

No one sat at the office desk. One man sat off to the side near the wall, his collar insignia that of a *zhong-shao*—what had been a major before the Confederation's Xin Sheng movement. Fitz placed him as the Nightriders' executive officer. Amanda Gahn-Skeeng stood at the window, ignoring Fitzgerald's entrance. The window looked out over the devastation that had once been a large portion of Yasu's merchant district; fires had claimed several square blocks. Fitzgerald winced. He'd been in the battle where those fires had started.

"So you are the Home Guard warrior taken prisoner at Chèng-hai?" the Nightriders' regimental commander asked. Her voice, husky and low-pitched, sounded different. "The one who claims to have *important information* right after making a run against my previous command post?"

Fitz shrugged, certain the gesture was missed by Gahn-Skeeng, but playing to the XO, who continued to watch him closely. "If that is what you call it when a lone tank flying a white banner drives straight up to the gates and pops its hatch," he said with a seriousness so heavy as to almost be sarcastic. "On Nashuar we usually call that a surrender."

Gahn-Skeeng turned from the window, her green eyes wide with curiosity. "I had not heard that," she admitted, and Fitzgerald reevaluated her attitude. "You were sent to parlay?" she asked.

"By Brevet-Colonel Nevarr," Fitz said, "military coordinator for Nashuar. Of course, he hoped I would gain more immediate access." A not-so-subtle reference to the ten days Fitz had been held a prisoner, trying to convince a paranoid company commander that he really had been sent to request an audience with *Sang-shao* Gahn-Skeeng.

"The last time a lone tank approached a battalion of the Nightriders," the executive officer said, "it cost us the lives of thirty-six good men and women to horrible deaths. So you *will* forgive us for being hesitant." His tone robbed the request of any politeness. "Enemy tank drivers are not well thought of among the Nightriders, or any regiment of Mc-carron's Armored Cavalry."

"I'm not a tank driver," Fitzgerald stated. "Not anymore. My latest ride is a *Men Shen.*" He noticed the sudden interest that peaked in the *sang-shao* and nodded. "The only one we've captured so far." He paused. "And I think you would agree when I say I understand what happened to you on Wei."

This shot hit home. Fitzgerald read it in the spine-stiffening postures of both Amanda Gahn-Skeen and her exec. *So they were upset by the nerve agent attacks against Nashuar.* He remembered thinking so months before, when the Nightriders stepped down the pace and ferocity of their attacks. He thought about pressing home this latest advantage but resisted. *If Nevarr is right about Gahn-Skeeng, she'll make the next gesture.*

She did, dismissing the guard and the *sao-wei* escort. Once the room was clear of all but the two Nightriders' officers and Fitzgerald, she said, "If you are hoping to trade on our previous run-in, I'd say we're even." But she hesitated, and obviously did not mind letting Fitz see her concern. "All right, Subcommander, what is it you propose?"

"Peace," he said simply, throwing the idea out on the table. "Peace on Nashuar."

The exec barked a short laugh at the declaration. Amanda Gahn-Skeeng quickly settled a hard mask over her face to hide her own thoughts. "Continue, Subcommander Fitzgerald," she said.

Fitz took this first use of his name as a positive sign. A promotion in credibility, of sorts. "With the battle for St. Ives joined, Nashuar is no longer important. You know that, and so does Colonel Nevarr. He proposes an immediate cease-fire. We will hold the planet in stewardship for whomever wins St. Ives."

Gahn-Skeeng tugged thoughtfully at a lock of her long, dark hair. "That is a risky wager to make, Subcommander. The Confederation cannot possibly lose the fight for St. Ives."

"Then Nashuar would be surrounded and overwhelmed," Fitzgerald said, ready for that argument. "We could not hope to hold out. In the end, it only raises the cost of lives on both sides. And any death is a horrible death, *Sang-shao* Gahn-Skeeng."

Still giving no sign of what she might be thinking, the Nightriders' CO tilted her head toward her executive officer. "We are to end resistance on Nashuar," he said carefully. "*Sang-jiang-jun* Zahn's orders were very clear."

Fitzgerald smiled grimly. "We would no longer be resisting," he offered. "Duchess Candace Liao orders us to deny the Confederation use of Nashuar, which would also be accomplished. No staging troops for the continued invasion of other worlds. We will shut down both recharge stations. Nashuar becomes a neutral world."

"And you think I would agree to this?" the *sang-shao* asked. "Why?" Her gaze never wavered. "Because I returned your courtesy on the battlefield one time?"

Feeling more than a little foolish, Fitzgerald nodded. "Pretty much," he said awkwardly. "But I have to say that my visit here has given me fresh optimism for the idea. Tell me, *Sang-shao* Amanda Gahn-Skeeng"—he nodded to the window, to the ruined city view—"did you take this as your office because you revel in the destruction brought to Yasu, or as a reminder to avoid it?"

Straightening, Gahn-Skeeng walked over to the window and looked out again on the destruction. She stood silently for several minutes, hardly moving. Fitzgerald wisely chose to remain silent, fearing that he could pressure her into a rejection as easily as acceptance. *This has to happen because she wants it to. Nevarr said as much.* The silence dragged on.

A knock on the door, followed immediately by the entrance of two junior officers. One stood by Fitzgerald while the other handed a missive to their commander. She read it quickly, green eyes narrowed in concentration.

"It seems," she said at last, her husky voice carefully controlled, "that while my second battalion, with Canopian support, engaged your Colonel Nevarr today, two Battle-Mech companies skirted our lines and are now moving against our position here. I can match then exactly, which promises a hard fight." She searched Fitzgerald's eyes. "What do you say to that, Subcommander?"

"I would say that *we*"—he stressed that last word with great care—"have a problem."

Danielle Singh, commanding from the cockpit of her *JagerMech III,* drew her forces up into two lines as they approached Yasu, one BattleMech company to each line, with two lances of armor support. *This has to be fast and furious,* she thought. Reports placed the Nightrider battalion falling back against her position, so her forces would have to fight their way back through heavy opposition to make Hazlet. *But if we can take the Nightriders command company down first—* She broke off the thought, not wanting to bet on "ifs" just now. Better to see what the final results were, and then worry about the next wager.

She stifled a laugh. *I'm beginning to sound like Fitz.*

"Nightriders," someone warned over the general combat frequency of the Home Guard. "Forming up in the fire zone."

Danielle's Home Guard company, supported by a second company borrowed from the mercenary Group W outfit, had approached Yasu from the northwest. That was where a battle between the Arcadians and House Hiritsu last year had set off a fire that gutted the northwest residential district as well as other portions of the town. *If we have to chase them into Yasu, I'd rather do it here where the battlefield is already clear of civilians.*

She fed sensor data to an auxiliary screen, counting the opposing forces. Two companies of 'Mechs, slightly heavier average weight than her own and lightly supported by infantry. No armor in sight. No sign of the new Confederation battlesuit infantry that reports from St. Ives warned of.

One armored vehicle in sight, she amended, noting the light hovertank that skirted along in the shadow of a *Yu Huang* assault 'Mech. Computer identified it as a J. Edgar. *Fitz' tank!* Her inquiries had found out that Fitzgerald had checked out his old J. Edgar for an independent recon, but he had never returned. *So the Nightriders got him.* She tightened her grip on her *JagerMech's* control sticks. *That much more I owe them.*

"Hovertank heading our way." That from Subcommander Cameron Long, now promoted to lead Fitzgerald's lance.

"This is Prowler One," a new voice called out over general frequencies, received by Home Guard and Nightriders both. "Danielle, respond please."

"Fitz?" She paused, watched the J. Edgar as its driver did some wild zig-zag as if in response to her question. "What are you doing out here?" She could think of nothing more intelligent to ask, dumbfounded that Fitzgerald had simply driven onto the battlefield from the Nightriders' position.

"Working for Colonel Nevarr. Danielle, you have to stand down. We have a cease-fire arrangement with the Nightriders."

A cease-fire? Not possible. "Nevarr planned this mission. He sent me here to take down the Nightriders command unit, if possible."

Fitz' reply was nothing short of exasperation. "Well, I was here first," he said in a child's petulant manner.

Danielle flushed. "Clear the field, Fitz. I don't know what you *think* you're doing, but this doesn't wash. I have my orders."

"You advance against Yasu, and I'll be forced to fire on you, Danielle." As if to back up his threat, Danielle's sensors picked up a targeting system lock-on from the hovertank. "Don't ruin this. Nevarr knows what he's doing."

"Nevarr can't be doing this," she said, unsure. "The Duchess will never stand for it."

"Ever know me to back the losing side, Danielle?"

Danielle Singh bit at her lower lip, trying to reason it out. The whole thing sounded like too big a gamble, but she knew that if Nevarr would risk something like this, of course he'd send Fitz. And *if* it were true, she might be about to make a big mistake. Anyone else out there, she would be thinking they had turned sides or been brainwashed. But dammit, she *knew* Fitzgerald. Finally, she keyed her transmitter.

"You'd better be right," she said. And then to her unit, "Stand down. Remain on high alert. Subcommander Fitzgerald," she requested formally, "would it be too much to ask to speak with the Nightriders' commander myself?"

"Easily arranged," he promised, "now that it's peacetime on Nashuar."

32

K'ris Plateau
Henan District, Ambergrist
Xin Sheng Commonality, Capellan Confederation
24 August 3062

"**E**nough of this!"

The exasperation and determination that *Sao-shao* Evans packed into that simple declaration attracted the attention of Ni Tehn Doh. It sparked memories of the Hustaing Warriors' first operation, in which those very words had preceded a piece of unorthodox but effective action on Evans' part.

And certainly something *is needed here.*

The Hustaing Warriors fought for their escape from Ambergrist, trying to reach their DropShips, which had found safe landing zones up inside the Hartford Mountain Ranges. Doh had already sent two battalions blasting spaceward. He and his command lance remained with Third Battalion, substituting for its usual battalion command, not about to flee themselves until seeing every last Warrior safely away. All it took was gaining the next pass. And that was not so easy as it might sound.

The Illician Lancers' first battalion held Hartford's K'ris Plateau by force and control of numbers. Doh had advanced armor; they countered with a 'Mech lance. The Hustaing Warriors tried to push forward a company, and the Illicians responded with two *and* aerospace fighter support. No places for concealment or flanking maneuvers, just a wide open no man's land that Doh's forces had to cross. Tactically, a hopeless situation. A lost cause. *How very Capellan,* Doh thought, until Evans spoke up.

The *sao-shao* began calling off lances, from his company and others. About half the force the Hustaing Warriors had left. "All of you form the first rank thirty meters out onto the plateau when I say. Everyone else, that includes all armor, second rank, just over the rise. Pack it in tight."

"We'll get clobbered," someone complained.

And another, "What about the fighters?"

Troops on the edge of panic. Doh had heard it before during his long career in the Confederation Armed Forces. Warriors ready to break and run, and be taken down piecemeal, instead of holding to the disciplined retreat that *might* save lives. He'd seen that before too. Unfortunately, most of what he'd heard and seen involved the tried and true conventional tactics that just weren't going to work here. So he felt more than comfortable allowing Evans to play out his idea.

"We *will* get clobbered," the young *sao-shao* admitted, "but that's no worse than staying here and waiting for reinforcements to hit us from behind. And let me worry about the fighters." He polled the lance commanders, and all reported back ready. "Colonel Doh, if you would join second rank, sir."

The regimental commander passed the order along to his command lance, then switched over to his private channel with Evans. "Lining us up like this will beg a strafing run from the aerospace fighters," he counseled.

"Na dui ma," Evans replied. *That is so.* "I'll just have to warm things up for them." He switched back to an all-hands frequency. "Advance at forty kilometers per hour," he ordered, naming the walking speed of the Warriors' slowest 'Mech. "Fire only on my command. Ready, advance!"

Three abbreviated companies of BattleMechs and the armored vehicles left to them ran out onto the plateau and shook themselves into two battle lines, as per arrangements. Already they were drawing sporadic fire from the Lancers, but no Warrior returned it. Then, to the likely surprise of everyone—and certainly to *Sang-shao* Ni Tehn Doh—Evans began a sing-song chant to a vaguely familiar tune.

> *Target their commanders, drop them to the ground.*
>   *First rank, fire! Second rank, fire!*
> *Hunchback on the right, let's all bring it down.*
>   *First rank, fire! Second rank, fire!*

The weapons fire was staggered at first, no one really knowing what to expect. The Arcade Rangers company picked up on the rhythm soonest, followed quickly by the rest of the battalion. Evans continued to chant as the battalion rolled forward on the Illician Lancers' position, calling off the broadsides by rank and inserting any special commands or targets into his words. The *Hunchback* he'd called attention to lasted through the second verse, but combined fire from ten 'Mechs on that side of the confined plateau ravaged its armor and sent it to the ground missing both legs and an arm.

Doh finally recognized the tune during the third verse, from the dim memory of a sporting event he'd watched back on Hustaing. It was the team spirit chant of the college from which most of the Arcade Rangers had been recruited, only instead of, "Go, team, go," Evans had substituted his call to fire.

The commander noticed also that Evans transmitted on an open frequency, meaning the Illician Lancers heard the chant as well. They began to respond to it, as targets being called out in the chant retreated or ducked behind cover rather than face the barrage-fire. So even without weapon exchanges, Evans was able to back Lancers away from their path. Doh almost laughed, and might have but for one problem.

He noticed the Illician aerospace fighters setting up for a strafing run.

Evans, though, was up to the task. Without missing a beat, he changed his chant somewhat to accommodate the timing of his counterattack.

> *Coming are the fightercraft, setting up their row.*
> *Arcade Rangers, grab sky, go!*

Set in the rhythm of the chant, no one missed what should have been the usual command to fire. A double-barrage went off, minus only the weapons of the Arcade Rangers company. Those 'Mechs took to the air. Evans having swapped out for all jump-capable BattleMechs months before. He had to have set up the plan beforehand, as each 'Mech angled its jump to come back down in perfect formation. At the height of their arc they targeted the strafing fightercraft with missiles, lasers, PPCs—everything at their disposal.

NOE runs, pilot jargon for *nape of the earth,* had little room for error. As a full lance of *Stuka* fighters swept in on the Hustaing Warriors, they were met by twelve airborne BattleMechs flooding their target zone with weapons fire. The first pair veered off, one miscalculating its escape path and slamming into a nearby butte. The second two attempted to run the gauntlet, one exploding under the combined fire of three different 'Mechs while the other made it to safety, but without having fired a shot of its own.

The cheers coming over the battle circuits did not keep Evans from continuing to call the barrages. Several Arcade Rangers also took up the fire order, turning it into a true chorus.

That was enough for the Illician Lancers. Their air cover shattered, the unnerving barrage-fire guaranteeing at least a one-for-one trade off with the Hustaing Warriors, they wrote the battle off as a lost cause when two minutes ago they had been so assured of a victory. *Sang-shao* Doh held his own fire and watched as the Lancers pulled back in orderly fashion, allowing no further losses. *But the pass is clear.* The Hustaing Warriors had evaded the trap set for them, and hadn't lost a warrior. Doh could certainly live with that, no matter the methods.

Once again, we get the job done.

Royal Palace
Tian-tan, St. Ives
St. Ives Compact

Though she didn't much feel like it, Candace Liao offered her son a brief smile as Kai joined her in her private sitting room. He accepted a seat in one of the large, high-backed chairs cushioned with ivory pillows. Despite his crisp military bearing, Candace still detected traces of weary frustration in the hard set of his gray eyes and in the frown he could not hide from her. "You should sleep," she said, doubting he'd rested in the last twenty-four hours. Kai lived in the field these days, his St. Ives Lancers the driving force behind the capital's defense.

"I'll be fine, Mother," he said, returning a wan smile. But he did settle back into the chair. "Your message said at once. I heard about Sasha Wanli. Have you located the breach in palace security?"

"Let's say I'm not worried for my safety because of it," she said. Finding Sasha Wanli dead, poisoned, had thrown the Royal Palace into an uproar for several days. No hard evidence as to the agent, but Candace had no doubt that it was on Sun-Tzu's order. *No worse than Wanli likely deserved.* Unfortunately, she could not return her nephew's favor of rumor management. Sun-Tzu's people had no reason to wish him dead. But certainly there were scores of suspects within the Royal Palace who might try to take their personal vengeance against the Maskirovka Director. "Better to let the matter fade quietly."

Kai sat forward. "Then you have another reason to wish me back?" he asked, shaking himself more awake.

Candace hesitated, not wanting to add to his concerns after seeing his state, but knowing it better from her than another source. "The trial ended three days ago," she said.

"I've put off a public address until you returned to Tian-tan. You will appear beside me."

He gripped the arms of his chair. "And Kali goes unpunished." Not a question.

"How do you punish someone who cannot even acknowledge the gross hideousness of her act?" Candace asked. "Sun-Tzu knew what he was about, sending her to trial. If a tribunal under the Star League's authority cannot bring justice to her directly, it is easier for people to excuse his lack of control over her."

Kai sighed, ran fingers back through his short-cropped dark hair. "I suppose so, but it makes it no easier to explain to Compact citizens." His shoulders sagged ever so slightly and he braced himself up again, but not before Candace noticed.

"Is it so bad out there?" she asked, referring to the battlefields where Kai had been living since his return to St. Ives.

Kai tugged at the sleeve of his field utility uniform, the ivory-trimmed, light gray jumpsuit that made his skin look darker by comparison. "No," he said. "Not so much. The Nova Cats see a good share of hostility, even from our own people, but that is to be expected. The fighting is still nowhere near as vicious as the reports we've seen off Ambergrist, or Nashuar before its defection."

Candace steeled herself, not wishing to add more to her son's plate. "Not a defection. Colonel Nevarr knows what he is doing."

Looking at his mother askance, Kai asked, "You approve?"

"I might have," she said slowly, knowing he would not let it rest but also that he would find it hard to accept what must be. "If·such an endorsement from Tian-tan would not have hurt the spirit of the entire Compact." She changed the subject back. "So the fighting is less savage. That is something anyway."

Kai looked grave. "It does not keep us from steadily giving ground."

Candace thought of the praise Caroline Seng continued to heap on Kai and his First St. Ives Lancers. Confederation forces did not try to force him back. They stalemated him, holding strong defensive positions or giving ground before him as they drove forward elsewhere. But even Kai could not be everywhere at once, though sometimes seeing his name on three different battle reports from three different areas in a given day told Candace how hard he tried.

"It may seem like shouting at the storm," she said kindly, "but we do what we must. And we cannot expect more aid."

"Victor would come," Kai said emphatically, defending his friend.

"He might," Candace agreed only to a point, "if you were to call for him." She paused, matching gazes with her son. Kai broke away first. "I didn't think so. Victor has his own concerns at the moment." Her tone darkened. "The crisis on Solaris has brought the trouble in the Federated Commonwealth to a head. Except for George Hasek, we cannot trust our intelligence on many districts now."

At the mention of intelligence, Kai frowned concern. "Quintus?" he asked after his brother.

"Silent," Candace said. "Nothing in weeks, but this would not be the first time he has been forced to lay low. Do not worry for him." *That is one of my duties.*

"So we are on our own." Kai nodded, accepting the role thrust upon the Compact, and him. He rose and came over to his mother, bending to kiss her on the forehead. "I will stay the night here, and fly back to my regiment in the morning."

In Kai's slow exit from the room, Candace read the heavy pall hanging over him. Like no battle against the Clans had done, this war was testing Kai to his limits. And without him, Candace knew, St. Ives might already be lost. *I wish I could give you hope, my son. But if there is to be hope for St. Ives, you must give it to me.*

And if not, there is still Cassandra.

=== 33 ===

Bào-feng Spaceport
Wuhan, Ambergrist
St. Ives Compact
6 September 3062

Standing at the center of his command post, careful not to step on the Free Capella insignia, Treyhang Liao continued to entertain Ambergrist's planetary diem with tales of military victories while watching Warner Doles' approach out the corner of his eye. Having expected the visit ever since the Blackwind Lancers' return to Wuhan, he spared a second's regret for the timing. Lady Ehn Wa'Tíng was no one to be brushed aside for a soldier, even a regimental commander. Rough about the edges, as provincial as Ambergrist itself, she still held power.

And Treyhang enjoyed cultivating such associations.

Everything in its time, everything in its place, he reminded himself. Doles had certainly earned an interview. *Curious, though, that he's wearing full dress uniform.* Trey did not miss the *dadao* hanging at the colonel's belt, the bribe Tormano had used to initially purchase Doles' support. The sword that Doles had used on Trisha Smithson.

"Ah, Lady. The hours I could spend recounting our recent drive to push the Confederation from your world," he said in his best courtier's manner. "But then I would be remiss in fulfilling the duties my aunt has set before me." A subtle way of reminding the diem that his family name carried more actual weight than her title. "I must get back to the war, but I have arranged for a well-laid dinner this evening, if you would join me." That meant pushing the mandrinn back to evening cocktails, he noted mentally. Sweeping up Lady Wa'Tíng's hand, he kissed it and then bowed a cordial goodbye.

"I interrupted?" Doles asked as soon as Lady Ehn Wa'Tíng had left the room.

Treyhang shrugged and shook his head lightly. "A fortunate coincidence," he said. "Much longer, and I would have had to explain Free Capella's failure to rout the Third Confederation Reserve. And let's not even begin to discuss the arrival of the Taurian Velites."

"You would have found some way to make yourself look good." Doles' comment was without rancor. Good-natured, almost. "You do enjoy this, don't you, Trey?"

A month ago, Treyhang would have been certain of reading Doles' thoughts. The lager man's command of himself had improved, making for a much more interesting game. Treyhang allowed his polite smile to widen into a real one. "To each his own, *Colonel* Doles." He leaned in, examining Doles' shoulder devices with exaggerated care. "Yes, I suppose they do suit you."

Doles flushed slightly, ruining his poker face. "They may, someday," he said. "Until then I'll do what needs doing, and try to settle some debts along the way."

Treyhang held the frown from his face. He had thought better of Warner Doles than petty vengeance. Nodding down at the sword Doles wore, he asked, "So, should I be concerned?" He hoped to remind the Lancers officer of the last "debt" he'd settled with the blade.

Doles grimaced and shook his head. "Not that way, no. My debts are to the Duchess, for failing her before. And to you, Trey, for reminding me who I was and who the enemy is." He drew the sword slowly from scabbard and offered it to Treyhang. "This isn't mine," he said. "Put it back on the shelf, or give it to someone who's earned it."

Accepting the sword, Treyhang left it cradled in his arm as he regarded the colonel with frank interest. "So is this your resignation from the services of Free Capella? Off to chase the Hustaing Warriors back to Indicass, are you?"

Shaking his head, Doles grinned humorlessly. "They aren't my enemy. And I have plenty of work to do right here on Ambergrist. You mentioned something about the Third Confederation Reserves, I think?"

"I believe I did," Treyhang said. "And the Taurian Velites."

"So does that mean you're sticking around for the duration?" Doles folded arms over his chest, returning Treyhang's earlier look of appraisal. "Dinners with Lady Ehn Wa'Tíng. Cigars with some Barduc Mandrinn and minor lords. Give you six months, you'll be the biggest media sensation Ambergrist has ever seen."

Treyhang feigned offense. "Six months? You give me no credit at all, Warner." He paused, shrugged. "I don't know about 'the duration,' but I'm certainly staying awhile longer. The solar yacht races over Marlette were cancelled anyway, thanks to the Commonwealth's troubles. Besides, Aunt Candace has officially asked me to remain at the head of Free Capella. She even offered me a formal title." He caught Doles' questioning glance. "Oh, I'm a lord already, I suppose. Tormano's legacy. But not landed, and certainly not of the sword nobility. Aunt Candace thought I might appreciate the formality."

"Just a minor consideration," Doles agreed with mock gravity. "So is it Lord Treyhang Liao or Mandarin?"

"Neither. I turned it down." Treyhang laughed at Doles' shock. "For now," he amended. "For now. Too many limitations seem to come along with titles. That's not my way. The responsibility of Free Capella is daunting enough." Then, as if reminded of its presence, he looked at the sword cradled in his left arm. "A beautiful piece of work, wouldn't you say?"

"It is," Doles said, nodding agreement.

Treyhang echoed the nod, a thin smile playing on his lips as he held the ring-pommel *dadao* up to admire with both hands. "Lady Aleisha Liao's sword would certainly be a worthy gift to someone with an appreciation for his heritage, and his duty." Then, without a hint of his intention, he suddenly brought the flat of the sword down across his knee. The blade snapped cleanly.

If Treyhang had wanted a better way to shake Warner Doles, he doubted he could have planned it with a month's preparation. *As is, only the last few days have been necessary.* "A replica," he said. "A fake." He nodded to an aide who brought over another sword—a ring-pommel *dadao,* this one partially wrapped in an ivory silk blanket to prevent hands from touching the polished blade. A few more nicks to the blade, this one. More worn. It made the sword somehow more real. "Here is the real one." The aide offered it to Doles, who stared at it blankly.

"Tormano's gifts were always ones to be looked at closely," Treyhang said, "for their real value and the strings attached. He wanted to buy the Blackwind Lancers, to buy *you,* and he paid in cheap coin, not caring about the old maxim of getting what you pay for." Treyhang nodded for Doles to take the sword. "You've earned it. Your Blackwind Lancers are a fine addition to Free Capella."

Doles carefully took the pommel of the sword in his left hand, then held it to his side while he accepted Trey's handshake. He paused, holding the grip while staring suspiciously at Treyhang. "How do I know this is the real one?" he asked. Not out of spite, but as someone who suddenly wasn't sure of the rules.

Treyhang smiled, laughed, and broke his grip after another vigorous pump. "Warner, you of all people should know by now." He plucked at one cuff of his uniform, straightening it, then brushed imaginary lint from it with a quick brush of his hand. "I do nothing second rate."

34

Celestial Palace
Zi-jin Chéng, Sian
Sian Commonality, Capellan Confederation
15 September 3062

Seated on the Celestial Throne, Sun-Tzu felt a chill wash over him as the throne room doors opened to admit his sister and her "bodyguards," though he betrayed no sign of emotion. Kali Liao wore a green silk gown, the image of her Hindu goddess namesake embroidered over her abdomen in heavy silver thread, reminding him of a spider's markings.

She moved with formal slowness, oblivious to the deadly men surrounding her. The four Death Commando warriors escorting Kali into the presence of the Chancellor wore full ceremonial dress; black chased with bronze, full cape and *dao* sword slung from a wide strap belted across the chest. Only the Mydron assault rifles they carried belied their actual purpose as guards rather than honor detail.

Sun-Tzu steeled himself against the performance he intended to give. Against *both* performances, he amended, noticing Naomi Centrella following the escort into the throne room. Though Kali had been ordered to the palace directly from the spaceport, he had not expected Naomi to follow immediately. He awarded her full marks for the preemptive maneuver, knowing he would just as easily rob her of the initiative.

Rising from his throne, Sun-Tzu then stepped down from the low dais to meet his sister on equal footing. The spectral presence of Romano, still plaguing his thoughts with re-membrances and the occasional whisper, demanded noth-ing less out of respect for her daughter's *courageous* actions. Sun-Tzu lent those demands very little weight. De-spite her madness, Kali was of House Liao and deserved every courtesy for her formal sentencing. *And besides—it robs Naomi of any advantage she might try to claim in a for-mal transfer of authority for the prisoner.* His mother's ghost only smiled.

"You are welcome back to Sian, Kali," Sun-Tzu said, as the escort halted their charge far short of the Chancellor's person.

Kali took two more steps forward, either ignoring the au-thority of the Death Commandos or simply unaware of it. She nodded a greeting, barely a bow but at least a small show of respect for the Chancellorship.

"Hello, my brother. It is good to be home." Kali's voice was silky smooth, unperturbed by the last several months' trial—literally—on Atreus.

"No longer," Sun-Tzu declared flatly, aware of the anger Romano Liao would have known in enforcing such an edict. "You are to be confined to the world of Highspire, until such time as you offer the Star League information leading to the recapture of the nerve agent still missing from the Wei graveyard." He watched his sister carefully for any sign of emotion. Her dark green eyes betrayed neither remorse for her previous atrocities nor any sign of anger at her exile. They remained flat, impassive.

"Our mother's world," Kali said finally. "Yes, I will be happy there. Thank you." She turned to leave, obviously considering the interview at an end, but then paused to glance back with something akin to pride. "I was right," she said.

Momentarily confused by Kali's calm acceptance of her

sentence and Romano's raging within his own mind, Sun-Tzu could only ask, "About what?"

"The Confederation still stands," Kali said with a light smile, "and stronger than ever. You found another way, as the omens promised. As I foresaw you would." That said, she surrendered herself into the care of her escort and retreated from the throne room, head high and staring into a future that obviously only she could see.

Sun-Tzu clamped down hard on the mask he wore, refusing to let his sister's mania disturb him and certainly not in front of Naomi Centrella, who stepped forward into the place vacated by Kali.

"Naomi," he said in greeting, remounting the dais and easing back into the hand-carved artifact of the Celestial Throne.

"Chancellor Liao." Her own greeting was formal, by comparison cheapening Sun-Tzu's casual acknowledgment. *She's learned well,* Sun-Tzu thought.

"So am I welcomed back to Sian as well?" she asked, a touch of humor and friendliness sweetening her tone. Naomi was well-schooled in matters of the court by her mother, the Magestrix of Canopus, an expertise Sun-Tzu wished to cultivate.

He nodded, the hint of a smile playing at one side of his mouth. "The Centrellas are as welcome on Sian as my own family, always."

That dashed Naomi's tentative smile against the rocks lurking below his easy words. "I would expect the invitation on slightly different stationary than you are offering your Aunt Candace at the moment."

Sun-Tzu conceded the point with a single nod. "As you say," he promised, though the *inner Romano* cursed at Naomi's presumption. Sun-Tzu decided to change the subject, wanting to wrap up the business at hand. "Your time on Atreus was well spent, it seems. I cannot say I enjoy being held directly responsible for Kali's future actions, but it was a necessary trade-off to make sure the trial stagnated."

Naomi could not as easily hide her own frustration, fidgeting and letting some of her anger show, a fact Sun-Tzu noted for future work. His influence over the heir to the Magistracy of Canopus was one of his most ambitious threads being spun out against the future.

"You cannot imagine," she finally said, "how difficult it was to sit in judgment over her. Holovids of the atrocities her followers committed in the St. Ives Compact were very compelling. In closed chambers, the Compact ambassador screamed for blood while Thomas Marik worked to find a path for justice."

And which did you want to back? Sun-Tzu wished to know, though he sensed the intrusion of Romano's own paranoia. He backed away from that line of thought. *I will not be ruled by paranoia my entire life. Not as she was.* "And instead, they were both forced to accept Kali's"—he paused—"*condition* for what it is. You have helped save the Capellan state." He looked at her directly, allowing a touch of his true resolution to show. A test, really. "I will not forget that, Naomi Centrella."

"The fate of my mother's Magistracy is tied to the Confederation." Naomi's black-gloved hand smoothed an imaginary wrinkle from the sleeve of her turquoise uniform tunic. The gaze with which she contemplated the Capellan Chancellor was intense. "We do not forget our *ally,* regardless of personal feelings."

How well Sun-Tzu knew and appreciated the practice of putting the state ahead of self. *Something my mother could never disentangle,* he thought with a measure of sudden vindication. *For her, matters of state were always a personal affront or a victory, to be treated as such with either rage or smugness.* Sun-Tzu wanted to believe he suffered no such delusions, though he still sensed Romano smiling at him from deep within his memories.

Preoccupied with his thoughts, he almost missed the emphasis Naomi placed on *ally. Singular, and certainly not a mistake.* He covered his long pause with another period of thoughtful reflection, studying the Magistracy heiress while tapping the ends of his fingertips together. Finally, he said, "The Confederation knows—I know—the difference between loyalty and a diplomatic solution of convenience."

That was vague enough to be read many ways, depending on which area Naomi was attempting to sound out. *If she wishes to pursue this, the first step must be hers.*

She did. Her dark blue eyes veiled, voice laced with sincere concern, Naomi pressed on in the best manners of court, be it Canopian or Capellan. "I would despise thinking that the Magistracy of Canopus no longer enjoyed the favor of the Confederation, in light of recent arrangements made." She paused, eyes narrowing. "No matter the depth of resolve to those arrangements."

She doubts my commitment to Grover Shraplen and his Concordat. And, by extension, to her own realm. His jade gaze fell on Naomi, measuring her worth. *And well she should,* a voice whispered up from his mind, the tone mocking him. Sun-Tzu blinked his irritation at the memories crowding him. Standing, he stepped to the edge of the dais and held a hand out to Naomi Centrella, letting the *inner Romano* glimpse his own sense of commitment. He could predict his mother's anger, the personal insult to her person, that he would consider treating so easily with a Periphery nation—especially one that had joined arms against the Confederation at its weakest moment in history.

How can you betray that memory? He sensed the question his mother would have asked, backed by a cohort of Maskirovka agents ready to test and reinforce his loyalty, no doubt.

Because the Confederation—the Capellan state—is more important than any historical footnote, any ideal and, under the proper circumstances, any number of lives. And certainly it was more important than the memory of a deceased Chancellor.

Naomi stepped forward cautiously, as if wary of a trap. Her hand slid into Sun-Tzu's, warm and soft, and he guided her up onto the dais. Equal footing, but instead of humbling himself, as was the Chancellor's prerogative in showing respect, he had instead raised her above all others who might stand in the throne room and hope for the Chancellor's recognition. Symbolism had its place in life, nowhere more so than the courts of Sian in the Celestial Palace itself. And in the rush of color to her face, her blue eyes wide with awe and fervor, Sun-Tzu also saw one other simple fact.

She understood.

Where Isis had not truly come to know the Capellan heritage she wanted to make part of her life, Naomi required no other words. Nothing more than the symbolic gesture, which said enough. So they stood in silence, both looking out toward futures of their own making. Sun-Tzu saw a strong Capellan nation—the Confederation reborn and renewed. *Xin Sheng*. And if Naomi looked upon a stronger Magistracy, Sun-Tzu would not begrudge her that.

For that too would strengthen the Capellan state.

35

HildCo BattleMech Yards
Tian-tan, St. Ives
St. Ives Compact
19 September 3062

At the northeast edge of Tian-tan, Hiritsu BattleMechs and Daidachi armor burst from the cover of trees that blanketed the low-lying hills they had hidden behind. The cyclone fence perimeter surrounding St. Ives' main production site of HildCo Interplanetary fell before the rush like wheat before the scythe. Sparks showered the feet of Aris Sung's *Wraith,* first to hit the electrified fence, but in the trampling that followed power was quickly lost. Both 'Mech companies and the armor support then moved against the real fortifications, a ten-meter-high wall of steel-reinforced ferrocrete mounting hardpoints of missile racks and overlapping banks of PPCs and lasers.

"You have . . . attention, *Lien* Sung." The broken transmission whispered into Aris' ear, cut apart by distance and interference. The voice was that of *Shiao-zhang* Ty Wu Non, who led the remaining Hiritsu company in a large battle west of Tian-tan under the command of House Daidachi. "Three companies . . . Lancers . . . Stars of Nova Cats falling back . . . Tian-tan."

And so now the word was out, that what had looked to be an all-out drive to assault the capital was only a diversion for a raiding force aimed at one of St. Ives' largest Battle-Mech production factories. Aris' plan, backed by Ty Wu Non, was to remove one of Tian-tan's primary support facilities and thereby make the siege of St. Ives' capital much more desperate for the defenders. Aris had convinced him it could be done with a minimum loss of life on either side, and without any need for fighting in the streets of Tian-tan. And so long as the larger assault diverted enough defending forces, Aris predicted low casualties to his own warriors.

In that he'd apparently been right. So complete was the surprise, the faster 'Mechs had cleared half the distance before the first fire returned from any defensive emplacement.

Too late for them now, Aris thought, caressing his *Wraith*'s main trigger and spattering one missile site with scarlet pulses from his large laser. A nearby *Thunder* added its withering autocannon fire to the assault, and between them they stripped most of the armor from the front of the battery. A *Raven,* moving at a full run parallel to the wall, threw a pair of medium lasers and a flight of missiles into the mix as it passed. Two of the missiles punched through, detonating inside and touching off the ammunition stores for the battery. Aris actually felt the shockwave of the blast as the battery effectively ceased to exist, the explosion taking a large chunk of the fortifications with it.

"There's our crack in the wall," the *lien-zhang* called out over the general combat frequency. "*Ji-song* units, force a breach."

The *delivery* lance, a *Cataphract* and a *Blackjack* from newly promoted Jené Silvers' company backed by both *Ti Ts'angs* from Aris', rushed the main wall as the others busied themselves with dodging the increasing weapons fire raining down off the wall-mounted armaments. The blue-white lightning strike of a PPC sliced into the *Wraith*'s right arm, flaying off armor and spoiling Aris' shot at a bank of lasers. The two forward *ji-song* 'Mechs slammed against the wall to either side of where the missile battery had been set, driving through the reinforced material and forcing a hole wide enough across that units could pass through two abreast. The *Ti Ts'angs* followed immediately.

All ground-limited machines, including the armor company borrowed from House Daidachi, converged on the break.

"Over the top," Aris ordered the rest, engaging his own jump jets and rocketing his *Wraith* skyward in a long-angle hop that delivered him just inside the wall but far off to one side of those emerging through the breach. The firefight had already been joined. An assault lance belonging to HildCo held the inner yard, a mix of *Victors* and *Pillagers* standing in the shadow of one of the large factory buildings. *To be expected, since those are the two designs produced at this site.*

The *Blackjack,* first through the wall, toppled as the combined fire of six Gauss rifles pummeled it to the ground. Poor target selection, Aris decided as he watched the *Ti Ts'angs* clear the rubble and rush the assault lance at TSM-augmented speed. The triple-strength myomer did more than increase speed, though. Running hot, the *Ti Ts'angs* could cause devastating damage with their hand-held hatchets. And they did. Both brought down the titanium-edged blades against a single *Pillager,* by far the most deadly design. One sliced deep into the assault machine's right leg. The other, having worked in toward the back, crushed through the armor protecting the *Pillager*'s rearward torso and obviously cut into the gyro support structure. With a violent shudder wracking its frame, the assault machine tumbled forward to land sprawled against the hard-packed earth.

Hiritsu 'Mechs continued to pour into the yards. A lance of Regulator tanks cleared the breach in the wall and fired a synchronized salvo at the remaining *Pillager* still standing even as the *Ti Ts'angs* turned against one of the two *Victors*. Three of the four Regulators' Gauss slugs bit deep into the assault machine, shattering armor and sending it raining to the ground in now-impotent shards. The *Victors* struck back at the *Ti Ts'angs*, threatening them, but their inability to concentrate fire left them easy targets for the smaller but deadly in-fighter Confederation 'Mechs. Besides weathering a scathing attack of medium and small lasers, one *Victor* nearly lost its right arm to a hatchet, and the other took a crushing blow against the left leg. Their initiative lost to greater numbers and more modern designs, the *Victor*s cut in their own jets and jumped back on jets of plasma to take cover behind the very buildings they had been defending.

As most fire now turned on the upright *Pillager,* Aris raced his *Wraith* forward at best speed to worry the flank of the fallen *Pillager* now attempting to stand. Between his pulse laser fire and the shotgun-effect cluster rounds from the Daidachi *Cataphract,* the *Pillager* was thrown off-balance again and crashed back to the earth. The second assault machine made a successful retreat back around the corner of a factory building, but not before surrendering at least four more tons of armor to the Regulators.

As suddenly as the violence began, it was over.

In the calm that descended over the HildCo site, Aris took stock of the situation. The *Pillager* on the ground had given up, shutting down rather than face overwhelming fire from House Hiritsu. Men and women were abandoning the wall, its weapons not designed to fire down into the factory complex itself. Twin *Raven*s and a *Men Shen* probed deeper into the complex, scouting further opposition. The *Blackjack* that had fallen earlier rose to shaky feet—gyro damage at the least, and from the infrared monitors it also appeared to be bleeding heat from its fusion engine. He heard *Lien-zhang* Jené Silvers order it to remain at the back. Silvers, in her captured *Penetrator,* stalked after the scout 'Mechs in search of prey.

"Phase one complete," Aris transmitted on his private circuit to Ty Wu Non. The *Shiao-zhang* would pass it along to House Daidachi, if the Regulator tank crews had not already. "Proceeding to phase two."

"Acknowledged, Aris Sung." The Hiritsu Master's voice sounded stronger. "Be aware . . . Lancers and Nova Cats are five minutes out from your location. We are circling in . . . support of your escape route."

Five minutes. Aris almost smiled. *We'll be done and*

gone in three. He had no doubt that HildCo had further defensive units in the yards somewhere, and they would be trying to mass for a determined defense. *But they won't be expecting us to move inside.*

Aris switched back over to a general frequency. "You all know your assigned buildings. *Ji-song* units force entry, and everyone follow. Regulators know where to cripple the production sites without destroying the entire complex, so BattleMechs concentrate on the pieces, parts, and partially assembled machines. Remember, everyone hauls out a piece of prime salvage."

For the benefit of those not yet accepting his practice of limited engagement, Aris continued. "Do not linger outside. You'll have no support if the assaults link up with their friends and come hunting us. Three minutes, we rendezvous at the south end of the yards. And you give the workers inside a full twenty seconds after wall breach to clear the immediate area. Move."

As if anticipating his command, the *Cataphract* and both *Ti Ts'ang* designs selected a factory building and plunged through the reinforced walls to open the way for others to follow. Regulators plunged in next, one lance to each lead 'Mech, and then the remaining Hiritsu war machines filed behind. Three minutes, and Hildco Interplanetary would be effectively shut down. Aris allowed himself a brief second of pride over his accomplishment, quickly overtaken by the memory of what it had already cost. Li Wynn had not been the only House Warrior to seek escape in a glorious charge once the House Master began to affirm Aris' new—or rather, old—policies.

"Contact," a new voice called out over the commset. It was Jené Silvers, voice full of anticipation. "The assaults are currently safeguarding the employee evacuation. The *Men Shen* spotted another lance moving up from the south side to rendezvous." A pause. "They won't find much left to link up with."

"Negative," Aris ordered at once. "Do not engage." There was no need. *They've lost, a circumstance they'll be aware of soon enough.*

Jené Silvers was not so easily put off. "*Lien* Sung, those assaults are heavily damaged. A few salvos will be all they can take."

Aris was saved from the argument by *Shiao-zhang* Non's intervention. "Which would be several more salvos than . . . people can take. HildCo is out of business, there . . . no need for further loss of civilian life."

Muscles tense, Aris waited for Silvers' acknowledgment. Would she accept the order, or decide to follow her predecessor into the next life? Either her survival instinct or loyalty to the House Master won out. "Disengaging," she said. "We're moving against building seven."

Aris breathed a sigh of relief, then walked his *Wraith* into the gaping hole left in one of the nearby factory complexes. Ty Wu Non was right. HildCo was certainly out of business and its shutdown would herald the fall of St. Ives. *A victory won by warriors, honorably and with due concern—due respect—for those we fight against. A victory won without violating the precepts of Warrior House Hiritsu.*

To Aris, that was the only victory worth winning.

Home Guard Staging Grounds
Hazlet, Nashuar
Compact/Confederation Stewardship

The meeting, held in Colonel Nevarr's office, strained the small room's accommodations. Nevarr sat behind his desk, with Danielle Singh and Maurice Fitzgerald flanking him to either side, their chairs set almost into the corners against the back wall. Colonel Torri Hughes, the ranking officer left to the Seventh Federated Commonwealth RCT, sat opposite Nevarr, with Precentor Darryl Burns of the 403rd ComStar Division at her side. Also present were representatives of mercenary forces on-world in the form of Major George Relant of Group W, and the Arcadians' Commander, Anya Trovich. The mercenaries sat in chairs carried in from nearby offices.

Fitzgerald glanced from Nevarr's partial profile to each of the allied commanders in turn, waiting to see who would crack first. He was betting on the Seventh RCT's Colonel Hughes. He won his bet.

"You are aware that in recent weeks the Nightriders have used your 'truce' to dig in on their side of the line." Hughes kept her self-control through an obvious effort of will. "Our reports are sketchy, but we estimate they've sent a battalion of Cavalry and another regiment's worth of various units to aid the Confederation push against St. Ives."

Nevarr let the not-so-subtle accusation hang unanswered for a moment. "Colonel Gahn-Skeeng forwarded an accurate report three days ago," he said, voice calm and eyes icy. "As a courtesy. The total is actually a battalion short of two regiments."

Precentor Burns laid a restraining hand on Hughes' arm. "Doesn't that violate the terms of your statement of neutrality? Using this world as a staging base?"

Nevarr inclined his head slightly toward Fitz, letting him field the question. "I have been in contact with *Sang-shao* Gahn-Skeeng," he said, using her title correctly. "Those forces have actually been sent back to Brighton, where I'm certain they will then be routed to St. Ives. The terms of the cease-fire hold."

"And we are to believe that Duchess Liao has sent no official word on the situation here?" Colonel Hughes scoffed. "No support for your decision, Colonel Nevarr? No condemnation?" She shook her head. "I am not part of the St. Ives military. If I find out that you've withheld orders from our legal commander—"

Again, it was the ComStar officer who attempted to put Hughes at ease. "Your legal commander," he pointed out, "is on New Avalon. However, your point taken, I can assure you that no message from Katrina Steiner-Davion *or* Candace Liao has been passed through ComStar channels."

"So we are alone in this," the Group W major said with a light shrug. "It sounds to me like your coup of neutrality will hold. So, do we depart for St. Ives as well?" He smiled lopsidedly. "Passing through Armaxa first, of course."

Fitzgerald appreciated the calm, matter-of-fact tone the mercenary adopted. *Then again, to him this is just another job. Group W is merely on loan from their Lyran Alliance contract. If there is no fighting here, they move on to the next world.* Fitz found the lifestyle unappealing, but knew he'd better start considering the idea. *When the dust finally settles, no telling what my prospects in the St. Ives military will be.* Certainly the young soldier had no intention of giving up being a MechWarrior.

"Only the Seventh RCT is heading out," Nevarr said, as usual keeping to his clipped speech. "They will eventually route toward St. Ives. If it is not too late." He nodded toward the mercenary commanders. "The Arcadians remain here, to hold the Compact side of Nashuar's stewardship. Group W forces are all heading toward Tantara, where they will reform at full strength along the Teng Front."

Precentor Burns nodded. "And I've received my orders from Precentor Martial Davion." He stood. "Good luck with your war, Colonel. I'm afraid you will need it."

Nevarr nodded his understanding. "Good luck with your own," he said.

"Not me," Burns said. "I'm bound for Kurita space, via the Free Rasalhague Republic." He paused, meeting Nevarr's gaze. "And after seeing the St. Ives conflict up close, I think I'm fortunate in my assignment." The Precentor left after a nod of farewell to all the commanders present.

That seemed to be the signal for the meeting to break up. Orders had been passed. Colonel Hughes was out the door close on the heels of Burns. Fitzgerald stood, stretched.

"I am curious on one score," the Group W officer said as he too stood. "Aren't you worried at all about Colonel Hughes' question? About Candace Liao's eventual reaction?"

Fitzgerald glanced from Nevarr to Danielle. Nevarr met Relant's questioning look with a wintry silence. Danielle Singh returned Fitz' stare with an uneasy look. "For my part," Fitz said slowly, feeling as if it defaulted to him to respond, "I'm not. I followed the colonel's suggestion freely, because I felt it the best resolution to our problems on Nashuar. We are just as responsible to the people we protect as we are to the leader of the Compact. At some point," he said with a light shrug, "the former can outweigh the latter."

The mercenary either accepted the explanation or wrote off the question as a bad investment. Regardless, he tossed Colonel Nevarr an easy salute and left with the Arcadian commander. Fitzgerald did not dismiss the situation quite so easily. He certainly recognized the dangers that could still result from their decision, but the die had been cast and he believed it worth the gamble.

For all the worry about Duchess Liao's reaction, Maurice Fitzgerald slept better at night knowing that peace had come to Nashuar.

══════ 36 ══════

Home Guard Compound
Lhasa, Tantara
St. Ives Compact
24 September 3062

Cassandra Allard-Liao stood before the window of her second-story office, gazing out over the Home Guard's parade grounds, currently vacant. Tantara's overcast morning sky hanging heavily over the deserted grounds colored her mood quite appropriately. Gray. Bleak. Gusting winds silently blew scraps of paper across the desolation.

One scrap for every member of my family scattered before the tempest, the storms brewing in the Inner Sphere. Kuan Yin working at her relief efforts somewhere in the occupied zone, the so-called Xin Sheng Commonality. Kai and myself living on battlefields worlds apart. Quintus buried in the growing trouble within the Federated Commonwealth. Mother . . . She glanced down to the lengthy missive clutched in her right hand. The numbers couldn't be argued with, though she certainly wished to try. She set the verifaxed message on a nearby table. *Mother—preparing to abandon St. Ives.*

And, perhaps most disconcerting of all, the idea of losing

their capital world did not surprise or shock Cassandra as she thought it should.

I should have been there, she thought, even knowing there would have been nothing she could really accomplish. Kai had achieved little more than a stalemate against the numerically superior forces of the Confederation on St. Ives, and then only on one battlefield at a time. Cassandra wanted to believe she might have made the difference, but, if nothing else, the conflict of the last two years was beginning to teach her of her own limitations.

We should have taken to heart Kai's earlier example and brought the war to the Confederation. Again, she argued herself out of the idea, recognizing it for wishful thinking. Even with the help of Victor Steiner-Davion's SLDF and ComStar troops, the Compact lacked the resources to defend its own territory, much less mount an offensive. Nashuar and then Taga forced into taking positions of neutrality awaiting the outcome of the battles on St. Ives. Milos lost, again—and likely for good. *Not much use in fighting on Confederation soil when there would be nothing, no world, to return home to.*

In that, at least, Cassandra could take the measure of her own victories and value to the Compact. *I've held the line. We have a position to fall back on—all is not yet lost.* From Spica to St. Loris to Ambergrist, the Compact controlled the Teng Front. *And with three-fifths of the nation's military production still available and feeding into less than half the territory, we could technically hold out forever.*

How long, Mother? Cassandra shivered, not with chill but in the realization of Candace Liao's ultimate resolution. All that time, Cassandra denied the resources to launch an offensive, pulled between worlds to coordinate the Teng Front's defense. *How long have you known we might be forced to this?*

Cassandra turned from the desolate view, resolved to set her mind back on work. The Cossacks needed supplies, as did Treyhang Liao's Free Capella Movement. There was a raid to plan against Indicass; to deprive the Confederation of the Ceres Metals production facilities if the world itself could not be retaken. The work might not be glamorous or glorious, not the single-battle solution she had thought to find so early on in the war for the St. Ives Compact, but work that needed doing nonetheless. And it fell to her.

Cassandra still knew her duty.

Sem-po Mountains
Vedray District, Ambergrist
St. Ives Compact

Rage spent. Anger faded. The desire for vengeance replaced with duty. The duty of a *janshi-warrior*.

The temperature in the *Emperor*'s cockpit jumped several degrees higher as Colonel Warner Doles triggered another full salvo of weapons while carefully walking the assault 'Mech down the rough, rubble-strewn slide area within Ambergrist's Sem-po Mountain Range. Lasers struck out against the fleeing *Marauder*'s rear, cutting deep into its right arm and all across its back. Cluster munitions from the LB-X style autocannon that made up the *Emperor*'s arms sanded away the remaining armor, a few fragmenting rounds seeking a breach but apparently not finding one.

Warner grunted his annoyance, then tensed over his controls as the Taurian Velites MechWarrior twisted about to bring his right-arm PPC to bear against him. The azure whip scored his left leg, sending armor runneling to the ground in a bright molten stream.

Across the rises and shallow valleys that made up the northern face of Mount Wei-shi-ji, the Blackwind Lancers pushed forward against the Taurian Velites' encampment. Having slipped a battalion through a pass recently abandoned by the Third Confederation Reserves, Doles had been able to surprise the Periphery unit with this dawn raid. Their picket company fell back against the bulk of the unit, which scrambled to mount up and engage. Even so, their outdated weaponry made for an uneven battle. *So much the worse for them,* he thought with little charity but no real malice. *This isn't their war to begin with.*

Doles restricted his weapon fire to his autocannon and a single large laser on his next salvo. No reason to overheat when the fight could so obviously only go in one direction. The *Marauder,* antiquated on today's battlefield but still a tough opponent, turned into the attack and absorbed the damage across its front side this time. Its own dual PPCs and autocannon spoke, the coruscating energy drawing twin scars across the *Emperor*'s right and left side while the autocannon hammered into his already-damaged left leg. A *Javelin,* a lightweight missile support design, popped up over a background prominence and let fly with two flights of short-ranged missiles. Corkscrewing in on smoke trailers, over half the missiles found their target and pockmarked the thick armor plating that protected the *Emperor*'s internal structure.

That evened the playing field. Against Doles, at least. Comm chatter hinted at more reinforcements showing themselves up and down the line, but still nothing to worry over yet.

"Hold your positions," Doles ordered, a hint of caution working its way into his mind. "Lateral movement only. We hit them, and then we fade."

A month ago—two, perhaps—he wouldn't have been satisfied with such a battle plan. *I would have wanted to hurt them, destroy them. And I might have risked my entire unit to do so.* Today, he did not feel the need. It no longer worried him that he might be losing his edge in combat. If anything, it made him that much more dangerous. No mistakes.

Like the *Javelin* had just made.

Feeling some amount of support now, the *Marauder* held position to trade volleys while the *Javelin* faded only slightly along the lateral line of the ridge that protected its lower half. Skin flushed with excitement as much as the stifling heat build-up, Doles drifted his targeting reticule away from the heavy Periphery 'Mech and over the *Javelin*'s upper half. The reticule flashed from red to the deep gold of target lock. The colonel rode out the heavy buffeting of two more PPC attacks, triggering his own weapons at the lighter machine.

A large laser and two of his mediums cored into the ridge protecting the *Javelin*'s legs, the ruby energy beams scorching the thin mountain grasses and setting the dirt smoldering. Everything else concentrated against the *Javelin*'s upper torso, arms and—most damaging—the head. Several sprays of fragmenting autocannon rounds spanged off the side of the domed cockpit area, chipping away at the armor and no doubt rattling the warrior inside. Doles winced in sympathy, knowing the beating the Periphery pilot would take, being thrown against his harness and seat.

Too much of a beating, it seemed. The *Emperor*'s tactical computers registered no armor breach, and Doles saw nothing to indicate such, but still the *Javelin* toppled back out of sight. Warner Doles did not envy that pilot the headache he would have on waking.

Still, the *Marauder* pushed forward to point-blank range, this time switching one PPC out for its medium lasers. Doles turned his assault 'Mech to the left, trying to protect his vulnerable leg. The *Marauder*'s autocannon still found the opening, peeling away the last of his armor over that location as its PPC cored into the still-fresh protection over the *Emperor*'s right leg.

A desperation attack, Doles judged of the opposing pilot, *or it has more backup on the way.* "Prepare to fall back," he ordered over the general frequency to his battalion. "Concentrate fire against vulnerable targets." In the slowest of his unit's machines, Doles would have to begin falling back early. But first, he intended to claim one more "kill." The Periphery warrior either couldn't understand or failed to acknowledge when he stood outclassed. The *Emperor* could deliver full salvos for a longer duration, carried fifty percent more armor, and could do one more thing the *Marauder* could not.

It could jump.

Shunting plasma flow from the fusion engine into his jump jet reaction chambers, Doles guided the *Emperor* into a ninety-meter spinning flight that landed him directly behind the *Marauder*. Realizing his error the Periphery warrior tried to turn into the attack, but too late. Lasers flared ruby energy into its already-weakened rear torso and sides, evaporating any remaining armor it might have claimed and then carving deep into internal support structure. The autocannon hammered its shotgun-like ammunition into the breaches, each fragmenting piece ricocheting deeper than the one before in search of critical components.

These they found in abundance. The tailings of his energy weapons fire actually sliced through the supports holding the fifty-millimeter autocannon up over the *Marauder*'s right shoulder, cutting the large weapon free. Gem-colored darts from his pulse laser worried engine shielding. Flames licked out the rents in the armor as the fusion reactor bled waste energy directly into the internal structure. Then the twin shotgun blasts from his autocannon tore out the gyro housing, and the entire machine dropped like an unstrung puppet, burning and broken.

So much for several million C-bills in Concordat state property, Doles thought, lumbering his massive *Emperor* around the fallen *Marauder* and then setting off the way he'd originally come.

Cresting the next rise, Doles surveyed the fragmented battlefield. His warriors had held to a fairly orderly line and were mopping up the picket company. In the distance, his tactical computer identified a full battalion moving forward. Symbols painted over his head's up display indicated heavy machines flanked by light support designs. He dropped his chin down, activating the mike built into his neurohelmet.

"Twenty seconds to full retreat," he said. "No heroes, no martyrs. If you need the time, begin pulling back now."

In singles and pairs at first, the heavier, slower 'Mechs of the Blackwind Lancers broke away. Then entire lances pulled back, forming into a solid rearguard line that Doles doubted the Velites could break even should they catch up with the retreating Lancers.

Doles nodded to his empty cockpit, satisfied with the

day's work and proud of his unit. Today they had claimed a victory, but Ambergrist's problems would not be solved in a day or likely even a month. There would be more battles to fight; advances, retreats and—too likely—brutal clashes where the Lancers might claim victory or be subject to harsh defeats. Warriors and machines would be lost, destroyed, captured, and in some cases even ransomed back to opposing units. That was simply the nature of warfare.

And that was his job. Nothing more.

37

Royal Compound
Tian-tan, St. Ives
St. Ives Compact
27 September 3062

At thirty stories in height, the *Fortress* Class DropShip *Xiang-ya Lei* dwarfed St. Ives' Royal Palace. Its bulk crowded better than half of the palace's open grounds, its trees and shrubs crushed beneath landing gear and the ground scorched nearly to glass beneath its massive drive. The ship proudly displayed the Compact's ivory horse's head insignia, six stories high and painted on three different facings. The duchess' DropShip.

Her escape vessel.

Candace Liao stood in its shadow near the foot of the main ramp as the last of the palace staff and guards filed onto the massive vessel, their families in tow, carrying all they would be allowed to bring from St. Ives. Her gray eyes showing concern but not defeat, Candace offered an encouraging nod or word now and then as she searched the final group of military commanders and advisors for her son. *Kai is not coming.* She knew it, felt it in the heaviness pressing down on her shoulders even before she spotted Caroline Seng.

"He refused to abandon his regiment," Seng said, even before Candace could ask about Kai. "He'd already worked out his plan of escape. If the First St. Ives Lancers can't make the spaceport, Kai has arranged with Kuan Yin to bring down another fleet of DropShips in the mountains to the north." Reading Candace's silence as concern, she added reassuringly, "He'll make it."

Candace was not silent out of worry for her son, but in contemplation. The sounds of battle were faint but still carried from the eastern edge of Tian-tan, where two regiments fought the final rear-guard action. To the west, she counted the drive flares of three new DropShips that shot spaceward to rendezvous with the flotilla of JumpShips holding at the nadir jump point. Even as she watched, a fourth vessel burned into the sky, a rising star dim in St. Ives' bright noon.

It had to be this way, Candace decided. *Fighting to the last minute. The dramatic escape. By coming for St. Ives, Sun-Tzu forces on me the choice I could not make after Black May.* Caroline Seng had outlined the problem six months prior; either full capitulation, or selling off the majority of her realm to keep the St. Ives Front active. *Now, instead, I allow St. Ives to fall and so save half of my nation. We are beaten, but not defeated. And so long as we fight, there is hope. The Capellan Solution, to fight on as best we can until finding our path of return. It worked for the Confederation, cut in half during the Fourth Succession War. It will work for the Compact as well.*

She said none of this to Caroline Seng. The Compact officer already understood.

"We should board," Candace said simply. "The sooner we lift off the sooner peace returns to St. Ives, if a Confederation peace." She looked back at her palace, unable to keep a trace of her grief from dampening her eyes.

"It is a world, Candace," Seng said softly, sensing the conflicting emotions in her sovereign and friend. "It is not the Compact."

Candace drew herself up tall, jaw set and speaking with conviction. "It is home," she said simply. "And we will return here." She breathed a deep sigh. "But not for a while. Possibly not in my lifetime." One last look, then. From now on this place would be only a memory, a cause behind which she would rally her remaining worlds.

She stepped up onto the ramp, a heavy step, abandoning the soil of St. Ives.

Aris Sung pressed forward, his *Wraith* one of the faster designs fielded by either House Hiritsu or Daidachi. He cut left, and shouldered his way into a light stand of hemlock and pine. An *Enfield,* belonging to the Fourteenth Donegal Guards and making for the same stand, pulled up short. Its large pulse laser stuttered emerald bolts into the forest while autocannon fire splintered branches, missing the *Wraith* for the trees. Aris suffered no such handicap. His own pulse lasers answered in ruby darts that ate into the *Enfield's* right side.

The medium-weight Lyran 'Mech faded back to the protection of its own lines, which held just outside Tian-tan's suburbs, while Aris' company moved forward in support of their commander.

The shift continued up and down the line, House Hiritsu guiding off Aris' company. House Daidachi, further south and not about to be upstaged by their rival/brother Warrior House kept pace. Only the Concordat Jaegers to the north were slow on the move, more interested in trading hard fire with the Donegal Guards than claiming ground.

Tian-tan's skyline sat low against the horizon except for one massive DropShip sitting inside the city. Aris guessed at its meaning, but began to worry the closer they pushed toward the suburbs. The signs were there, to be sure. The DropShip sitting next to what Aris was sure would be the palace complex. Other vessels further west, blasting out of Tian-tan's spaceport with regularity. The First St. Ives Lancers led by Kai Allard-Liao giving ground for a change, trading meters for time. It all spoke of an evacuation strategy, and *Shiao-zhang* Non agreed, but much longer and the fighting would be pressed into Tian-tan itself and that Aris hoped to avoid. *There is simply no need.*

As if sensing their backs being pressed to the wall—literally, in the case of the city buildings not a kilometer behind them—the Donegal Guards and First St. Ives Lancers surged forward in a coordinated press. Aris cut in his jets, springing back from the trees as they came under intense concentrated fire. Airborne, he managed to score again against the same *Enfield* as before, the medium-weight machine thinking to lead the charge. *Too eager, that one.*

"Barrage Lance, swing south," he said quickly, sensing the opportunity. He knew a split second's hesitation, calling down such a strike against the under-armored Lyran warrior, but then, "Target the *Enfield*."

Nearly half a kilometer north and east, four heavy LRM carriers swung over and launched an impressive umbrella of missiles against the *Enfield*. The carriers were a recent purchase from the Canopian Regiment on St. Ives, and the Hiritsu infantry were still learning the intricacies of commanding the slow-moving vehicles. Still, one could not call the demonstration of raw firepower subtle. Over three hundred missiles took flight, cloaking the carriers in the cloud of smoke raised at the launching and then saturating an area of over two hundred square meters centered on the Lyran machine. But as Aris had expected, the infantry's inexperience with the support vehicles and the *Enfield*'s decent speed curve made for above-average misses. Only a quarter of the missiles actually came in on target, not enough to annihilate the *Enfield* but stripping nearly every last shred of armor and hammering deep into its internal framework. The *Enfield* stumbled, went down.

After such a display, the Lyran press sagged back and quickly forced a halt to the advance. Aris' company again surged forward, Aris calling off targets for concentrated fire. Between himself and a *Men Shen* OmniMech, the *Enfield* failed to rise from the earth. Raven Clearwater's *Huron Warrior* cracked open the left-side armor of an opposing *Stealth* with her Gauss rifle, and Aris' scout lance savaged it with medium laser and short-ranged missile fire. The *Stealth* also went down, bleeding heat and chunks of burning metal through the holes blasted into its engine shielding. Both MechWarriors ejected, gliding their parafoils toward the back line, where fast hovercraft streaked out to pick them up.

And the DropShip lifted.

"There she goes!" sang out *Pai-zhang* Julie McDaniels, from her cockpit in one of the two *Ti Ts'ang*s in Aris' company. Aris wasn't sure if the "she" referred to the vessel or its likely passenger.

"That's it." It was Ty Wu Non's voice, strong and hard even over the comm unit. "They are fading." As called out, the Compact forces abandoned the fight all along the line and broke for the city. *Shiao-zhang* Non switched over to the officer's circuit, tied in through all three regiments. "It would seem that Duchess Liao has surrendered St. Ives. I doubt that the Lancers or the Donegal Guards will put up any resistance anywhere between here and the spaceport."

Aris nodded agreement with his House Master's evaluation. "Second Company," he ordered, selecting a channel to his unit, "form up for parade. We march into Tian-tan in good order."

"No pursuit?" That from the Concordat Jaegers' CO.

They're running, Aris said to himself. *Let them go.*

Ty Wu Non put it more succinctly. "No." He selected a command-wide frequency. "Does no one else have a desire for a victory parade? House Hiritsu follows Daidachi in," he said, bowing verbally to the senior Warrior House. "The Jaegers after us. Aris Sung, since your command is ready, you will lead House Hiritsu. Straight to the Royal Palace, and strike the colors of the Compact when we get there.

"St. Ives is ours."

Aris reveled silently in the Confederation's victory. He wished Li Wynn could have lived to see this—lived, and understood. *It took me nearly two years to rediscover that a warrior's glory lies not in triumphs and conquests, but in the* conduct *of warfare leading to them.* There lay the true challenge, warriors holding true to their own ideals and beliefs and still able to submit to the orders of the State.

I am a warrior of the Capellan Confederation, in the best sense of the definition. Aris throttled his *Wraith* into a walk, leading House Hiritsu into Tian-tan. *And that can indeed be glorious.*

Epilogue

Celestial Palace
Zi-jin Chéng, Sian
Sian Commonality, Capellan Confederation
2 October 3062

Zhong-qiu-jie. The Autumn Moon Festival.

Those important to the Confederation's efforts against St. Ives, or influential enough to warrant inclusion regardless, had gathered in the Celestial Palace's third-floor ballroom at the invitation of Chancellor Sun-Tzu Liao. Servants distributed wines and spiced ciders and the festival's traditional moon-shaped cakes. Through the large window that made up fully one-fourth of the ballroom's eastern wall, Sian's primary moon, Fu Hsi, rose in majestic fullness, the reflection off the satellite's copper-rich soil lending it a shade of amber. Conversations were spirited, and people clustered in tight knots as they do at most large gatherings.

"But not by caste," Sun-Tzu whispered just loud enough for Talon Zahn to hear.

Sun-Tzu Liao walked the floor with Zahn at his side, then turned toward the dais set against the northern wall but in no hurry to get there. He was dressed in golden robes with silver dragons chasing down both wide sleeves and coiling around ivory horses' heads. Two large Death Commando guards trailed in his wake.

"Chancellor?" Zahn asked. His dark eyes flicked about as he sipped from a glass of cider, searching, and then he understood his master's reference without needing further explanation. "Yes, that is"—he paused, obviously for effect—"different."

The pause leant "different" the meaning of "strange." Sun-Tzu agreed, though it pleased him to see it. Where at any other time the islands of people would be broken down by caste, tonight that did not hold true. Directorship and Intelligentsia mingled, sharing conversation and ideas. The *janshi*, warriors, mixed freely and at times were sought out by the nominally higher castes for opinion or simply for recognition of their services.

And, best of all, there were no uninvited guests. Romano Liao lay silent. No ghostly whispers. No arguments. *As is only right,* Sun-Tzu thought, jade eyes narrowed in contemplation, *for a woman ten years dead.* Returned to memory and accepted as such, but never again to throw her dark mantle over his rule of the Confederation. Several reasons lay behind Romano's final death, he knew, not the least of which was the ultimate success of his Xin Sheng movement. Truly a *new birth* for the Confederation.

"For the first time in over thirty years," Sun-Tzu said softly, keeping his conversation with Talon Zahn private, "the Capellan people no longer feel the broken nation Hanse Davion left behind in the wake of the Fourth Succession War. We have won back that which was once ours."

Zahn took another sip from his glass. "The final solution may yet take awhile," he reminded his Chancellor. "The worlds remaining to the Compact might hold out another six months, or longer."

Sun-Tzu waved away the concern. "Six months or six years, it hardly matters. The fall of St. Ives bought the Xin Sheng movement capital enough to last a lifetime."

He hesitated in his walk as conversation in a nearby knot of warriors and administrators ceased and all rendered him a formal bow not called for in the social setting. Sun-Tzu returned their courtesy, his gaze making contact with each person in turn to let them know their Chancellor had acknowledged them. Those few who flinched from his gaze he took note of for future reference.

"Yes," he murmured, "a lifetime." He smiled as glasses were raised in another nearby group. Although the *zhong-qiu-jie's* ostensible purpose was the celebration of autumn and hopes for good harvests, nearly every toast Sun-Tzu heard celebrated the return of the St. Ives Commonality.

That, too, pleased him. *Not the subjugation of an enemy,* he noted, *but the return of a lost Commonality.* With the fall of St. Ives the Chancellor had been quick to reclaim the true name of the Commonality, a promise to the Capellan citizens there that they were welcome home. To hear the name toasted so easily gave him hope for fully mending the Confederation, for a complete reconstitution of the Capellan state.

The final knot pulled free.

Ion Rush and Nancy Bao Lee passed nearby as Sun-Tzu closed on the dais. She wrapped into an emerald silk dress, he dashing in the ivory and green of House Imarra's dress uniform, and both so obviously uncomfortable in the company of the other. *A good match,* Sun-Tzu thought, pleased with his command that they attend the celebration together. *Each a brake against the other.*

They stopped and bowed to Sun-Tzu. Nancy Bao Lee held eye contact with the Chancellor as she did, giving him a thin smile. A reminder of her success in reaching Sasha Wanli on St. Ives. Sun-Tzu allowed the Maskirovka agent her touch of pride. He never should have let Sasha live to begin with, regardless of his attempts to throw off Romano's legacy. *Mother may have been cold to her people, ruthless in her direction and even at times unbalanced in her reasoning—but that does not mean she could not occasionally be correct in her actions.*

Accepting that fact had also gone a long way toward the banishment of Romano's specter. *Never,* he promised again, *will I allow her memory to impede my judgment, in any form.*

Following close on the heels of Rush and Lee came Naomi Centrella, flanked by two hereditary nobles of the Confederation's House of Scions. Her low-cut evening dress of turquoise and black stood out against the colors her escorts had chosen, reflecting her Periphery allegiance rather than a Capelian heritage. Another positive sign, Naomi being so well-accepted within the room. They all three nodded formally, first to Chancellor Liao and then to *Sang-jiang-jun* Zahn.

When Sun-Tzu paused to recognize them, Zahn spoke for both himself and the Chancellor. "Ambassador Centrella," he said, awarding Naomi her formal title in the Sian court rather than the military one she adopted for command of Magistracy forces operating in the Confederation. To the nobles he simply said, "Sirs." A member of the Barduc, the sword nobility, Zahn did not have to address them with full titles.

Keeping his expression neutral, Sun-Tzu lifted a fresh glass of wine from the tray of an attending servant. "Naomi, again the Confederation's thanks for your people's recent assistance in reclaiming St. Ives."

He offered the glass to her, pretending not to notice the sudden stiffness in the accompanying nobles or the silence that overtook some of the nearby conversations. Though his gesture was not exactly improper toward the representative of an allied nation, Sun-Tzu wanted to gauge Naomi's reaction to the awkward situation. One of dozens of such tests he'd performed this night.

Naomi rose to the challenge. She accepted the glass—for to refuse would be a slight against the Chancellor—taking it with both hands from his one. Sun-Tzu nearly smiled at the subtle implication of his greater strength.

Naomi bowed. "Your acknowledgment is appreciated, Chancellor Liao, but not necessary. The Magistracy is merely showing its commitment to the alliance." She then offered the glass to Talon Zahn. "If you seek to reward anyone for the victory on St. Ives, it must be *Sang-jiang-jun* Zahn."

Zahn set his half-empty cider on the tray of a passing servant and accepted the wine from Naomi with another light bow.

Not too badly done, Sun-Tzu decided, taking a glass of dark plum wine for himself from the tray. Over Naomi's shoulder, he saw Nancy Bao Lee frown. But whether it was personal dislike of Naomi Centrella or a mere desire for such honor to be shown to her, Sun-Tzu could not be sure. *Either will suit my purposes,* he thought, *but I will have to discover which it is. Tomorrow.*

Sun-Tzu ended any further conversation by turning away and mounting the low dais. Allowing him an additional thirty centimeters, the platform gave the Chancellor a commanding view of the ballroom. Conversations melted away to silence as everyone turned his way. Capellans all, but for Naomi. *They look to me as Chancellor. Liao. The voice of the Capellan people, who are the nation.* This was Sun-Tzu's karma, to serve the state to the best of his ability. Nothing else mattered so much.

"To the St. Ives Commonality, now forever known as Xin Sheng Commonality," he said, raising his plum wine in a toast, "and to the Capellan Confederation and the Trinity Alliance." He held his glass in the air, drawing out a moment of silence as everyone reflected on the events of the past two years.

From the first rank surrounding the dais, Talon Zahn then came to strict attention and also raised his glass in salute of the Chancellor. *"Xin Sheng!"* he barked out, his commanding voice rolling throughout the ballroom.

Beneath a wave of upraised glasses or fists thrust upward in salute, a hundred voices answered back, *"Xin Sheng! Xin Sheng! Xin Sheng!"* Each time louder than the last, the shouts echoed throughout the great room.

Everyone drank after that except Sun-Tzu Liao, who allowed himself to get caught up in the moment and enjoy a touch of pride at what he had started. *They are not celebrat-*

ing me, but themselves. What we have accomplished. Anything left to be done paled in comparison.

Sun-Tzu finally lifted the glass to his lips. *Nothing can stand in our way.*

The Capellan Confederation has returned.

Loren L. Coleman is an on-again off-again resident of the Pacific Northwest state of Washington. He started writing as a hobby in his high school days, but it was during his five years as a member of the United States Navy, nuclear power field, that he began to write seriously.

His first year out of the military, Loren joined the Eugene Professional Writer's Workshop and within a few months sold his first fiction story. He has spent the last five years working as a professional freelancer, writing source material and fiction for companies such as FASA, TSR, and Wizards of the Coast. His BattleTech® novels include *Double-Blind, Binding Force, Threads of Ambition,* and now *The Killing Fields*.

Loren L. Coleman currently resides in Washington State with his wife, Heather Joy, two sons, Talon LaRon and Connery Rhys Monroe, and a new daughter, Alexia Joy. He works in the company of three Siamese cats, who collaborate in his writing by offering the frequent paw and occasional body check against his keyboard.

Glossary

Officer Ranks

Capellan (Han)	Old Ranking	Equivalent
Sao-wei	Subcommander	Lieutenant
Sang-wei	Commander	Captain
Sao-shao	Captain	Major
Zhong-shao	Major	Lieutenant Colonel
Sang-shao	Colonel	Colonel
Jiang-jun	Senior Colonel	General
Sang-jiang-jun	Nonexistent	Senior General

Warrior House Ranks

Zhang-si	Infantryman	Lance Corporal
Ban-zhang	Squad Leader	Lieutenant
Pai-zhang	Lance/Platoon Leader	Captain
Lien-zhang	Company Leader	Major
Ying-zhang	Battalion Leader (infantry)	Lieutenant Colonel
Shiao-zhang	House Master	Lord Colonel

Wraith

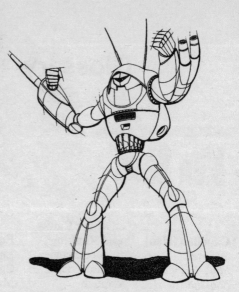

Cestus

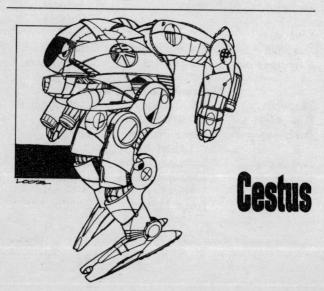

Men Shen

Yu Huang

Helios

Ti Ts'ang